WELCOME TO
MALLARD POND

TARYN L WAGNER

Welcome to Mallard Pond
Copyright © 2022 by Taryn L Wagner

All rights reserved. No part of this publication may be reproduced, distributed, or transmitted in any form or by any means, including photocopying, recording, or other electronic or mechanical methods, without the prior written permission of the author, except in the case of brief quotations embodied in critical reviews and certain other non-commercial uses permitted by copyright law.

tellwell

Tellwell Talent
www.tellwell.ca

ISBN
978-0-2288-8336-4 (Hardcover)
978-0-2288-8350-0 (Paperback)
978-0-2288-8351-7 (eBook)

This book is dedicated to
my parents Phyllis and Robert,
and my friends Carole and Ralph.
Without you this book would never have been
more than a file on my computer.

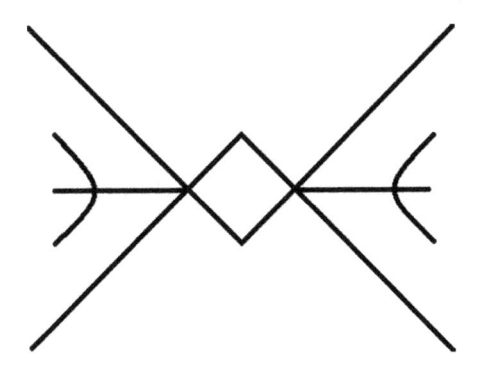

CHAPTER 1

"I still think this is crazy!"

Everleigh's mother had been following her around her apartment since she had arrived an hour ago, repeating the same things over and over: "You haven't thought this through," "you'll be so far away," and "you don't know anything about the place or even where it is."

"Mom, stop." Everleigh sighed. "You're right. I've never seen the place, not even a photo, but I have thought it through. I want to do this. Grandma left me her cottage. I at least want to see it."

"Mallard Pond is nothing more than a few shops and a handful of houses. There's nothing there. What will you do?" She threw up her hands in frustration. "Do you know how they named the town? Some kid saw ducks swimming in the pond and said 'duckies.' That's as much thought as they gave to the name of their town."

"What does that have to do with anything? I would know more about it if you would tell me what you remember instead of keeping it all some big secret." Everleigh was getting tired of the same conversation. Every time she saw her mother it was the same. "I have three months left on my lease and I've already talked to the management company. They've agreed to wait until the last week to sign for another year or get out."

"You're not moving there, so I don't see why that would be an issue. What about work?"

"It's my business, Mom. If I want time off, I can take it. Besides, Bess can handle the flower shop, and she has my number if she needs me." Everleigh hugged her mother tight. "I know you're worried."

"What about Donald?" Amelia asked softly. "Don't you want to be here when he's released? He loves you and he's going to need a place to stay—"

"Have you lost your mind?" It was Everleigh's turn to lose her temper. "If you think I'm going to let that man anywhere near me, you're the crazy one."

"Everleigh, he said it was just an accident. A misunderstanding," Amelia pleaded.

"NO!" Everleigh stood to her full height. "Leaving me here like that was no misunderstanding. I'm going and that's that. So, help me pack and let's talk about something else." She was forcing herself to take deep breaths and calm down, but her eyes fell to the floor behind the couch.

"No, you're 22. I'm not going to help you throw your life away." Amelia pulled away from Everleigh and headed for the door but stopped suddenly before opening it. "You may not like what you find there. You don't know what she was like to grow up with."

"Maybe it's time I find out. You could tell me about her."

The door slammed and her mother was gone. Everleigh sat down on the arm of a chair and listened for the familiar engine sound of her mother's old car. Yup, she was leaving. Everleigh slid down into the chair and saw the pile of papers on the table and the letter that had started this adventure.

Everleigh felt sick thinking her grandmother had been so close and she had no idea. She remembered the old lady who used to frequent her shop. She always wore a long blue dress and gray shawl. She had long, silver hair but what Everleigh remembered most were her shining green eyes.

The old woman would wander the shop longer than anyone else who came in. She knew all the flowers by name and would even offer advice for caring for the ones in pots.

Everleigh hadn't seen the old woman in a long time. Had even asked Bess if she had seen her, but the woman had just stopped coming in. In her heart, she had felt something must have happened to her but, without knowing her name, there had been no way to try finding her.

* * *

The day the lawyer called her shop asking her to come to his office regarding her grandmother's will brought back so many questions about her grandmother, questions her mother had always refused to answer. He wouldn't say more than that over the phone, so of course she had agreed.

The Adams and Adams Law Firm had a nice office. It was well decorated and welcoming. The receptionist that had greeted her was a very friendly older woman. She had walked Everleigh back to his office where he stood immediately to greet her introducing himself. "You can call me Mark. With two Mr. Adams here, it gets confusing." He had a bright, friendly smile.

He indicated for her to sit on the gray couch away from his desk and he took the matching chair. Between them was a glass table with a black box on it.

He told her that a woman by the name of Lilli Miller had come to see him several years ago. She had asked him to help her with her will.

"I can't help but wonder what this has to do with me. I've never heard that name before," Everleigh told him.

"You may not have heard of her, but she certainly knew you," he assured her. "She was your grandmother on your mother's side. Your mom's mom. Before you say anything, she also told me your mother and she had been estranged for many years." Mark gave Everleigh a moment before continuing. "She gave me this box to give to you upon her passing, which I am sorry to tell you happened a week ago. I was told it was peaceful."

Everleigh sat staring at the box on the table. It was too much to take in all at once. She had so many questions, none of which he had answers to.

"The box contains a letter she wrote to you, along with a set of keys to her home. She left everything to you."

Tears were filling Everleigh's eyes. "I don't even know where she lived." It wasn't meant to, but it came out as a whimper.

Mark moved to the couch beside her. "This is a lot for you all at once. I can't even imagine myself in your shoes right now. If you want to leave the box here, go home, and think about it, that's ok. I'll put the box on my shelf, and we can talk again next week, if you like. Give it all a chance to sink in."

Everleigh couldn't take her eyes off the box or her mind off the letter it contained. Mark's offer was nice, but there was no way she was leaving his office without the box.

Mark led her over to his desk and showed her where she needed to sign for the estate. "I'm going to copy these. I'll be back with a copy for you in a moment."

It was more than she could resist. Everleigh lifted the top of the box off. The first thing she saw took her breath away. She slowly picked up the photo. A smiling woman was looking at her with a little baby in her arms.

Mark came back and hurried to his desk. He grabbed a tissue box and offered it to Everleigh. She hadn't realized she'd started to cry. He joined her on the couch and looked at the picture.

"Is that the woman who came to you?" She was almost hesitant to ask, but she had to know.

"She was much older, but that's her. She wore a blue dress and gray shawl just like that. She had long gray hair and lovely green eyes. Much like yours, if I may say so." Mark smiled. "Is that you she's holding?"

"I think so." Everleigh smiled, wiping away her tears.

Everleigh took the box back to the shop with her fighting the urge to open it again as soon as she got to the car. It was almost time for Bess to go for her lunch break, and she had promised she would be back on time.

Bess left for lunch with the promise that Everleigh would tell her everything when she got back. She went into her office and sat down. Carefully she removed the top of the box, and this time took out the letter tied with a ribbon.

Hello little one,

>*I know you must have more questions than I can possibly imagine. Let me first tell you, though we were not able to spend a lot of time together, I treasured my visits to your shop. I wore the same clothes I had on in the photo so that in the end you would know it was me.*
>
>*The people here in Mallard Pond are wonderful, so loving and kind. As I could no longer do tasks for myself, there was always someone asking if they could do it for me. They agreed to allow me to stay in my cottage until it was my time to leave this world, and that is what I wanted.*
>
>*You must be wondering why I didn't tell you who I was. The honest answer is I did not want to anger your mother and disrupt your life. Time moves on and what's done cannot be undone.*
>
>*I am leaving my cottage and all its contents to you, little one. You are my only grandchild and the only one who will understand the importance of what you will find there. It is yours now to do as you wish. The choice will be yours as it was your mother's, and as it was mine a lifetime ago.*

Go to the village of Mallard Pond. There you will find a man named Jack Killian. He is the one who drove me to see you. He will help you, guide you and protect you. If you have trouble finding it on a map, close your eyes and say out loud, 'The way is clear' and look again. This will all make sense when you get there. My journals are yours. I hope they answer more for you. I left one on the table in the kitchen. Start there.

Know that I loved you every day of your life, my dearest Everleigh Lyn Roberts.

Love, Lilli

* * *

Her grandmother had been right. Even Google had trouble finding the place until she closed her eyes and said, 'the way is clear', which if she was honest was only adding to the mystery and intrigue of the little village. Her mother was no help on the issue insisting she let the whole thing go and forget about it.

She couldn't put her finger on it, but there was something odd about this whole thing. She knew asking her mother wouldn't get her anywhere so the only way to find out was to go there. She wasn't sure why, but she was very careful not to tell her mother about the box or the letter.

Everleigh had carefully planned for her time away. She had moved all the plants from her apartment to her store, Little Flower Shop. It would be easier for Bess to take care of them for her. Her neighbors, Sam and Dom Noah, were going to pick up her mail and care for Grayling, her little gray cat.

Grayling landed on her chest, bringing her back from her memories. He stretched out, purring loudly as she stroked his fur. "I've almost done packing, Gray," she told him, "and if I leave by 9:00am, I should arrive by dinner time. What do you think? What are the odds I can get there without getting lost?"

Grayling meowed loudly in reply and jumped to the table beside her chair. She watched him walk in front of the clock. She hadn't realized how long she had been sitting there. Almost an hour had gone by in a flash. The sunset on her side of the building had tricked her into thinking it was late afternoon when in fact it was closer to dinner time.

"Better get moving hadn't I, Gray? Gray?" The little cat had jumped up on top of one of her packed suitcases and curled up for another of his many daily naps.

She grabbed her bag and keys, picked up the suitcase without the cat on top, and headed out the door. She popped the case in the car, made sure it was locked and continued walking down the street.

As she walked, she realized how little she knew about where she had lived the last five years. She exchanged friendly greetings with the people she passed, but really knew nothing about them. She passed two tall, brown brick buildings before reaching the pizzeria where she had a standing order every Friday night, a medium pizza with mushrooms, green olives, pepperoni, and a Coke.

"Hello, Everleigh. I was wondering if you were coming by tonight. You're late; is everything alright?"

"Hi, Gino. Sorry I'm late. I got sidetracked." Everleigh smiled.

Gino laughed. "That sounds like you, my dear. I've got your order nice and warm."

"Thanks, Gino." Everleigh paid and turned to leave but stopped. "Gino, I have to cancel my order for the next couple months. I'm going to be away. I'll come by when I get back."

"Well, have a safe trip, my dear. You'll have to tell me all about it when you get back." Gino smiled.

The shop was busy tonight. Almost every seat was taken. She glanced at the TV in the corner away from the counter. A game was on, and from the smiles and cheering, Everleigh could tell the right team was leading.

The chime rang out again and a laughing couple came in. The man held the door for her, and she thanked him and left. Everleigh walked home a little faster with the warm pizza starting to feel hot on her arm.

She tucked the pop in her pocket so she could open the door to her building. The familiar smell of floor cleaner greeted her. It was a strong chemical smell she was glad didn't find its way into her apartment. The building had six apartments and was unusually quiet tonight, something she was grateful for, since she was hoping to go to bed early.

Grayling, sitting next to his empty bowl, began meowing loudly his disapproval evident as he stared at her.

"I'm sorry, Gray." She set the pizza on the table. "You first, buddy." She picked up his bowl, put his favorite wet food in, and returned it to the mat. A flick of his tail said he was still displeased at having to have waited what he felt was too long for his dinner.

Everleigh laughed as she went to open the sliding door to her balcony. She could hear the cars on the main road beyond the trees. There was music and laughter from the party next door. It was a lovely summer night, not too hot, with a nice breeze.

Sitting on the floor, her back against the couch, she popped open the pizza box and wondered what the night would sound like tomorrow. She wondered again how big the village would be. Her mother kept saying there was nothing there but a handful of shops and houses, but that was years ago. How much could a village that is so hard to find change over the years?

She also started wondering why the village was so hard to find one minute and right there on the map the next.

A knock at the door awoke her from her daydreaming. She seemed to be doing that a lot lately. She got up and noticed half her pizza was gone, and her pop with it. 'I don't remember eating all that,' she thought, but shook it off.

"Hi, Eve. Sorry to bother you so late, but your light was on," Sam said, smiling shyly. "You haven't given me your key yet and I didn't want you to forget. Are you still leaving tomorrow?"

"Hi, Sam. Sorry, I meant to drop it by. I guess I forgot." She handed him a set of keys from the small table by the door, one for her mailbox the other for her apartment door. The tag on the ring had her name. One of those impulse buys from the souvenir store. Seemed silly at the time she bought it, but it turned out to be a handy thing to have around for times like this.

"Thank you for looking after my mail, and Grayling won't be any trouble, will you buddy?"

Sam picked up the cat circling his legs. "I'm sure he won't be. Tell her we'll be fine." He turned the cat around and raised his voice. "Sam's right, we'll be fine. Catnip parties every night."

Everleigh laughed as she took the cat. "You boys better behave yourselves while I'm gone." Grayling curled into her arms. "And seriously, thank you for looking after him and the mail. You can toss it on the table. There shouldn't be much more than fliers."

"Hey, it's no problem. I best be off. You have a long drive and I have to be at the hospital first thing. Have a safe drive. Goodnight."

Everleigh said goodnight, sat Grayling down on the table, and picked up the pizza box. The other half would be a good road snack. It was getting late and, if she really was going to drive all that way, she knew she should get to bed.

She turned off the lights. The streetlights outside gave plenty of light to see by. She checked the door and closed and locked the sliding door. It was quiet outside now, only the cars on the main street, which was always busy, no matter what time it was.

She set the ambient sounds app on her phone to crickets and went to the bathroom to get ready for bed. When she returned, she took a quick look at her alarm clock. It was 11:30pm. "Well, so much for going to bed early."

Grayling didn't move when she crawled into bed. She pulled the covers up tight and looked out the window at where she knew the stars would be twinkling beyond the streetlights.

She drifted off, wondering if she would be able to see them from her bed in the cottage.

* * *

"Wake up little one." It was a soft familiar voice. "It's time to wake up."

"I'm up, Grand—" Everleigh gasped when she opened her eyes. There beside her bed was an old woman in a long blue dress and gray shawl.

As Everleigh stared at her, the old woman she now knew as her Grandma Lilli smiled sweetly and faded away. She sat for a moment wondering if she was really awake or if this was some sort of lingering dream. She decided she must be awake, because she wasn't waking up again.

Grayling meowed. He was sitting next to her. "Did you see her?" Everleigh asked. The little cat purred and tilted his head.

There was a sharp knock at her door, and she jumped out of bed. Rattled from what she still wasn't sure she had seen, she went straight for the sound.

"Sam! Hello, good morning." She was out of breath when she reached the door.

"Good morning," Sam stuttered back. "I was just coming home from work. I forgot something and noticed your car still here." By the confused look she gave him, he could tell she had still been sleeping. "The power went out last night and when I saw your car I thought—"

"Oh my goodness! What time is it?" Only then did she realize she had gone to the door in her PJs and it was making Sam a little uncomfortable. "My alarm didn't go off. I think I overslept."

"It's almost 10:30am," Sam answered, grateful to be looking at his watch. "Have a safe trip. I hope it goes better from here, but I must get back to work."

"Yes, of course. Thank you for checking. I was still in bed. I couldn't get to sleep. Too excited I guess," Everleigh stuttered.

They exchanged a nod, and she closed the door laughing to herself. She went back to her bedroom and looked around. There was no one there. She took a deep breath and decided it must have been a dream. A very clear, very real dream.

She decided to dress for comfort as she was going to be in the car for most of the day. Gray leggings would do the trick, along with her Dan's Law t-shirt that read 'Shut up and do something'. Appropriate for the day, she thought as she tossed her PJs into her last open suitcase and closed it up. She went for one last look around for anything she might have forgotten but didn't find anything.

She took her pizza from the fridge and moved it into a plastic container. The box she took to the balcony and, with a practiced aim, dropped it perfectly into the recycling bin below.

Carrying the last suitcase in one hand, and her snack bag in the other, she walked down to her car. With every step, she was flooded with renewed excitement. She had never done anything like this before but somehow it felt like the right thing to do.

She put her hand on the black box in the passenger seat beside her, double-checked the directions she wrote out were there too, and backed out onto the road.

Her mother and friends, her apartment and the constant rushing of the city were all in the rearview mirror. She was leaving it all behind for a cottage in a village called Mallard Pond, a village that a month ago she hadn't even known existed. Despite all the arguments her mother had tried to make that she had lost her mind, Everleigh enjoyed a good mystery. This was the biggest mystery she had ever been handed. Not only that, this was one she had been trying for most of her life to solve.

For the last eight years, it had been her and her mom. Her dad had been very sick, and by the time they found what he had, it was too late. "It's hard to know you're sick when you don't feel sick." This is what her dad had told her to help her understand, but he passed soon after.

Everleigh stopped at a green light. With no one behind her, she sat and watched it turn red. "This is it," she said aloud to herself. "The last traffic light."

She was almost out of the city. A few stop signs and she would be out completely. She rolled slowly through the neighborhood and passed the elementary school she had attended. With the window down, she could hear the kids laughing in the yard. Rows of houses and side streets were replaced by tall trees.

She had reached the farthest part of the city. The conservation area surrounded a man-made lake where she used to go to day camp in the summers with her friends while her mom was at work. Everleigh tried but couldn't remember ever being farther out of the city than that.

According to the directions she was able to get from Google, she had about two hours of farmland before she reached the first town. Then every hour-and-a-half to two hours there was another until she reached a town called Strawsburg. There, she was going to have to ask locals for directions and hope someone could help her.

"Well, Grayling, what do you think of the country so far?" The little cat had jumped onto the front seat and was looking out the window. "Wait? Gray? How did you get here?"

The little cat curled up on the seat next to the box and purred himself to sleep. Everleigh sighed and made a mental note that she was going to need to buy cat food and bowls before heading to Mallard Pond. If her mother was right about the place, they may not have a pet store and she didn't want to take the chance.

They passed town after town. They had to stop once for gas and a washroom break for herself and Grayling. The station was small, only two pumps and a snack bar. The young man tending the pumps was very friendly. He told her there was no pet store in town and the general store was closed for the afternoon.

"A long-time employee passed away and the owner decided to close the store so anyone who wanted to could attend the funeral. Can I ask why you need cat food? It seems an odd thing to run out of on a road trip."

"I have to agree." Everleigh laughed. "I wasn't intending to bring my cat along, but he snuck into the car somehow, and I was too far along to take him home when he appeared. Would you happen to have any milk in your coolers?"

She followed the young man into the station store. She bought a small carton of milk and two bottles of water. Just because she was curious, she asked if he knew how much farther it was to Mallard Pond.

She wasn't surprised when he said he had never heard of the place. He did know she had another five-hour drive to Strawsburg. He had family there, so he knew the drive well.

"Stay on this road. It's a straight shot. There is a nice pet store. It's a big city compared to our little town. Safe drive!"

"Thank you. Have a nice day," she called back as she left the store and returned to the car.

"Well, Gray, he didn't have any kitty food, but I got you some milk." She shooed him from her seat and set the bag down. "I saw a sign for a park a little farther. We'll pull off and have a rest."

It was a lovely little park. Kids were happily playing on what looked to be a new playground while parents watched from the benches. There was a large, open field with goal posts for football or soccer and tall trees offered lots of shade for the picnic tables.

Everleigh went to the back seat where she had put her bag of snacks. It was lying on its side and her container of pizza was on the floor. She closed her eyes and sighed. It was still closed, but she knew how Grayling had made it to the car.

She had left her hiking boots in the car from a previous trip, so she pulled out one of the laces to make a DIY leash for Grayling, who was not impressed with the idea. They walked over to the shade and sat down on the grass. The little cat bit at the shoelace trying to free himself. Everleigh used the pizza container's lid to pour some milk in and he settled down right away. Everleigh finished her pizza.

With his belly full, he curled up in her lap for a nap as she stroked his soft gray fur. "We have five more hours to drive, Gray. That puts us in Strawsburg around 8:30 tonight if we leave now." Everleigh sighed.

Grayling was happy right where he was, so she had to carry him back to the car. With everything put back in the bag, and her passenger in his own seat, they were back on the road again.

The sun was beginning to set in her rearview mirror. She was grateful not to be driving towards it. It had set completely by the time they reached Strawsburg. It certainly wasn't a city like London, where she was from, but she could see why the young man had called it that.

She could see glowing signs for stores she recognized. She saw a pet store and decided she should get supplies for Grayling before trying to find a place to stay for the night. He was going to want more than just milk soon.

She looked at her watch: almost 8:30pm, right on track. Sam should be home by now, she thought, as she searched her contacts for his number.

"Hey, stranger!" Sam's voice was calmer than it had been when she saw him at her door that morning. "You haven't been gone a day and you're checking on me?"

"No, Sam, I totally trust you. I just didn't want you to worry about Gray," she replied.

"What about him? I'm just leaving the hospital now. Another bad car accident had the ER too busy for me to leave." Sam sounded tired.

"That's what makes you such an awesome doctor. Gray's with me. I think he was in my bag when I tossed in some snacks. I didn't see him and, well here he is." Everleigh looked at the little cat watching her carefully.

Sam started laughing. "Guess he didn't want to be left behind. Thanks for calling. I would have been in a panic thinking I lost your cat on my first day."

They chatted a little longer before saying goodbye. Everleigh picked up her little stowaway and went into the store.

"Good evening. What a sweet little kitty," she was greeted as they walked in. "I don't want to rush you, but the store is closing in a few minutes. Is there something I can help you find?"

Everleigh explained how he ended up on her road trip and that she had nothing for him but milk. The story attracted the attention of a couple of other employees, who were giggling when she finished.

"Well, I think we can get you set up. My name is Sara, by the way. Let's start with some food and work our way around from there," she said and grabbed a basket.

The store was well laid out, but it was a lot faster with Sara leading the way. Grayling loved the attention. Everyone stopped to give him a pat and say what a lovely kitty he was.

At the end, he had several cans of his favorite wet food, a bag of dry food and bags of treats, as well as new bowls, a litter box, his very own kitty seat for the car, and a new set of his favorite toys.

"You are one lucky kitty, Grayling," Sara said as she gave him a cuddle while Everleigh worked the debit machine.

"Yes he is," Everleigh agreed. "Can I ask one more thing? I need a place that we can stay for the night. Do you know of any motels that are spoiled kitty friendly?"

"I'm sure there are, but let's ask Mike. He'll know for sure." Sara led the way to the door, where Mike was waiting to lock up.

"Hi, I'm Mike. I own the store, and this must be the little one who invited himself on your road trip." He smiled as Sara passed him the little cat and said goodnight.

"Yes. Thank you so much for letting me get all this stuff. Sara was so helpful!" Everleigh was starting to feel tired from the long day.

"It's not a problem. We're happy to help out when we can. Sara is one of the best we have. She has three cats of her own." Mike held the door for her and carried the little cat out to the car.

Everleigh loaded the bags into her now very full car and put Grayling on the front seat, where he curled up in his new cat sized booster seat.

"So, you need a place for the night?" He smiled and gave her directions to a motel not too far away. "A friend of mine owns it. I'll let him know you're coming."

"That would be wonderful! So many places don't allow pets." Everleigh was relieved. She had expected it to be much harder to find a place for the night. "Just one more thing, if I may? Do you know how much farther it is to Mallard Pond?"

"To be honest with you, I've never been there. I do know someone from there. He picks up supplies here once a week; it's a big order." Mike was looking at his phone. "He should be coming in sometime tomorrow. Could I give him your number? He's a good guy. I've known him for years. I know he'll help you out. His name is Jack Killian."

"That would be great, Mike. Thank you." She wrote her phone number down with her name and the words 'Lilli's granddaughter'. She thanked him again before getting in the car and driving to the motel.

The motel wasn't very big. The office was simply decorated; there was a counter where the guests were greeted, with had a bouquet of flowers on it and guest book with pens. The walls had a few simple paintings of landscapes done by a local artist, which the motel manager was very proud to point out.

The manager walked her down the row of doors to her room and opened the door for her. He offered to help her with her bags, but she thanked him and said goodnight.

Her room was just as simply decorated as the front office. There was a bed, table and chairs and a small dresser with a TV on top. A lamp was on each of the bedside tables.

Mike was right. The manager had been fine with her bringing Grayling in for the night. She fed him and set up the litter box before bringing in her bag from the car.

Everleigh hadn't realized how tired she was until she had her PJs on and sat down on the bed. She lay down and was asleep in no time with her little Grayling curled in a ball next to her.

CHAPTER 2

Everleigh woke up late in the morning. It was another beautiful day. The sun was bright, and the air was warm without being overly hot.

She checked her phone. A couple of text messages from her mother, but no phone call. She had been worried that she missed Jack's call by sleeping so late. Everleigh had remembered the name as soon as Mike said it: this was the man Lilli had asked her to find and she had to believe he would have at least some answers to the many questions about her grandmother and Mallard Pond.

She got dressed and packed all their things back into the car. Grayling, who had stayed curled up on the bed while she packed, was now sitting on the edge looking at her. Everleigh clipped on his leash and the two walked out the door.

Everleigh had noticed a picnic area while she packed the car, so they headed over to it. She put Gray's bowl on the ground, and he was happy to see his breakfast. She sat at the table, fingers tapping next to her phone.

"What do you think we should do?" she asked. "We have to find someone who knows the way from here. Or should we wait here, buddy?"

The car wasn't far away. With the little cat eating, she had time to retrieve her box before he finished his food.

When she returned with the box, Grayling was cleaning his paws. She sat back down at the table and slipped the leash around her wrist. She took the top off the box and pulled everything out setting it in the lid. Piece by piece, she began looking through the papers for directions she may have missed. She knew there was nothing, but she had to do something.

Carefully she picked up the photo. "I could really use some help. I wonder what I would have called you. Grandma? Nana?"

"My guess would be Gran. At least that's what she liked the kids to call her." Everleigh turned on the voice behind her. "Sorry, didn't mean to scare you. Mike told me you might be here. He also told me you're looking for Mallard Pond?"

"Oh yes. Hi, you must be Jack." She stood to greet him. "My name is Everleigh and—"

"Yes, you're Lilli's granddaughter. You have her eyes. Do you like cheeseburgers? I hope you do. Lilli did. I know it's a bit early but there's a place not far from here that makes the best burgers. I always stop there when I come into town." Jack handed her one of the bags he was carrying.

Jack was tall and thin but, by the look of the black t-shirt he was wearing, very strong. Jeans and work boots rounded out his look. He had a friendly, honest smile and bright brown eyes. Brown hair that reached just past his shoulders was tied back from his face. She had been expecting someone older, but he appeared to be around the same age as her.

"Thank you," she answered, accepting the bag. "I do like cheeseburgers. Can I pay you for it?"

"It's hard to treat a pretty girl to lunch if she buys it herself." Jack laughed as he sat down on the bench on the other side of the table. "Before we dig in, could I see the picture you were looking at?" Everleigh passed it to him. "You know, I wondered what happened to this. It was in a frame on Lilli's wall of memories for as long as I can remember. Then one day it was gone, and she wouldn't tell me what happened to it. I guess now I know." Jack passed the picture back and started opening his bag.

Everleigh returned the picture to the box and closed it up. "Obviously you knew her well to notice a missing picture."

"I did. I run the Travelers Inn in Mallard Pond. We don't get a whole lot of visitors, as you might imagine, but the locals like to come in for drinks. It's more of a tavern than a proper inn. We have dart tournaments, quiz nights, that sort of thing, just for a laugh. What about you? You own a flower shop if I remember correctly."

"I can't help but think you have me at a disadvantage. You seem to already know a lot about me." She wasn't really surprised. Knowing her grandmother had been visiting her in secret, she had to assume she had talked to someone about her visits.

"I guess I should explain. Lilli was very strict about one thing and that was that I never introduce myself to you unless you came looking for me or Mallard Pond. I'm the one who drove her to London to see you. We would drive up and spend the night. On the way home, we would stop by your shop. I would go to the bakery and get some treats for the ride back and she would go to see you."

"I wish I had known who she was." Everleigh's heart ached again, but knowing how her mother would have reacted to finding out they were meeting behind her back, she understood why it had to be secret.

"I stopped driving to London after Lilli took ill. It started as a cold, but I think she knew it was something more. She took care of herself, always had. Made us all promise not to take her out of her home. It wasn't easy for any of us, but we wanted to respect her wishes." Jack let his head fall. "She wasn't alone when it happened. I mean Mia was with her. She brought the news to the Inn."

"She was well-liked then?" Everleigh felt a lump growing in her throat but wanted to know more about her mysterious grandmother.

Jack's head popped back up with a smile. "Liked her? No. Everyone loved Lilli and she loved us right back. There wasn't a lot she didn't know about all of us. By us, I mean the entire village. Birthdays, anniversaries, she kept them all written in her calendar, and everyone got a card. She took care of us, and it was only right that we took care of her."

Everleigh finally had someone who wanted to tell her about her grandmother, and she was taking full advantage. They talked into the early afternoon. The manager noticed them and came to collect the key to the room so it could be cleaned but welcomed them to stay at the tables as long as they liked.

The clouds had started to roll in and the wind was picking up. Grayling didn't like the change in the weather and started meowing and pulling towards the car.

"I think Grayling has the right idea. We should get going. It's a half-hour drive to the Pond and it looks like rain." Jack stood up and grabbed the empty bags from their lunch. "You can follow me there. It's not easy to find if you don't know the way. The cottage is ready for you. A couple of the girls cleaned it up. If you'd rather stay at my inn, you would be welcome, and Grayling too."

"I would like to go to the cottage first. I'd like to see it before I decide." Everleigh hadn't actually thought about how she would feel staying in the cottage.

Jack gave her directions to get to the road that would take them out of town. "In case we get separated at a light or something. I'll pull off and wait for you. Here, I wrote down my number if you need it." He handed her a torn piece of the paper bag from lunch and tossed the rest into his truck.

"It won't be hard to find you. Your truck is huge." Everleigh wasn't used to trucks this big. Living in the city, there wasn't a need for them.

"I know. A lot of folks in the village thought it was too big, but I didn't hear a lot of complaining come wintertime. We even pulled some of the small trucks out of the ditch last winter." He smiled and patted the open door. "If you're ready, let's ditch the big city."

It was clear Jack was proud of his truck. It was a shiny, dark blue pickup. Everleigh got the feeling it was a strategic purchase as much as it was a toy for showing off.

"I'm right behind you." Everleigh climbed into what felt like a very little car and clipped Grayling into his seat. She remembered how proud she was when she drove her little silver Mazda to her mother's for the first time.

She followed the big truck out to the main street. Traffic was light for a Saturday afternoon, so she didn't have much trouble. It was a nice little town, and she couldn't imagine how small Mallard Pond must be if he referred to this as the big city but decided it must have been a joke. Or perhaps her mother was right, and she was heading to a handful of houses and a duck pond.

"You know, Gray, I think there is a lot more to Jack than just an inn owner. What do you think?" The little cat was purring softly in his seat next to her.

Another twenty minutes on the road again and Everleigh was tired of driving. Jack turned onto a road so narrow she would have taken it for a farm lane had she not been following him. Lined on each side with midsummer corn fields and a grass shoulder, the road itself was two dirt strips separated by a line of short grass. It was a bumpy ride and Grayling was not happy about it.

Jack slowed down and moved his truck off to the side, and she followed. Another large pickup rolled up heading in the opposite direction. Jack exchanged greetings and she saw the other driver point at her. He smiled, laughed, and they started driving again. He smiled and waved at her as he passed, and she did the same.

"I guess there is a purpose for these big trucks after all, Gray." Everleigh couldn't see much around the truck, so she drove a little slower for Grayling as well as for her poor car. It wasn't used to this kind of off-road driving.

The road widened enough for two vehicles to pass easily where the fields ended, and the road continued into a dense forest of tall trees. They crossed a well-maintained bridge made of wood. She could see where sections had been repaired by the colour of the wood not that long ago.

On the other side of the bridge, Jack pulled over again. Everleigh stopped behind him. He got out and waved to her to do the same. As she walked up to join him at the front of his truck, he bowed extending his arm and said, "Welcome to Mallard Pond, my lady."

It was a bit dramatic, but then, so was the view. From the top of the hill, she could see the whole of the village. It was nothing like what she expected to see. She expected the pond of course and, from that distance, the river looked like a blue ribbon running through the village into the fields.

The little river connected the pond to a much larger river that followed the curve of the hill and emptied into a large lake. The road where they had parked curved its way around to the bottom, where there was another bridge over the larger river.

The village itself was sitting in a huge valley protected on all sides by the hill they were standing on, which made the road they were on the only way in or out. The dense forest they had passed through also encircled the valley and covered the hillside reaching down to the valley floor giving the impression of being a very large green bowl.

"The big building over there—" Jack was pointing off to the right, "—is the Great Hall. Nothing fancy, really. It's like a big dining room for festivals and big events. A little farther is a big field for outdoor festivities and such.

The lake is good for swimming if you're so inclined. Most of the other buildings are homes. We have a few shops, but for most things, we go into town. The most important building is that one with the red roof just to the far side of the hall. That is the Travelers Inn." Everleigh almost laughed and he gave her a smile before continuing. "Then you have the pond, of course. To the left is where the farms and the barns are. The prevailing winds come in over the lake, so there isn't normally any farm smell." He was pointing now toward the left side.

Everleigh was trying to take it all in, but this was going to take time. "This is so much more than I imagined! From the little my mother said, I was expecting maybe a handful of buildings. This is amazing! Over there, the big building on the far side of the pond, what is that one?"

"Oh, that one...that one is best left for another time." Jack's voice seemed to change. For a second he sounded nervous, but quickly changed the subject. "I have saved the best for last. Would you like to see the cottage?"

Everleigh's heart skipped a beat. "YES! Oh my goodness, yes." She could hardly contain her excitement looking at Jack to see what direction he would point.

"I hate to do this to you, but you can't actually see it from here." He could feel her heart sink in disappointment. "See where the river bends around behind the fields and back into the trees? There is a waterfall back there that feeds the rivers. Your cottage is on that bend, hiding behind those trees."

"Then what are we waiting for?" Everleigh asked feeling her excitement rise. She was so close she could feel it calling to her. Without realizing it, she began walking down the hill towards the bridge.

Upon reaching his truck, Jack noticed her and called out, "It might be faster if we drive."

As if waking from a trance, she turned around quickly and walked back to her car. As she passed Jack, she laughed. "You're right. I don't know what I was thinking."

Jack pulled away and Everleigh slowly followed, taking a last look from above. She let Grayling jumped up on the dashboard for a better view. "What do you think, Gray? This is a whole new world to explore." The little cat meowed and jumped back down to the seat.

Everleigh followed slowly behind trying to take in every detail. Listening to her mother talk about this place, she expected to see a village lost in time, but this was nothing like that at all. The buildings looked old, made of beams and field stones, but with modern shingled roofs. The lawns, flower beds, even the trees, were well-cared-for. The road, though unpaved, was very well-maintained. Everywhere she looked, she saw a mix of old and new, and the two blended perfectly.

Jack's truck had disappeared around a bend in the road. When she caught up, he had pulled up in front of a little cottage tucked in behind tall pine trees. He was pointing for her to park beside him.

"Welcome home, Everleigh," he said, as she stepped out of the car with a furry gray scarf flicking his tail against her cheek.

"This is it? This is mine?" she asked as if stepping into a dream.

Jack followed, allowing her to take her time. She walked slowly down the well-worn cobblestone path toward the front door with Grayling watching carefully. Large plants lined the path. Some she knew, others she didn't. The cottage was constructed with field stones and a gray, shingle roof. They passed a large window and came to a door. The path continued curving around where the wall was built farther out. She could just see where the path was joined by another to the left but couldn't tell where they led.

"Well, what do you think?" Jack asked. "Should we walk around the outside or start on the inside?"

"Oh, I left the keys in the box on the passenger seat," she said and turned to go back to the car.

"Here I have a set." Jack reached into his pocket and pulled out the keys. "I guess I should give these to you."

"Can I ask why you have them?" she asked.

"I had two extra sets made. One was for me and the other went to Mia. We had them in case something happened and we had to get in. Fortunately, we never needed them for that reason." Jack smiled, unlocked the door, and stepped back. "She locked herself out once in awhile, but that was all."

Everleigh stepped into a rather dark room. All the heavy curtains had been pulled and there was a bit of a musty scent starting to take hold. Jack pulled back the curtain from the large front window and Everleigh couldn't believe what she saw.

The room was much larger than she expected it to be from the outside. Dark wood shelves lined with books on the top shelf, and large crates and cauldrons on the bottom, ran along the walls. Their tops were covered in bowls, dried herbs, and all sorts of things Everleigh couldn't identify. There was a large stone hearth on one wall with a short oak table and comfortable-looking couch in front of it. Two equally comfortable-looking chairs sat on either side, making a cozy spot to entertain. On the far wall was a writing desk covered in papers and other things you would expect to see, along with more strange items.

The closer Everleigh looked, the more she saw that she didn't understand. There were markings carved into objects that looked familiar, but now was not the time to dig into these things with so much more to see.

Jack busied himself opening more curtains, allowing more light in, and opening some windows to clear the air. He didn't say anything, just allowed her time to look around, and she greatly appreciated that. Grayling had jumped off her shoulder and made himself comfortable in one of the chairs.

Next to the door they had entered through was a row of coat hooks with her grandmother's gray shawl hanging there. Her handbag was sitting on a bench with a pair of shoes and slippers set neatly underneath. The rest of the wall was covered in nails for drying herbs and framed photos.

"Lilli's wall of memories," Jack said standing next to her. "She always said pictures were the best kind of magic." He pointed to an empty frame. "The picture in your box, that's where it was."

"I always heard stories were the best kind of magic," Everleigh commented. "But I guess they are sort of the same thing. They both allow us to relive memories and remember those we've lost."

Everleigh turned away from the wall. She took a deep breath and started moving around the room again. The wall of memories was about half as long as the room and at its end was an oak dining table with four chairs. There was a brown, leather-wrapped journal on the table next to an empty vase.

Turning the corner, she found a simple but very modern kitchen in comparison to the rest of the cottage, which had a very old feel to it.

Jack opened the rest of the curtains and must have seen the confused look on her face. "Almost twenty years ago, a few of guys in the village did a huge renovation for Lilli. I'm told they put electrical outlets all over the cottage. She chose to use very few of them." He laughed. "She wanted the stainless-steel appliances because they are silver and she liked the colour. It's all safe and up to code so you don't have to worry about that. I should also tell you we tossed out the food. We didn't know when, or even if, you would come."

"Good to know." Everleigh smiled. "What are these rooms?"

"The far one is the bathroom, bedroom is in this corner and this is, or was, her shop."

Everleigh head whipped around to the closed door. "Her shop!" she repeated.

"Yes." Jack had his hand on the doorknob. "You have a lot more in common then you know." He knew there was no stopping her, so he opened the door and went in first. He crossed to the large window on the far side and pulled open the curtains. He heard her gasp and gave her a moment to look around before saying anything.

The walls were lined with jars. Each was labeled according to the contents, and many of them Everleigh knew from her botany classes or her own personal interest studies. Others seemed to be blends, though she didn't know exactly what they could be for. In the center of the room was a table with two chairs. The wall behind the counter held all kinds of candles in different colours and sizes.

"Lilli was an apothecary," Jack said in what he hoped was a gentle tone. "Everyone came to her first before going to a doctor in Strawsburg. She kept records of everything under the counter. Every family has their own binder, and each person has their own section in it. What she gave us, how much, if it helped. She always checked on us a day or two after to make sure we were getting better. Even if she told us to go to the doctor, she always came to make sure we were on the mend. She wasn't a fan of technology."

Everleigh knelt down behind the counter and pulled out a large wooden board. It had a flower of life grid burned into the wood and the same strange markings she had seen carved on things in the other rooms. "My grandmother was more than an apothecary."

"Yes, she was much more but—"

Everleigh walked past Jack, dropping the board on the table as she passed. She went to the door next to the large window, unlocked it, and went outside. She could now see where the second path went and followed it to a U-shaped driveway she hadn't noticed before. One end connected to the road and the other to the section of driveway where they had parked. She turned back toward the cottage to see Jack closing the door and walking towards her.

He had a leather-bound journal in his hands and an unreadable expression. "I was hoping you would read this before asking too many questions."

"What is it?" Everleigh asked.

"Lilli made me promise that if you did come here, I would show you around. I don't know why she picked me. This is one of her journals. The last one she wrote and the first one she wanted you to read. She made sure we all knew to leave it on the table for you." Jack was working hard to keep his voice steady, but it wasn't working, and he knew it.

Everleigh took the journal and held it to her chest.

"I will try and answer all your questions, but I think you should read it first. I don't know what she wrote in there, just that it was important to her. I understand if you want to go somewhere else for a bit. I can take you to my inn. You can have something to eat and stay there tonight if you want. Grayling is welcome to come too." Jack realized he was rambling but couldn't stop himself.

"Why not show me around the outside? Did I see a garden out back?" She really wasn't ready to go back inside yet, even though Grayling seemed perfectly at home.

"Sure, we can do that. Let's go around this way." Jack led the way around the bedroom side of the cottage. "This is the old well. I wouldn't drink from it. It hasn't been maintained and who knows what's growing down there. The plumbing inside works fine and there is access to the river just over here. Both are safe to drink from. The dock needs repair, which I'd be happy to do if you like. Lilli didn't use it."

From the well they followed another cobblestone path, just like the one at the front, to where a meter high stone wall encircled the garden. Jack pushed open the lovely wood gate and waited for her to enter.

A small greenhouse and a shed of equal size were in each corner of the garden with rows and rows of large healthy plants. Lavender, thyme, sage, bergamot, and many others were growing in the center. Everleigh knew most of them by sight or smell. Against the cottage wall, a bunch of large pots held different varieties of mint plants, which, considering how fast these plants spread, made perfect sense. Aside from where the plants grew, the garden walkways were all gravel to cut down on mud and the extra maintenance that grass required.

She took a quick look in the greenhouse and wasn't surprised to find it full of healthy plants as well. These, however, had been carefully chosen because they were all plants that would not survive being outside through the cold winter months. On the other side of the stone wall was a compost pile set off to the edge near the trees. The rest of the yard was an open lawn that extended down toward the river. It wasn't fast moving, but it was steady, and the rushes and grasses grew tall. A little dock poked out into the river, but it looked in rough shape just as Jack had said.

Jack had followed her down to the dock. "There's one last part of the garden I think you should see," he said with a smile. "Ready?"

"I guess so," Everligh said, wondering what surprises were coming next. They walked down another worn cobblestone path through a thick growth of well-trimmed trees that opened into a clearing. This time, a much higher iron fence greeted them with a heavy lock on the gate. Jack started to open it when Everleigh stopped him.

"Do you know what's in there?" It came out as more of a statement than she had meant it to be. A much larger greenhouse stood in the center with a large sign on the door that read, 'Everything in here will kill you!'

"I'm guessing this is where she kept the poisonous plants," Jack answered, trying to lighten what was for the second time becoming a rather tense moment in the tour.

"Why? Why would she have poisonous plants to begin with?" Everleigh had no intention of going inside until she had a better idea of what was in there. "Who else has a key to this?"

"As far as I know, I have the only other key. I assume she gave you hers along with her keys to the cottage." Jack smiled and closed the lock again giving it a tug to be sure. "I know what I'm doing in there. I was the only one she ever allowed in there with her. I've been caring for those plants on my own for a couple years. I don't know them all by name, but I do know how to care for them."

The first few drops of the long-threatening rain were finally starting to fall and the two hurried back to the cottage. They went in through the back door that opened into the kitchen.

Everleigh dropped down into one of the four wooden chairs and set the journal down. She noticed it was the same journal she had seen sitting there before they went into the shop. Jack must have grabbed it before joining her outside. She was also reminded of the part in her grandmother's letter which spoke of a journal sitting on the table.

Her head was swimming with questions. Jack sat quietly in the chair across from her, allowing her time to organize her thoughts. Finally, she gave up. "Tell me what to do, Jack. I just don't know where to start."

Jack's heart sunk. He could hear the uncertainty in her voice, and he didn't really know how to help. There was so much he wanted to tell her, but he didn't know how. "This is a lot and, if I'm honest, you've only just seen the surface. Why don't I help you bring in your things from the car? That is, if you want to stay here. You're welcome to a room at my inn for as long as you want it."

"No, I would like to stay here. You've done so much already. I can unload my car. I need to get Grayling set up first." She looked around but he was still curled up in the chair. "Is there a place I could get some food? For me I mean. Even just some fruit for the night?"

Jack looked at his watch and shook his head. "I do have an idea. Sera Mason, the girl that works with me, is a great cook and I think she's making Shepherd's Pie tonight. You can work on getting settled and I can bring dinner to you in a couple hours."

"That sounds like a lovely idea, Jack. Thank you." Everleigh was starting to feel a bit better.

The rain outside was falling harder now, so Jack helped her get her things into the cottage before he left. She watched him drive away before closing the door. She stood for a moment looking at the gray shawl hanging on the hook before opening one of her bags and hanging her gray hoodie on the hook next to it.

She went to the bedroom and opened the closet. All her grandmother's clothes were there. She stepped backwards until she felt the bed behind her and sat down. Something crunched beneath her. It was a note:

Dear Everleigh,

I know this must be a hard time for you. I didn't feel right about taking Lilli's things out of the cottage. I laundered her clothes, and the pillows and bedding are brand new as our gift to you. Welcome to the Pond. I hope we get to meet soon.

Mia Millstone

Grayling hopped up on the bed next to her. He always had a way of knowing when she needed a cuddle. She scooped him up. "People here seem so nice, Gray. I haven't even met anyone other than Jack." The little cat meowed and enjoyed a few more pats before he jumped to the floor and walked out of the room.

Everleigh pulled out her clothes and laid them on the bed. Then she went to the closet and removed one item at a time, looking it over carefully before removing it from the hanger. She folded it and piled them up on the chair at the end of the bed. She hung her clothes on the hangers and put them away. Her suitcases she tucked under the bed. When she was done, she went back to the kitchen.

Grayling was sitting on the table with his front paws on the journal.

"How long have you been sitting there?" she asked. She picked up the little cat and the journal and carried both to the couch. She unwound the leather wrap, opened to the first page, and sighed. It was too dark to read. With the late hour and the cloud-filled sky, it had grown darker earlier than it should have.

There was a lamp on the desk in the corner and, to her genuine surprise, it was plugged in and working. With Grayling content to wander the cottage, she settled herself into the desk chair and opened the journal again, making a mental note to ask Jack if he knew where the outlets were around the cottage.

As she began to read, she realized the first pages were simply sitting on top. They were not actually part of the journal. It was a second letter.

Hello little one,

I guess I should start by saying welcome home, Everleigh. There is so much I wish I could have told you and, more importantly, taught you over the years. You were little more than a baby when your mother left the Pond.

It is my hope that you have met Jack by now. He has been a wonderful help to me over the years. I must ask you to trust him. There is a large greenhouse set away from the cottage. It houses my collection of poisonous plants: belladonna, nightshade, oleander, and the like. Jack understands them and knows how to care for them. As a favor to me, let him. I know you can do it yourself, but for now let him help.

Everything I have in the cottage, and outside, has a purpose, and through my journals it's my hope I can teach you everything you will need to know. As I have no way to predict what Jack may have already told you I'll start with the most basic.

To most of the village, I am an apothecary. They come to me before making the drive into Strawsburg to see the doctor. Most ailments - coughs, colds, headaches - can be cured by the herbs in the garden. There are binders under the counter in the shop. Each family has their own, alphabetical by last name. Everything I have provided them is noted, dated, and in great detail, as you'll see.

I am sure you have guessed by now, I am more than an apothecary. I am a Witch. I use magic, along with my knowledge and skills, to help others. Magic was in my blood, and it is also in yours. It is our birthright passed down from our grandmothers of old.

Each of my journals is numbered in the top corner of the first page. I'm almost certain I've left them in order for you. The first four are about my plants. One for each greenhouse and one for the garden and what grows wild in the forests around the village and where to find them. I also included what is grown on the farms, not always as useful, but good to know. The fourth is what I have found growing in the rivers, pond, and lake as well as in the well beside the cottage.

The rest are my recipes, all the blends, potions and spells that go with them. This journal is my Book of

Shadows. I want you to read through it first. It will help you understand all of my workings here in the village.

There is one more thing I would ask of you. Get to know the people who live here. Spend time at the Travelers Inn. Attend events at the Great Hall. The more involved you are, the more you'll see the beauty of the village and the people who call it home.

Love always, Lilli

CHAPTER 3

Everleigh sat staring at her grandmother's words. Did the village really think Lilli was a witch? Will they think I'm a witch? Is magic real? If it is, am I a witch? The questions circled as she took out the loose papers, set them aside, and started flipping through the journals' pages. Alignments, guides, totems, elemental power, she wasn't sure what to make of it all.

It wasn't like she had never heard the words before. Bess studied magical lore and loved to talk about it with anyone who would listen. Suddenly she wished she had paid more attention.

There was a crash from the other side of the room and a yowl from Grayling, who ran across the floor and stopped under the couch. Everleigh walked to the bookcase he had jumped from.

"Really, Gray?" She found an upturned bowl and Burdock berries scattered around the floor. She pushed up her sleeves and scooped them back into the bowl. "Come here, silly kitty," she laughed. "Let's get those out of your fur before they get too tangled. Burdock isn't a good toy for cats."

She sat on the floor with the wiggling cat, trying to carefully remove all the small, barbed berries tangled in his fur, grateful he was a short-haired cat. When she had them all out, she let him go. He immediately hopped up onto a chair and began to groom his fur back into place.

Everleigh put a second empty bowl over the one full of Burdock and went back to the desk. The quiet of the cottage being broken so suddenly had made her jump and knock the journal to the floor. As she picked up the journal, more loose pages, which had been folded in half, and tucked into the journal, slid out. She picked them up and opened them finding another letter.

My dearest little one,

> *It is my hope that reading this has given you a better understanding of my life's work here in Mallard Pond. The choice to carry on where I have left off is one you have to make for yourself and not one you can make lightly, as I'm sure you now understand.*
>
> *There is one last thing I need to pass on to you. A second choice you will have to make. Unfortunately, there is no way to know when you will have to make it.*
>
> *Near the pond, there is a large building, Eldaguard Hall. It is the oldest building in the valley. The village has grown around it. The whole of the valley is a sanctuary for the Darkvale Warriors, but the Hall is the most sacred. The Warriors are defenders for all that is good in this*

world. They are the protectors of magic. They will ask for your help as they did mine. This is the decision that your mother couldn't live with.

By agreeing to help them, there was a chance, a very remote chance, that I was putting my life and that of my family in jeopardy. As I became more involved in their efforts, your mother felt I was being reckless. She refused to be part of it, and when you came along, she moved you and your father far away from me and the danger she perceived. I don't blame her for wanting to protect you, and you shouldn't either.

For my part, I helped by providing potions for various things. To ward off infections if they were injured, to ease the symptoms of poisons until they were able to find help, I gave them vials to take with them and I cared for them upon their return. I did what I could to aid in their cause because I believed in it. In time, I asked them to build the green house away from the cottage and began growing the poisons plants. I created poisons for them but there are other uses for them, as you will learn.

They will ask for your help, but the choice will be yours. Do only what you are comfortable with, and they will respect you, whatever choice you make. I know as you get to know them, what they do, and why they do it, as I did, you will want to help them.

My dearest Everleigh, you know everything you need to know to start. Use the journals I wrote for you and the record binders in the shop. Learn as you go, and you'll be fine.

I had a single regret in my long life. I was not able to teach you these things in person and for that I am truly sorry. I want you to know I was always proud of you.

All my love, Lilli

Everleigh sat slumped in the chair with Grayling winding himself around her legs. She set the second letter on the desk with the first one and went back to the couch. She took the top off the black box, picked out the photo, and leaned it against the box.

Grayling had curled up on her lap and was purring against her chest. "This is so much more then I could have imagined. Why couldn't Mom have just told me something, anything?"

The headlights from Jack's truck lit up the room for a second. Everleigh went to the door and waited for the sound of the truck door closing before opening the cottage door for him.

"Hey, I'm back. Did you miss me?" Jack laughed, but quickly changed his tone. "What's wrong? Did something happen?"

"No, nothing happened. I was just reading." She closed the door behind him and followed him to the table. "Wait. What did you think could have happened?"

"Nothing, you just seem...distracted." Jack smiled. "I hope you don't mind but I brought some for me too.

I thought we could eat together. If you don't mind of course."

"Of course, I don't mind, Jack. You're always welcome here." She went to the cupboards to retrieve plates and cutlery from the exact places Jack said they would be. As she reached for them, she caught a glimpse of her tear-stained face in the reflection of the fridge door.

She hadn't realized she'd been crying but, at the same time, wasn't surprised. She set the plates on the table and excused herself to freshen up. When she returned, there was a lovely meal set with candlelight.

"It's a little more romantic then I intended, but we have limited lighting choices." Jack smiled and pulled out her chair.

"It's lovely, Jack." Everleigh smiled and took her seat.

While they ate, they shared stories. Everleigh told him about her Little Flower Shop, her apartment, and her mother. Jack told her stories about following Lilli around looking for plants he had no way to identify himself.

"There is something I want to ask you about," Everleigh said when the conversation had died off. "Can you tell me anything about Eldaguard Hall or the Darkvale Warriors?"

The question hung heavy in the air, and she noticed for the first time Jack was having trouble looking at her.

"You're a fast reader. I thought we would have had more time to get to know each other, maybe meet some of the people who live here before we went there." Jack's voice was deeper than it had been. He reached into his jeans pocket and pulled something out that he held so carefully it could have been made of glass. "I guess since you know, there's no point in hiding it." He extended his hand and in his palm was a ring.

Everleigh took it and Jack's smile returned. It was a silver ring with detailed engravings around the band. On top was a blue stone that seemed to sparkle from within. It seemed lighter than a ring that size should be.

"This is a Darkvale Brotherhood ring. They are given to us by the Elders in our Brotherhood when we complete our training." Jack took the ring back and slipped it onto the ring finger of his right hand.

"I should tell you; I didn't read the whole journal. It fell on the floor and a letter fell out. I read it before I realized it was meant to be read after the journal." Everleigh sighed. "So, I guess you're one of them? A Darkvale Warrior I mean?"

"Yes, for five years. Maybe it's good you know at least a little about us." Jack smiled. "It makes me feel better not having to hide my ring to avoid questions. I can't help but notice you're not packing up and running for the door."

"No, I'm not going to do that. I want to know more about everything. There's more going on here than I can imagine, and I understand why Lilli wanted me to learn about it in a certain order." Everleigh collected their plates and took them to the sink to wash. She started the water and turned back to Jack. "I know you can't be here to help me all the time and Lilli said I should get involved and meet people. Would you mind if I study some of this stuff at the inn?"

"I think that's a wonderful idea." Jack joined her at the sink and started drying the dishes she washed. "You can meet people as they come in and ask all the questions in the world."

They were almost done when they heard a truck pull up fast and stop suddenly on the gravel. Jack put down the tea towel and started for the door. Everleigh let him go. She could see the change in his demeanor and instinctively knew he was in protection mode.

As she finished cleaning up, she could hear the muffled argument outside. It was a man who had arrived, and it sounded like whatever he wanted, he wanted it now. She sat back down at the table but didn't have to wait long.

Jack came back in visibly shaken. He sat down across from her at the table wringing his hands. "Something you should know about us is that much of what we do is kept on a need-to-know basis until it's over. Who goes is decided by the Elders based on our strengths and what will be needed for success. Does that make sense?"

"It does. Can I ask? What are your skills?" Everleigh was genuinely curious.

"There will be time for that later. I promise I will tell you everything you want to know." Urgency was creeping into his voice that he had been trying to hold at bay. "Outside, that was Scott Mason. He was sent out with John. I don't know where or for what, but John is hurt. He was cut badly across his upper arm. I know you haven't even been here a day but..." He looked hopefully at her.

"Let's go!" Everleigh was on her feet and heading for her jacket. She put it on, grabbed her keys and locked the door. "He'll likely need something for pain and something for infection." She turned, heading for the shop, but suddenly froze, looked at Jack and asked, "I'm not going to be expected to stitch the wound, am I?"

"No of course not. That will be done already. But he is in a lot of pain."

Jack led the way into the shop and pulled a basket out from behind the counter to carry the jars Everleigh had started pulling off the shelves.

"Ready?" Jack asked, picking up the basket.

"I'll need something to bind the herbs to his wound with," Everleigh answered, still looking around.

"We have all that stuff at the Hall. Is there anything else?"

Everleigh took a quick look in the basket. Satisfied she had everything she may need, the two headed out the door to Jack's truck. He opened her door and passed her the basket.

The late hour made it impossible for her to see which roads he was taking. She could just make out the shapes of buildings as the headlights passed them.

"It certainly gets dark here." She hadn't meant to say it out loud.

"You'll find not many people wander out at night. Not because it isn't safe, but because we don't have streetlights, and porch lights don't reach very far." Jack's voice had calmed somewhat. "I have a table near the door in the inn just for lanterns and flashlights. People bring them when they know it will be a late night and they'll need to be walking home after dark."

They crossed a small bridge and pulled up to a huge stone building. Long, narrow windows ran vertically starting about halfway up the wall and almost to the roof line. In the dark, she couldn't tell how many there were.

They walked around to the front of the building where light was pouring out through stained glass making the path glow different colours. Solid wood doors, with heavy locks, stood open just enough for a sliver of light to escape. For a moment, Everleigh wished it was lighter out so she could see the markings on the doors better.

Jack knocked before pushing the door open. He was greeted by a young man, no more than maybe sixteen if Everleigh judged correctly. He had short, cropped, straw-blond hair and bright blue eyes. He looked to have been crying. His eyes were red and so were his cheeks, but he greeted Jack warmly.

"This is Everleigh Roberts. She's here to help your dad."

Before Jack could say more, the young man threw his arms around her. "Thank you so much! He's in so much pain, ma'am."

"All the more reason for us to hurry." Jack pulled Everleigh away from him. "Justin, why don't you go home to your mom and tell her what's happened." The young man nodded. "Someone will come around soon with an update."

Jack closed the door behind him and led Everleigh down a short hall to the left of the entry way. Jack was walking quickly, so there wasn't time to take a proper look around. He stopped suddenly in front of a door. They could hear muffled voices on the other side.

"Wait here a minute," Jack instructed, and Everleigh nodded, holding tight to the basket.

Until that moment, she hadn't felt nervous at all. She also hadn't stopped and thought about what she was doing or what these men expected of her. 'Don't start worrying now. This man needs you to keep it together,' she told herself.

The door opened and Jack smiled his most reassuring smile and waved her in. "There'll be time for introductions later. This is John Millstone." He indicated the man lying on the bed.

John smiled weakly at her. His brown eyes were ringed red, and every muscle looked like it was strained to its limits. His shoulder-length brown hair was matted and soaked with sweat. He was breathing hard, trying to manage the pain he was in.

"Hi, John, my name is Everleigh. I'm Lilli's granddaughter, but I bet you already knew that." As she hoped, he managed a smile. She set her basket on the bedside table and pulled out some of the jars. She looked up at the others in the room. "Would someone be so kind as to get me a glass of water and an empty glass? I will also need clean bandages."

She didn't have to wait long for the items to appear. She carefully measured the herbs, added them to the water, and mixed them. Letting it sit for a moment, she slowly and carefully unwrapped the bandages from his arm. John's sharp intake of breath told her they were stuck in the drying blood on his arm and it was going to hurt no matter how careful she was.

Like they knew what she was going to ask for next, a bowl of warm water appeared on the bed next to his wounded arm, a clean cloth beside it. She went back to the glass, took a small strainer from the basket, and poured the water through it into the empty glass.

"I know it's going to hurt, but I need you to sit up. This is going to dull the pain very quickly after you drink it." She smiled at him, and he smiled back trying to do as she asked.

Scott, who was standing next to him, helped him up. John's breathing became ragged with the effort but quickly calmed. He was holding his arm still, so Everleigh put the glass to his lips and slowly poured a little at a time until it was gone.

Scott helped him back down again and returned to where he had been watching from. She noticed for the first time that there was an older man sitting in a chair watching but didn't give him much thought.

"It was sweet," John said after catching his breath again. "Lilli's was always very bitter."

For a second, she worried she hadn't made it right, but she could tell by the relaxing of his muscles it was working. "I added a little honey. You're in enough pain." She smiled. "Now I'm going to try soaking the bandages before I pull them off, but it will hurt."

"No worries. You do what you need to do to patch me up." John was strong and hid the pain well. He tried to stay as still as possible for her. Everleigh had the feeling this was not the first time he'd been through this sort of thing.

Once she got the soaked bandage off, Jack took it and tossed it into a large bin. The wound bled less than she had expected. It had been cleaned and stitched by someone who knew what they were doing. She went to work, mixing the contents from a few other jars into a paste, applied it to the wound, and wrapped it back up in the clean bandages.

John was breathing normally again but he was wide awake. "Would you like something to help you sleep?" she asked him, and he nodded.

She mixed the contents of a couple jars and handed the tiny bowl to Jack. "Mix this with hot water and we will have a sweet-tasting sleep draught." Jack was out the door before she could thank him.

John thanked her as she packed her jars back into the basket. She held up a half-full jar of yellow and green herbs. "This is for tomorrow. Add a spoonful to hot water to make a tea. It will help you heal and ward off any infections. It will also hurt, so I added a little extra kick." She winked at him and sat the jar on the bedside table.

Jack returned with the tea and again Scott helped him to sit up so he could drink it. John drank gratefully and slumped back down into the bed.

Everleigh finished packing up and the little group moved out into the hall so John could rest. The older man sent Scott to talk to Mia and Justin. "Tell them he will be fine and likely home before midday," to which Scott inclined his head and left.

"Lovely work, Everleigh Roberts, granddaughter of Lilli Miller," the old man said very officially. "You know more than I expected you to."

She wasn't sure how to take that, but she thanked him anyway. Neatly combed white hair and an equally trimmed white beard made her wonder if this was one of the elders Jack had mentioned earlier. His sky-blue eyes were fixed on her, but she didn't feel uncomfortable.

Jack stepped closer. "This is Marcus, one of the Darkvale Elders." He inclined his head and stepped back.

"Yes, of course I am. I do apologize, my dear, I forget things, you see, age creeping in and all that." He walked to the alcove at the end of the hall and sat down. "Come sit with me a moment. Jack, you go talk to the others in the Hall. They'll be waiting for news."

Jack was hesitant to leave them but did as he was asked. Everleigh sat down and set the basket at her feet.

"Less than a day and you're in Eldaguard already." He smiled. "Your grandmother held out for almost a year before she agreed to join us in here. She wasn't one of us in the strictest sense, of course. She didn't train or go out on official business, but she did take care of the lads when they came back. No matter what shape they were in, Lilli looked after them."

Everleigh let Marcus continue his rambling. Some of what he was saying made sense, while other parts led her to more questions than she already had. When Jack returned, she wondered if she looked as tired as he did. There were two other older men following him.

"This is Everleigh," he said as the three reached the alcove. "Everleigh these are the other two Darkvale Elders, Tom and Carl."

"It's nice to meet you." Tom spoke first, extending his hand. Everleigh stood to shake it. "The last time I saw you, you were little more than a baby."

Tom was a tall man. The top of his head was bald and the hair circling it was trying desperately to hold on to the chestnut tone it once had. His eyes were a soft brown and Everleigh noticed he was missing the fingers, from tip to knuckle, on his right hand.

Carl was slower to join them, as he walked with a noticeable limp. He, too, was older with graying brown hair. His eyes were such a soft blue they were almost gray.

"Yes, welcome back, young lady. I hope we will be able to welcome you into our Hall as we did your grandmother." Carl had a soft voice but there was an edge of seriousness to it.

"One step at a time, Carl. We need to allow her time to get settled." Marcus rose and the three men inclined their heads. He held out his arm to Everleigh and she linked her arm with his. Together they walked back to the heavy wood doors in the entry way.

"Jack will see you home my dear and we will talk later. Once you've had a proper tour in daylight, of our village." Marcus stopped and Tom stepped up beside him. The two continued to walk towards another set of doors that led further into the Hall.

Jack, basket in one hand, opened the big door for Everleigh to walk through. It had begun raining again so she ran to his truck and hopped in. Jack was right behind her. He passed her the basket and closed the door.

He hopped up in the driver's seat. "This has been quite a day for you, I imagine."

She could tell he really didn't know what to say, and in truth, she didn't either. A quick look at her watch and said, "I don't suppose the Inn is still open for a drink?"

Jack put the truck in gear and smiled. "I think I can get us in. I know the owner."

Everleigh sat quietly trying to process the day. It wasn't a long drive to the Traveler's Inn, but the rain was coming down harder. Jack told her to wait in the truck until he got the door open. "The key sticks sometimes. I've been meaning to fix it."

Once inside, he took her jacket and hung it up with his on the hook next to the door. "Have a seat and I'll get the drinks."

Everleigh sat down at a table next to what she imagined had been a large, crackling fire earlier in the evening. Most of the lights were off, so it was hard to see to the far end of the room. She could see lots of round tables down the center and rectangular ones along the walls. The bar was about half as long as the room with lots of stools for people to sit. Stone walls reached up to tabletop height. Drywall rose to the ceiling, where she could just make out wood beams.

Jack returned with two pints, and they sat sipping at them for a long time in silence. A large clock, by the sound of it, chimed twice: 2:00am.

"What is this place?" Everleigh asked a little louder than she meant to. "You can only find it if you already know where it is? I wasn't sure what you meant by Darkvale Warriors, but it sure wasn't men limping and missing fingers. And John! That cut is deep and was stitched by a pro. Couldn't have been a doctor or he would have had a painkiller and antibiotics. That's not even the half of it! I have a green house full of poisonous plants and that building has more weapons on the walls then a museum."

Jack sat drinking his pint, allowing her to get it out without interruption. He had to admit this had been a day of surprises for her.

"It's a lot to get your head around all at once. I get that. I really do. I see Marcus told you a few things out of turn but, if I may say, you handled yourself better than I expected." Jack waited until she looked at him. "Would you like me to try and explain this place?"

Everleigh nodded, as she didn't trust her voice not to betray her.

"Well, I guess I'll start at the road. It's narrow and meant to look like a field road for tractors. It's sort of our first line. Most people drive by and don't even see it, or they ignore it. For anyone who does come down uninvited, at the first bridge there's a barrier spell. It encircles the whole valley. Around the top of the bowl, as Lilli liked to call it. It makes people want to turn around and go back the way they came, whether they are driving or walking. That's why the road is so wide right there. No one has come into the village without knowing the phrase that clears the distraction from their mind."

"The way is clear," Everleigh said. "That was in her letter to me. It even said to say it out loud and that it would help me find my way."

Jack gave her a half smile. "That sounds like Lilli. Telling you a tiny bit of what you need to know and letting you figure out the rest. That's sort of how she worked. We trusted her. No one needed to know the ins and outs of everything she did because she took care of it." Jack was staring into the dying fire. "I guess we ignored that she was getting older. I know I never thought about what it would be like without her here."

The fire cracked loudly and made them both jump. "You know, Everleigh, I'm sorry for how this day turned out. Lilli wanted you to take it slow, and here you've been dumped into so much, without any warning or preparation." Jack finished his pint. "I can't imagine what must be going through your head right now."

"I'm too tired to think right now, but there is one last thing I'd like to know." Everleigh finished her pint. "Is what Lilli did here important? And if it is, why did she not just train someone here? There had to be someone willing to learn from her."

"Lilli didn't want someone; she wanted you." Jack's voice took on a low tone, reliving a memory he would rather forget. "There were others she tried to teach, but no one measured up. The one she thought might didn't want to live a life so isolated, so she left. The day I picked her up from her first visit with you, she was happier than I'd seen her in a long while. At first, I thought it was just seeing you, and that was a big part of it, but she saw in you what she didn't see in anyone else."

"Are you saying I'm magical? That magic is real?"

"I'm saying did you notice how fast John's pain went away when you gave him that drink you made? There is nothing I am aware of that works that fast. And before you ask, no he didn't have anything before that. Tom is the one who stitched his arm. Before he joined Darkvale, he was a field medic; that's why he knows what he's doing." Jack said softly.

"You mean he stitched his arm with without anything for the pain?" Everleigh said a little shocked.

Jack nodded in reply. "I don't understand how or why magic works; I just know that it does, and I saw it tonight working through you." Jack offered her another drink, but she declined. He took the glasses back to the bar and leaned heavily on it.

"Eldaguard isn't magical, and neither are the warriors that train here. In our long history, we never have been. This valley is a safe haven because women like Lilli, like you, who carry magic in their blood, have made it so."

"Are there other places like Eldaguard?" Everleigh desperately wanted to know but was starting to have trouble focusing her thoughts. It was late and she was too tired.

"There are. Some have magical protections, others do not." He yawned and saw her do the same. "Maybe we should call it a night. I'll take you home and we can pick it up tomorrow. I have to go back to Strawsburg. One of the orders wasn't ready. You could come with me, and we can hit up the grocery store and anywhere else you need."

Everleigh stood up and stretched. "I'd like that, but not too early, right?"

Jack helped her into her jacket. "No, I was thinking around 1 o'clock or so. I don't know about you, but I think I'll be sleeping in."

"I like that idea." She smiled and they walked back out to the truck. The rain had stopped long enough, she hoped, for Jack to get home.

Everleigh walked into the cottage grateful she had forgotten to turn the desk lamp off. It was the only light in the cottage other than the bathroom. She used the light on her phone to navigate her way to the table, where she set down the basket.

"Grayling! Grayling?" She couldn't see the little cat anywhere. She turned off the lamp and walked to the bedroom, happy she had taken the time to hang up her clothes. She knew exactly where to get her PJs.

She curled up in bed and turned off her phone light. Every part of her body was tired. Grayling jumped up next to her and curled up between her arm and side, his usual sleeping spot. Everleigh was sleeping in no time as the rain began falling heavily again.

CHAPTER 4

Morning came far earlier than Everleigh had hoped, but Grayling was demanding to be fed and refusing to be ignored. She got up, still tired and aching from the late night and lack of sleep. However, she had a lovely garden of plants that she knew would help her feel better.

With Grayling happily eating, she went out to the garden. The day was warm and the garden being in direct sunlight was almost dry. She meant to only be a minute, enough time to grab something to make a tea for her headache, but several hours later she was very dirty and feeling much better.

"So, this is where you're hiding." Jack came around the corner. "I was coming to see if you were ready to go into town, but it seems you've found something else to do today." He sat down on the gravel near where she was working.

"Time gets away from me when I'm surrounded by plants." Everleigh sat back and tried to brush the dirt from her hands. "I can be ready in a few minutes."

"Actually, I called the store, and the order is delayed another day. Something about mechanical trouble with the truck, so they're going to move the order to a new truck. Should arrive late in the day, but they need time to unpack and sort through it. Have it ready first thing in the morning, from what I'm told." Jack had begun pulling weeds as he talked. He heard Everleigh trying to stifle a giggle and looked up. "What's so funny?"

"Nothing," she said as she smiled. "I've never met anyone who couldn't resist pulling a weed or two."

Jack looked down at his hands and smiled. He tossed the weeds into the pile she had made.

"Jack, would you take me into the greenhouse?"

He knew the one she was referring to and nodded. "Been doing a little reading, have you?"

"I have. I'll get the journal and be right back."

Everleigh got up, collected her pile of weeds, and added them to the almost-full basket on the other side of the stone wall. She went inside, cleaned up, and found the journal that described each plant she would find inside what she had dubbed the "killer greenhouse."

She returned outside to find Jack leaning against the wall with a little gray cat standing with his back paws on his shoulder, front paws his chest, and rubbing his face against Jack's purring happily.

When Jack saw her, he walked the little cat to the door and put him down on the floor. "I think I made a new friend." He was smiling when he looked at Everleigh. "Another new friend." He extended his arm to her. "Shall we?"

Everleigh smiled back, closed the door, and accepted his arm. "Yes, we shall."

They walked the old cobblestone path through the trees to the clearing where the killer greenhouse was. Jack opened the heavy lock, waited until she passed him, and locked it again from the inside, exactly as described in the journal's first few pages. This was not a place to be taken lightly.

Everything listed in the journal was there and exactly where the journal said it was located. There were large, healthy plants filling the shelves around the walls. A coat rack held everything she needed to handle the plans. A heavy apron, with a set of thick, rubber-grip gloves, was tucked into the front pocket and a face shield hung on each of the two hooks. Everleigh took the shorter apron leaving the longer for Jack.

Next to the rack, there was a large worktable with a full set of hand tools for repotting, pruning and taking cuttings. The journal was very clear that the tools not be removed unless they needed to be replaced or repaired. There was also a set of instructions on how to clean the tools before letting anyone else handle them.

Everleigh placed the journal on the table and opened it to the first plant. She read the description and, without looking at the part about where she would find it, started looking for it herself. She wanted to learn to identify each of the plants by sight, just like her grandmother. When she thought she found it, she double-checked the journal.

While Everleigh wandered between the journal and plants, Jack busied himself watering them. She was happy to see that he was careful, wearing the second set of safety gear. When he was finished, he took a seat on one of the two bar stools at the worktable and watched her.

A few minutes later she closed the journal and sat down next to him, taking off her face shield. "Wow, there's a lot of detail in this journal, and from what I can tell it's all dead-on. She must have spent hours out here."

"Not unlike you." He smiled, showing her his watch. "There is one thing I would like to ask of you. I don't know if Lilli mentioned it in the journal or not, but she never ever came out here alone."

"I'm sorry I've kept you so long. It's sort of becoming a habit, taking up your time. She didn't mention anything about coming out here alone." Everleigh wasn't sure if he was angry about the time, but his voice had become very serious.

"I didn't mean it the way it sounded. I'm happy to spend all day out here with you if you want." His voice softened as he continued. "I just meant that if you came out here and something happened, how would we know? Lilli always told me when she needed to come out here. If I wasn't around, she would ask someone else. They would wait outside the door with the key to unlock the gate. She told them how long she would be and if she didn't come back out by that time, they were to knock to make sure she was alright."

"Or go for help." Everleigh knew where he was going with this. "I'll do that, too. It's a good idea. Would you like to be my first call?"

"I would like that."

"Well then, first call, what do you say we get out of here?" Everleigh picked up the journal.

They hung their gear back on the rack and walked out the way they had come in. Jack locked the door and gate as they passed and double checked each was locked tight. They walked to the front of the cottage where Jack's truck was parked.

"Thank you for coming by." Everleigh smiled, holding the journal to her chest.

"It's my pleasure to help out." Jack got into his truck and rolled down the window. "You should come to the Inn tonight. Sera set up a quiz night. Half the village usually turns up for it and you can get a good meal. I could come around and get you if you like?"

"That sounds like fun. I'll be there, but I think I'll drive myself. Have to start finding my way around here."

Jack smiled and nodded.

It was late in the afternoon, so she had a snack from what she had brought with her and settled on the couch with another of her grandmother's journals. Her phone rang.

"Hi, Mom, how are you?" She tried to sound pleasant. She had hoped it would take longer for her mother to start calling.

"Why haven't you replied to my texts? I've been worried!" Her voice sounded more worried than it should have.

"It's only been three days and I'm fine. How are you? Is everything ok?" Her mother had never worried about her before.

"Yes, everything's fine. When are you coming home?" Her voice had gone from worried to angry very quickly.

"I planned for three months off, and I intend to take it. I'm only three days in." Everleigh tried to match her tone. "We talked about this before I left."

"I told you I thought it was a bad idea. I want you home!" Her voice was becoming demanding.

"Stop it, Mom! I'm staying here and that's that. Is there anything else you would like to yell at me about?" Everleigh could feel her heart pounding and started taking deep breaths to calm down.

"What are you doing there?" her mother asked.

Everleigh made an effort to try and remain calm. "I'm going through Grandma Lilli's things."

"What? Why are you going through them? You should be throwing it all away—"

"Goodbye, Mom." Everleigh hung up her phone.

She was tired and her head was starting to hurt again. Her phone rang again. She looked at the name, and ignored the call, setting it to silent. She thought about going to the garden for some peppermint leaves. Remembering what happened that morning, she went for a glass of water and her headache pills instead.

She went to the bedroom to lie down, and Grayling jumped up, curling in next to her. Everleigh stroked his soft fur and fell asleep.

* * *

When she woke up, it was dark outside, very dark, and someone was knocking on her door. She turned on her phone light and saw 29 messages, but she ignored them and went to the door.

"Miss Everleigh, you are here. Jack sent me over. He was afraid you got lost on your way to the Inn." Justin was smiling and wringing his hat in his hands.

"Come in, Justin." She closed the door behind him. "I fell asleep. Am I late for quiz night?"

"You are. That's why Jack sent me. I think he's worried about you." Justin's face turned red, and he quickly added, "But that's not my place to say, Miss."

"It's ok. I won't tell you said so. I'm going to quickly change. Would you feed Grayling for me? There's a tin of cat food on the counter and here's his dish."

"I can do that, Miss." Justin took the dish and went to the counter.

Everleigh went to her bedroom, closed the door, and shouted out to him. "How's your dad today?"

"He's well, Miss, thanks to you. Ma won't let him come out tonight. He wanted to, so he could thank you himself, but Ma insisted he rest." Justin popped the top off the can and noticed he was being watched by two little green eyes behind the bread box.

He put the dish back on the mat next to the water dish and looked back at the counter. The eyes were gone.

"Good kitty. Gray, I'll be back later." Everleigh patted his head and looked at Justin. "Are you alright?"

"Yes, I am. You only have one cat, right?" He was sounding nervous again.

"It's just Grayling." She laughed. "He moves very fast when he wants to and he's very quiet."

Justin smiled back and they walked out to her car. He gave her directions to the Inn. It wasn't as far from her cottage as she thought. It would have been an easy walk if she weren't late.

They parked next to the Inn. On the way to the door, Everleigh stopped. "There is just one more thing I would like to ask of you, Justin."

"Anything I can do to help, Miss Everleigh."

"Call me Everleigh. Miss makes me feel like a teacher." She smiled. Justin smiled back and held the door for her.

The Inn was loud with laughter and conversation. There was a large, crackling fire in the hearth with bright electric lanterns mounted around the walls keeping the feel of the old building.

Justin went to the bar and spoke to someone who rang a loud bell; the room fell silent.

"We're going to start the quiz in a few minutes," Sear shouted.

"Everleigh, come join us. We need a fourth for the quiz." At a table near the fire sat the three Elders, Marcus, Tom, and Carl, each with an empty pint glass and bowl in front of him. "With someone else on our team, we may have a chance at not being in last place all night this time." Carl and Tom laughed.

"I would be happy to join you in a moment. I just need to say hi to Jack." Everleigh inclined her head and made her way to the bar.

Jack was busy refilling glasses and laughing with the people at the bar. He saw her watching him and called to Sera to come out.

"Come with me to the back." Jack took her hand, and they went into the kitchen. "Is everything alright? I thought you would be here earlier."

"I lay down for a bit and I guess I overslept. That smells amazing!" She hadn't realized until that moment how hungry she was. "Am I too late for something to eat?"

"Of course not. Sera kept a bowl for you. Have you found a place to sit?" Jack went about getting her stew.

"The Elders ask me to join them."

Jack almost dropped the bowl. "The Elders?"

"Marcus said they want to do better in the quiz." She wasn't sure why Jack seemed so surprised.

"The only thing is, don't call them Elders. Use their names. Titles are only used within the walls of Eldaguard. Same with any questions relating to the Hall or Warriors." Jack smiled and tried to be reassuring. "They come to have fun, but their kind of fun is usually limited to drinking. You're going to be doing the work tonight, I'm afraid. Go join them; I'll bring the stew out to you."

Everleigh went back to their table and sat in the empty chair between Carl and Marcus. She noticed the bowls were gone and there were now three empty glasses and three half-full glasses sitting on the table. She wasn't sure if these were the same glasses that were there when she came in but assumed in all likelihood they weren't.

"Well, gentlemen, how does the quiz work? I never played games like this."

"There you are." Carl clapped her shoulder. "You take this notepad, and we tell you what to write. You write it down and show it to the lad Justin there. He has a look, gives us a point, and we win."

"I thought you said you lost most of the time." Everleigh was slightly confused.

Tom laughed. "We know the answers, but we're a few pints in and we can't write them down."

The three men laughed out loud like that was the funniest thing they had ever heard.

"See what I mean?" Jack set a bowl of beef stew and glass of Coke on the table. "Good luck tonight."

"Jack! Just in time. My glass seems to have a hole in it," Tom announced, to another round of laughter.

Jack collected as many glasses as he could carry. "Back in a moment, gents."

The quiz started, and true to their word, they did know many of the answers. But as the pint count rose, Everleigh found them less and less helpful. With a second-place finish, the prize was a round of pints on the house. To the three men, that was a better prize than the large basket of home-baked cookies, muffins, and other goodies that the first-place team received.

The Inn began to empty, and many people stopped to wish the three men good night. They also introduced themselves to Everleigh and said things like, "We're glad to have you here" and, "We should have you to dinner soon."

Jack and Scott joined them at the table as Marcus put his hand on Everleigh's shoulder. "Would you stay and have a chat with an old man?" he asked.

"Would be a pleasure, sir." Everleigh smiled back at him.

Jack and Scott helped Tom and Carl get to their feet and up the stairs to their rooms.

"How do you like it here?" Marcus asked.

"I do really like it. It's a slower pace and everyone has been so welcoming. Not like the city at all." Everleigh surprised herself a little. The last few days had been anything but slow.

Marcus was quiet for a moment. "I really liked your grandmother. We used to sit and have long talks on the bench by the pond. It's a shame I knew her better than you." His voice drifted off. "Not right, not right at all."

Sera had returned and was busy picking up dishes from the now empty tables, taking them to the back.

"I feel like I am getting to know her through her journals and people's stories." Everleigh waited until he looked at her. "I'm sure you have a few."

"That I do, my dear, that I do." Marcus went on to tell her a few stories that had both of them laughing. "I am going to miss her, but I'm also looking forward to getting to know you. You are going to stay here, aren't you?"

"Yes I am." Everleigh sat back shocked by what she had just said. She hadn't even considered it and now she was agreeing just like that?

"Well, that is wonderful! I'll take your petition to the others first thing tomorrow and we'll have an answer for you in no time." He was on his feet and swaying badly.

"Jack, a little help out here!" she called. Everleigh knew she wasn't strong enough to hold the big man up if he started to fall.

Jack came running and took Marcus' arm. He smiled at her and walked him up to his room.

"Those three can be a handful on a night like this," Jack said when he returned. "That's why they stay here.

They live in private rooms on the upper floor in the Hall. That is, when they haven't had so much to drink.

"I was surprised by how much they know about what's going on in the world. I feel sort of disconnected not having a TV or internet," Everleigh admitted to Jack's genuine amusement.

"Most people do have both." He smiled and pointed to the large TV on the far wall. "I have a computer in the office. Sera and I use it for bookkeeping, placing orders, and the odd bit of poking around when it's not too busy in here."

Everleigh tilted her head and smiled. The large TV had been behind her, and she hadn't noticed it.

"That's where Sera got the questions for tonight. It was Lilli's choice to not have or use it." Jack smiled back.

"Just like the electrical outlets hidden behind bookcases," she sighed.

"She was old school. There's no doubt about that. I would also add that it doesn't mean you have to be." Jack wrote down the village Wi-Fi password and gave it to her. "Can I ask you what you said to make Marcus so happy?"

"He asked me if I was staying and I said yes," she replied, still a little surprised by it herself. "He mentioned something about taking my petition to the others. Do you know what that means?"

"You've been here three days and you've decided to stay!" Jack couldn't hide the surprise in his voice, but she nodded back. "You have to petition the Elders for permission to move here. It's not just the Hall that's protected, but the whole village. We must petition before we bring anyone to live here or even visit. It's a deep dive into who you are and who you know."

"So, they could toss me out?" She tried to sound worried, but Jack saw through it.

"We both know that's not going to happen. If you really are serious about staying, they will pass it in a flash."

Jack walked Everleigh out to her car and asked her to text him when she got to the cottage. "It's dark and the first time you're driving in the village alone."

"You think I'll get lost?" she answered teasingly.

"No of course not," he replied innocently. "But it is a possibility."

They both laughed, said goodnight, and she drove to the cottage. When she got there, she sent Jack a text and got a smiley face back with, 'I'll pick you up in the morning and we'll go to Strawsburg'.

She sent back a smile and 'can't wait'.

Everleigh sat for a moment longer before going inside. She used her phone light to see her way to the desk and turned on the lamp. Grayling hopped up and meowed.

"Hello, buddy." She patted the little cat. "Tell me something. How did grandma live here with only two lights?"

She sat down on the couch with Grayling in her lap. "What do you think about staying here, Gray? Three days and, without thought, I agreed."

She looked at her phone again. The messages from her mother were piling up. Most of them were the same 'don't ignore me' and 'get your butt home'.

There were so many questions swirling around in her head. How do I tell Mom I'm moving here? What am I going to do about the shop? How do I move my stuff? What do I do with Grandma's stuff?

It was all happening too fast. With Grayling purring in her lap, she looked at her phone again. 'I need to charge this thing', she thought.

"It's the right decision, little one."

Everleigh's head popped up from her phone. "Grandma?" Seated in the chair to her left was an old woman in a blue dress and gray shawl.

"Now that's a name I've never had. You just call me Lilli." She smiled. "This village needs you or it won't survive. If the magic fails, it will be attacked and Eldaguard will fall. Many will die fighting to protect it, but it will fall in the end. You must cast the barrier spell before it snows. It's the only way to protect it."

"But I don't know how."

"When you're ready, the journal will find you, child. Follow the directions as I've laid them out and you'll know what to do."

Everleigh looked away for a moment but, when she looked back, Lilli was gone. The chair was empty, and she was alone with Grayling purring in her lap.

CHAPTER 5

Everleigh woke with a start that bounced the little cat to the floor. He turned and hissed at her before walking away tail flicking.

"I'm sorry, Gray," she said breathing heavily.

She looked at the chair and slowly closed her eyes again. This time when she opened them, they fell on the photo she had propped up against the box the night before and picked it up. "Are you helping me, Lilli?" she asked the image in the photo somewhat worried it may answer her back.

Everleigh looked at her phone. She had meant to charge it overnight, but it hadn't happened and now it was dead. The sun was up, but not too high, so she guessed it was still early. She walked over to the wall of memories, took down the empty frame and replaced the photo. "If you are helping me, thank you."

Everleigh set out some clean clothes and hopped in the shower. She left the bathroom wrapped in a towel and went to the kitchen to start the kettle while she dressed. She looked out the window and saw Jack in the back garden calling for her.

"Jack," she called opening the door just enough to talk to him and still hide behind it.

"You didn't answer your phone, or the door, so I thought you might be in the garden again." He smiled as he walked toward her.

"Sorry, I didn't hear you. I was in the shower." She smiled, trying to hide her embarrassment.

"No, I'm sorry. I'll wait by the truck."

When she walked out the front door, Jack was talking to a woman holding a jar.

"Mia, this is Everleigh Roberts." He smiled when he saw her walking over. "This is Mia Millstone, John's wife. She needs to talk to you before we go."

"I hate to bother you. I know you're on your way out, but it's John's arm. He says it really hurts." Mia looked as worried as she sounded. "He's in the car. Would you have a look?"

Everleigh agreed and walked over to the passenger side of the car. John was wearing a muscle shirt that showed off his well-toned chest nicely. "Good morning, John."

"Good morning." John smiled. "We really are going to have to meet sometime over a drink instead of wound."

"I would agree to that, but for now let's have a look." She stood in the opened car door and John shifted so his arm was easier to see. "It looks good to me. It's not showing signs of infection. You should get the stitches out. You're healing faster than they are dissolving. That's likely why it hurts."

"Can you take them out? I understand if you don't want to. The clinic in Strawsburg will be open later and Mia can—"

"No, I can do it for you. I took some out of my leg once. It hurt, but it felt a lot better when they were out. Come inside. I'll bind it again after." Everleigh smiled. She knew he would rather she do it than go into town.

She walked back to where Mia waited with Jack by the truck. "I'm going to pull the stitches out for him. Do you mind waiting, Jack?"

"Not at all." Jacked dropped the tailgate and sat down. "I'll be here." He took Everleigh's bag and set it beside him.

Mia joined John and Everleigh went to open the shop door and collect what she needed. A half-hour later the couple left, followed a few minutes later by Everleigh.

"Well?" Jack asked as she neared the truck.

"I wouldn't want to put them in, but taking them out isn't so bad."

Jack hopped down and handed her bag back. He opened her door, walked back and closed the tailgate, and they were off.

* * *

When they got to the second wooden bridge where the road narrowed, Everleigh asked him to stop for a second and he pulled the truck off to the grass.

"Is this where the barrier spell is laid?" The question hung in the air. "When does it start to snow here?"

She was looking out the window and didn't see Jack looking at her. "It won't start to snow until late November, but it's usually mid-December before it starts piling up."

"What happens if it isn't laid in time?" Her voice was starting to sound farther and farther away.

"The barrier creates a circle that protects the valley from the outside world and those who would destroy it, if they could find it." Jack spoke softly. "We've had magical protection for so long we're not prepared if it were to fail."

"Eldaguard would fall."

"In time, yes and we, the Warriors would fall defending it." Jack moved as close to her as his seatbelt allowed. Her breathing was very slow, and she wasn't blinking. "Come back, Everleigh."

As if waking from a trance, Everleigh slowly sat back in her seat and looked out over the hood of the truck. "I need to be here." Her voice was little more than a whisper.

"Everleigh?" Jack unhooked his seatbelt and move closer. He touched her hand and she jumped and stared wide eyed at him. "Good Lord, are you all right? You look like you've seen a ghost."

"I saw... No, I was there. I could feel the heat from the fires. I could hear the screams." She looked at Jack with terror-filled eyes. "Eldaguard, the village, everything was burning."

Jack hit the button on her seatbelt and took her in his arms. When she was calm, he reached for his phone and made a FaceTime call. "Hey, Martin, you wouldn't happen to be up at your barn by any chance?"

"Jack! Good to see you. Yes, I am at the barn. What can I do for you?"

"Could you turn your phone around so we can see the village? I know what I'm asking, and I promise I'll explain later. Everleigh needs to see the village." He could tell the old farmer was not sure about his request. "I'll buy the first round of drinks for you and the boys."

"Since it's you asking. Just don't go telling anyone about this." Martin turned his phone and gave them a panoramic view of the entire valley. Everything was as it should be. No fire, no one hurt, just a beautiful view of the valley.

Jack's arm was still around her shoulders. He could feel her breathing settle and she stopped shaking. He thanked Martin and put his phone away.

"It was so real," she said.

"But it wasn't. It was just a vision of—" He stopped himself short of saying it.

"Of what will happen if I don't lay the barrier spell." The panic was rising in her voice again. "I have to stay. I have to figure out how to place it."

Jack squeezed her tighter. "Yes, but right now you have to go shopping with me." He felt her laugh and rubbed her back. "We'll figure it out, together."

Everleigh sat back in her seat. "You're right. One thing at a time."

They put their seatbelts back on and Jack started down the road. The rest of the drive into town was very quiet. Everleigh was writing in a notebook she had pulled from her bag. Jack was curious as to what had claimed her attention so completely, but thought it better not to ask.

When they got to the first stop, a hardware store, Everleigh waited in the truck while they loaded the order Jack had been waiting for.

The second stop was the Burger Bar, where Everleigh insisted on paying for lunch.

Their last stop was the grocery store. Everleigh walked every aisle, with Jack pushing the cart behind her. They loaded everything in the back of the truck and climbed in the cab. "Ready to head home?" Jack asked.

Everleigh smiled. "I am."

She settled herself in the truck's soft bucket seats and tried to relax. She pulled out the notebook again and started reading over it, adding more notes as she went.

"Jack, do you know how I can move the stuff from my apartment?" She was tapping the pen on the notebook. "I don't imagine I can just call up a moving company."

"No, that wouldn't really work too well. Who knows where your stuff would end up once they got too close to the barrier?" He laughed. "I would bet there are few guys in town that would be willing to help. Once you're packed and ready, they can drive up one day and back the next. We could even rent a truck if we need to. Someone from the village would have to drive it, of course, but it could work. You really want this to happen fast?"

"It needs to be as fast as possible. If my mother finds out, let's just say I don't really know what she'll do. She didn't even want me coming here to visit." Everleigh told him everything on the drive home. About her mother, the fights over leaving, and about the dreams she started having about Lilli.

"Are you sure they are dreams?" Jack asked as they rolled to a stop in front of her cottage. "You could ask Marcus, but I think Lilli saw things sometimes. She didn't really talk to me about it but, if she said anything, it would have been to him."

"Maybe I'll do that. I think my brain's on overload today," she told him as she rubbed her forehead.

"Don't tell me that just started today." Jack laughed and they walked back to meet at the tailgate. "You haven't had the subtlest of welcomes to our little village."

"No, I guess not." Everleigh took a bag and started walking to the cottage to unlock the door. She stopped and turned back to Jack. "But you know, since I've been here, it's felt like home. I never felt like this in the city. I truly feel like this is where I've been meant to be all along."

"That is good to hear," Carl said, walking up the driveway to join them. "This, Miss Everleigh Roberts, is for you."

Everleigh took the paper and read it over. "It's the deed to the cottage with my name on it," she said a little shocked and looked up at Carl.

"It's all yours now." Carl smiled. "I'll be on my way. It looks like you two cleaned out the store." He nodded to the bags in the bed of Jack's truck and started back down the driveway.

She showed the paper to Jack. "The Elders are the only ones who can grant this permission. It's usually a long process of digging into everything about the person, but I guess for you they made an exception."

They took all the bags inside and, when they were done, walked back out to the truck.

"I'll leave you to it. I have to get this load out to the training yard." Jack closed the tailgate and his eyes. He knew what was coming next.

"Training yard? What's that?"

Jack smiled to himself. "You'll find out soon enough. Best get those groceries in the fridge." He jumped up in the truck before she could ask any more questions.

Everleigh laughed and waved goodbye before going inside to put things away.

With that job done, she started looking around the cottage. A little gray streak launched at her from the back of the chair. "Grayling, one day I'm not going to catch you in time." The little cat curled into her arms and started pawing at her hair.

"Where do we start, Gray?" she asked. "There is just so much in here. I would hate to get rid of something important."

She set the cat on the chair and went to the shelves along the wall. "First thing I need to do is find a place to charge my phone." With the shelves being so heavy, she gave up trying to move them and opted for the outlet under the desk.

"There, that's done. Now what's next, Gray?" She watched the little cat walk in to the bedroom, hop up on the bed, tilt his head and look at her. "Ok, buddy, the bedroom first."

She went through her grandmother's clothes again but, as Lilli had been shorter and a little more around the middle, the only item she decided to keep was her gray shawl, which she was going to leave on the hook by the door next to her jacket.

She moved the clothes and everything else she thought should be donated to the chair in the living room. In the end she had two big piles on each of the chairs, one of clothes, the other of things that she couldn't identify.

Everleigh chose one of the items, took a picture of it, and sent a text to Bess asking if she had any idea what the markings meant.

Grayling joined her on the couch. "Now we wait, buddy. If Bess can tell me what the markings are, maybe we can figure out a few of these things on our own."

Her phone rang. "Hi, Jack. Did you get that stuff where it needed to go?"

"Yes actually. I'm still here. We're starting to build it now and, before you ask, I'll show you when it's done. I wanted to ask you; how soon do you want to move? I mean officially, like get your stuff from the city and bring it here?"

"Sort of a strange way to put it, but I would say very," she said looking around the room at the ever-growing mess.

"I was talking to the guys here and they are all willing to help. That would be five pickups and strong men to help." Jack waited but there was no reply. "Are you still there, Everleigh?"

"Yes, I'm here." She took a deep breath. "When are we doing this?"

"Whenever you're ready. They just want to help, and I thought that would be one thing to check off in your notebook."

He was right about that. "Give me a couple days to keep going through things and I'll have a better idea then. Will you thank them for me?"

"Hang on, you're on speaker now."

"Hi, Everleigh, it's Steve. Would you like some boxes? I've got some from the order I picked up the other day.

They're in good shape. I can drop them by on my way home when we're done here."

"That would be great, Steve, thanks! And thank you all so much for offering to help." Steve and Jack both said goodbye.

Steve was right about the boxes. They were the perfect size to pack clothes in, with a bunch left over for other items as she worked her way around the cottage.

It was getting on to the dinner hour, and Everleigh was in the midst of making one of her favorites, when she heard the text message tone from her phone. Hoping it was Bess, she picked it up.

"Mom," she sighed. "What now?" She opened the app and read the message. Another argument as to why she should come home. Fighting the urge to tell her about her plan to move, she instead sent 'Tell me the real reason you want me home so badly or stop'.

There was also a message from Bess. 'I recognize the markings. They're called runes. They are written from the Nordic language. Very old. I can't read it, but I can translate it for you when I get home tonight.'

'Thanks that would be great,' she replied. She asked about the shop, and everything was going well. Orders were in and out on time and Jen loved the extra hours.

The shop. She hadn't considered what to do about the shop. "I can't run a flower shop from so far away," she told Grayling, who was watching carefully from the back of the chair every time she was near his tins of food.

Grayling was happy with his dinner and Everleigh sat down at the table for hers, with her notebook and her head swimming with things she would have to look into, though the larger looming question remained her mother.

There would be no easy way to tell her she was leaving London without the meltdown to beat all meltdowns her mother was going to throw. She was going to need time in the city, and it was all going to have to be done quickly.

"That's it!" Everleigh shouted out loud. She often wondered if she was the only one that spoke to their pet like a person. She grabbed her keys and almost ran to the Inn.

"Everleigh, I didn't know you were coming tonight." Jack came out from behind the bar to greet her.

"I wasn't planning on it, but I need to talk to you." She was looking around to see how many people were at the Inn but, compared to the night before, it was almost empty.

"Is this a private talk?" Jack asked watching her look around.

"Not private like has to be kept a secret. More like family drama type of private."

"Sure, right, because that makes perfect sense." Jack smiled and passed her a pint. "Sounds like you need this."

Everleigh laughed. She had to admit that even to her that had sounded stupid. She waited until he returned from delivering a tray of drinks.

"So, what's on your mind?" he asked taking the stool next to her.

"I was thinking. I'm going to need time in the city. I'll have to sell my shop and that may take time. Then there's Mom. She's not going to be happy about it and I'd rather not tell her right away." She showed him the dozens of new text messages her mother had sent.

"I haven't known you long, but I'd bet you have a plan," he said handing her phone back.

"I think I should go back alone. An army of trucks will draw too much attention too quickly. I'll pack up and get it all ready. Then when the shop is sold, I'll call you. The only thing I need is someone to feed Grayling while I'm gone."

Jack sat listening to her plan, nodding and smiling. When she finished, he stood up and took her hand leading her into a smaller side room with a table and six chairs. He pulled out a chair on the far side of the room for her and took a seat next to her where he could still see the group in the other room.

"Everleigh, you can't go alone." He could see her confusion and continued. "The same people who would see us and Eldaguard burn would take you as a prize for themselves."

"What does that mean?" Everleigh was getting frustrated with all the secrets.

"That means you are valuable. In broad terms, women like you, witches, seers, healers, whatever title you want to use, have always been sought after. When we, Darkvale, find them, we always give them the choice to join us or not. In exchange for their help, we offer our protection to them. If they choose not to, we honor that choice. We would, of course, help them if they were in trouble. The only choice the Balordran offer is to join willingly, by force, or die."

"You offer your protection as in my cottage?"

"Not just that." Jack was relieved. At least for the moment she wasn't asking about the Balordran. "When Lilli started coming to see you, Marcus felt you might be in danger. Especially if she was right and you were, as you are, a witch. Lilli was adamant that you be left alone. She said you would be safer if we didn't draw attention to you. Normally there would be a Warrior living nearby who would be charged with your safety, if you agreed, of course. But that meant you would have to be told, and I guess now I understand better why she wanted it that way."

"Why is it you always give me more questions than answers?" Everleigh asked with a sigh. "What exactly are you saying? You believe someone may come after me?"

"I don't want you to be fearful of leaving the valley. There is more that is safe than isn't. You just have to be smart about it." Jack smiled. "I want you to be aware that's all."

"I'll be careful." They got up and Everleigh gave him a hug.

"Talk to Justin," Jack said, sounding more worried than he had intended. "I bet he'll take care of Grayling for you. He's really good with animals."

Everleigh turned back to him and waited until he looked at her. "Would you go back with me?"

"Look, I didn't mean to frighten you. I honestly don't know what I was thinking." Jack was starting to feel embarrassed. "I know you'll be fine."

"Please come with me." Everleigh suddenly felt very uncomfortable with the idea of going by herself. "I want you to come with me. If we work together, I could get back here faster."

"There are a few things I'll need to take care of, and I'll need permission from the Elders to be away. We don't know for how long, and I'm guessing you want to leave tomorrow." Jack's smile had returned.

"I would like to, but maybe the end of the week would be better?" Everleigh couldn't get the vision of the valley burning out of her head. She wanted to get back so there would be lots of time to study the spell that made the barrier around the valley, and she had to find it first.

Jack reached out and took her hand again. "Can you stay for a while?"

Everleigh nodded and they walked back out to the main room. The group at the far table was leaving. They exchanged good nights and Jack locked the door behind them. They collected the glasses and took them to the kitchen.

"We can work together, and you can ask me whatever you want. Wash or dry?" Jack asked as they rounded the corner to the kitchen.

"I'll wash and you can put them away as we go." Everleigh smiled. "Now what should I ask you about? There's so much!"

"Why not start with Lilli?" The voice from behind them startled them both. "I am sorry I let myself in. The back door was open. I would like you to know why Lilli decided to stay here. Jack, if you would be so kind, could you fetch a chair for me? I find these stools too tippy."

"I can do that, Marcus." Jack did as he was requested.

"Everleigh, I want you to know what happened. You deserve the truth. You need to know why Amelia doesn't want you here. You two work and I'll tell you how I met Lilli." Marcus sat in the chair Jack set near the hearth and stretched out his legs.

Jack poured a coffee, and passed it to him, before joining Everleigh who had started washing the piled dishes.

"Back when I was a young man, four of us were sent to a plantation house in the middle of nowhere. It was a hold like Eldaguard, but for the Balordran. We were sent to find a relic, but we also found a young woman, a witch, chained to a wall by an iron collar around her neck."

A plate fell from Everleigh's hands, landing on the floor with a crash. Jack dropped his towel into her hands and steered her to a stool at the small table next to Marcus.

"I'm so sorry, Jack," she mumbled with a shaky voice before sitting down and handing the towel back.

"It's only a plate. I have plenty more." His voice was calm and reassuring.

"I'm sorry, my dear. Maybe this isn't the time to tell you this, but you should know."

"Please go on, Marcus," Everleigh pleaded.

"We freed her, and she asked if we could find her daughter. We separated. Two went looking for the relic, and my partner and I went after her little girl. She told us exactly where both would be, and she was right." Marcus looked into the fire. "We were on our way out when Amelia started screaming. Lilli picked her up and we ran for the gate. We fought our way through with Lilli's help. That's where I got this." He lifted his shirt revealing a large scar that stretched down below the belt of his faded trousers.

Everleigh sat with her eyes closed, fighting back the threatening tears. "Did the others make it back?"

"Yes. Though not without scars of their own. But we retrieved the relic and saved Lilli and little Amelia."

Jack joined them at the table. "Why was Amelia screaming?"

"She asked where we were going. Lilli told her they were leaving, and she didn't want to go. Lilli thought she would be a prisoner for life. She had no reason to think anything else. Her husband, your grandfather, was killed because he fought back when the Order came for her. They took Amelia in the hope she would be a witch too. Lilli told me that when they were together, the collar was taken off and they were in a locked room under guard. Amelia was taken out with the other children to play in the garden while Lilli was chained and forced to create whatever they demanded."

"Mom never saw what they were doing to her? How they treated her? All she knew was she was being taken from her home a second time." Everleigh's heart ached for her mother.

"Yes. She was happy here until she got older and met your father in Strawsburg. Our restrictions and rules were too much for her and she didn't understand their importance." Marcus took a long drink from his coffee. "It came to a head when you arrived. Your mother was determined you would have a better childhood then she had. A few months later you and she were gone, and we never saw you again."

"They just left. That was it?" Jack seemed genuinely surprised.

"I had a feeling there was more to it, but it was only a couple years ago that she told me what she had done." Marcus sat up in his chair and reached for Everleigh, who willingly took his hands. "Lilli did what she felt she had to do. She created some kind of potion, and the day your mother left, she slipped it to her somehow. That night when she went to sleep outside the valley, she forgot about Mallard Pond and her magic was gone."

"Did she do anything to Everleigh?" Jack's concern had him sitting straight up with fists clenched.

"Of course not, Jack. She was only a baby at the time." Marcus leaned back in his chair still looking at Jack. "I guess you were too. The two of you would have grown up together."

There was a knock on the door and Jack went to answer it.

"Everleigh, I loved your grandmother very much. We spent much of our time together. I often thought I should have married her when I had the chance."

"Why didn't you?" Everleigh smiled.

"I didn't think it was fair to tie her to someone who, one day, may not return. There is always a chance that when a Warrior leaves, he may not return, or he may return wounded and recover, but that isn't always the case." Marcus' voice was getting quieter.

"Why do I get the feeling this is turning into a warning?" Everleigh moved her stool closer to Marcus. "Do you think my mother would reconnect with the people she knew as a child?"

"I don't know. We are looking more carefully into it now. If she had, I have to believe Lilli would have known before she left you all her things, including the cottage and instructions on how to find us." He tilted his head, still smiling at her.

"Marcus! This is not what we agreed!" Tom was visibly angry.

"You mean it's not what you dictated to Carl and me. That is not how our Brotherhood handles decisions." There was a menacing tone to Marcus' voice that Everleigh would not have guessed him capable of.

She felt Jack's hands on her shoulders and his lips at her ear. "There is a staircase behind me. Go upstairs. First door on the right is my room. Lock the door behind you and stay there until I come up."

Immediately she did as he instructed. Taking a quick look back, she saw the two elders standing toe to toe with Jack at Marcus' shoulder. She reached the door, went in, and locked it.

The room was nice. There was a hearth with a table and comfortable looking chairs in front. A large wardrobe with the door open, full of clothes, and another closed with a lock on it. His bed was in the center of the far wall neatly made with light summer blankets.

She sat down in one of the chairs listening to the muffled voices from the kitchen below. It got very quiet for a moment, and she wondered if it was over.

"It's just me." She heard Jack call from the other side of the door before it swung open. "I need to get something." He crossed the room to the locked cabinet.

"What happened?" she asked seeing the urgency in his movements.

"I don't have time right now. I have to go to Eldaguard." He turned sword in hand and saw her eyes widen. He tied it around his waist and went to her. "Everything will be fine, but I would like you to stay here. I'll explain everything when I get back."

Everleigh agreed.

"I'm going to lock the doors downstairs. There's a washroom at the end of hall should you need it. If you get tired, you can lie down. I don't know how long I'll be." He hugged her tight. "If I had more time, I would take you home."

"It's alright. I'll be fine," Everleigh said as she hugged him back.

They stood a moment longer and he was gone. She sat back down in the chair. A quick look around told her he didn't spend a lot of time in his room. There were no books, no magazines, nothing.

She went back downstairs. It was only 8:30pm, but with the hill and the trees, the sun set far too early in the valley. There was still enough light to see men running in the direction of Eldaguard Hall, each of them armed.

Everleigh felt a knot in her stomach tightening as she watched. With so many armed men, she didn't want to imagine what was going to happen. She decided she needed to get her mind off it. She went to Jack's office, where she remembered he told her he had a computer. Luckily it wasn't password protected. She signed into her work email just to see if there was anything new.

Sure enough, there were a couple of inquiries. She answered them and added that she was on vacation and for further assistance to contact Bess or Jen and included their emails. Suddenly she felt the knot in her stomach again. How was she going to tell them she was selling the shop?

She had hired Bess a month after opening the shop and they had become very good friends. Jen was a university student who helped part time with larger orders for weddings or funerals, but she enjoyed it so much she asked for more time and both Everleigh and Bess agreed it would be a welcome help. This was not going to be easy for them.

Everleigh brought up the website. She had paid a fortune for the design, but it had been well worth it. Her first order had come in the same day the site went live. It was an anniversary bouquet. When he came to pick it up, she had explained it was her first order, so she added some extra flowers as a thank you. He was very grateful and had ordered from her regularly ever since.

"Funny the things you remember," she said out loud before remembering she was alone in the Travelers Inn, waiting for a sword-wearing Warrior to come and take her home.

Four days. That's how long it had taken. Four days and nothing in her life would be the same.

Everleigh pulled out her phone. There was a text from Bess. 'The runes in the picture say 'strength'. To use it, burn it like the sage bundle I gave you a while back.'

'I remember that bundle. Thanks so much,' she replied. She searched a few websites and emailed herself the addresses of a few she wanted to spend more time on.

After a few hours, she found her eyes were starting to feel heavy. She went back upstairs and turned on the bedside lamp. Jack's bed was softer than she expected, and she took her shoes off and lay down. Hoping he would be back soon, but with the soft lamp light behind her, she fell asleep quickly. Grayling was going to be pissed.

CHAPTER 6

When Everleigh woke up the in the morning, she found herself covered by a warm blanket. Jack had moved the chairs so he could put his feet up and was still sleeping, a blanket over his legs and his arms folded across his chest.

Everleigh folded the blanket back across the bed, slipped out of the room and down to the kitchen. She was setting the table when she heard him coming down the stairs.

"You've been busy this morning," he said with a smile.

"Good morning. I was just going to come up and get you," Everleigh greeted.

They sat down and ate quietly at the little table. She could see his knuckles were cut and bruised and he seemed to be having trouble chewing. A knock at the door made him turn his head, revealing a dark, purple bruise on his jaw under his ear.

He got up and walked slowly to the door.

"Good morning, Mr. Jack. Ma asked if I would check with you about when you needed Dad's help."

"Good morning, Justin. I'll have to let you know. I haven't had a chance to talk to Everleigh about it yet."

Justin nodded and Jack closed the door and returned to the table.

"Should I ask what happened?" Everleigh asked softly.

"No." Jack's answer was clear he was not going to talk about it.

"Are you alright?"

"We have a rule that, when these disagreements happen, we suffer with the pain. It's a reminder to us that we cannot allow disagreements to divide us," Jack said with a sigh as he lowered himself to the chair.

"Well then you sit there and let me clean up." Everleigh washed up the dishes and cleared everything away while Jack watched silently from the chair he had brought in for Marcus the night before. He was glad he had not taken the time to put it back.

Everleigh could see the pain he was in building, and she didn't want to leave him alone. However, she also knew Grayling would be starting to think she was going to let him starve to death.

"You stay there. I'll be right back." Jack was too tired to question her, and Everleigh took the stairs two at a time.

She dug through his wardrobe and found a soft pair of pants and t-shirt comfortable for sleeping in. She also took a set of clean clothes as he had come down in the same clothes from the day before. She tossed it all in a rucksack that was sitting next to the wardrobe. She picked up his shoes and keys and went back down.

"Put your shoes on. You're coming with me." She could tell he was going to say something, but she cut him off. "No arguments. You're coming home with me."

She went to the truck, opened the passenger door, and tossed the bag in the back. Jack was walking slowly, and she allowed him to take his time. She locked up the Travelers Inn and walked back to the truck.

When she got to her cottage, she drove in the U-shaped driveway so she could back the big truck up making the passenger side closer to the door.

"I'll get the door. You take your time." She grabbed the bag from the back of truck and opened the front door of the cottage.

Grayling stood up on the chair and hissed at her angrily. "I'm sorry, buddy." She tried to pet him, but he swatted her hand away. "You're going to have to wait a little longer."

"Would you like to shower before you change?" she asked as Jack reached the couch and leaned heavily on its back.

"Yes, that might be a good idea." He slowly turned and headed for the bathroom.

Everleigh darted around him, got the water started and clean towels and set his soft clothes on the counter.

"Don't worry about the mess; I'll get it when you're done," she told him.

When he came out, he was moving a little faster, the hot water having loosened up his stiff and aching muscles. He sat down on the couch, which luckily was long enough for him to lie down on. He allowed Everleigh to add pillows behind his head and under his knees.

"Thank you. I've never had someone care for me like this," he said as he settled in and closed his eyes. He was asleep before she could reply.

Grayling, having been fed an entire can of his favorite wet food while Jack was in the shower, hopped up on the couch. He curled into a ball over Jack's stomach, making himself comfortable. He hissed at Everleigh again before curling his head in and purring himself to sleep.

She smiled at them both before heading off to tidy up the bathroom. She tossed the towels and Jack's clothes in the washer and closed the sliding door to soften the noise. It was almost lunch time but, seeing as they woke up late and had a late breakfast, she had decided not to wake him.

With both of their phones on silent, it made for a quiet afternoon. Everleigh spent her time sorting through the books on the shelf nearest to the window. Many of them were very old but in good condition. Flipping through the pages, she noticed handwritten notes, and not all of them in Lilli's writing. She counted at least three different people who had made notes in the different books.

A truck pulled up and she hurriedly set the books aside to get to the door before they could knock.

"Hi, sorry to bother you but, is Jack here?" Sera asked.

"He is, but he's sleeping." Everleigh could see Scott behind her moving as carefully as Jack had been.

Sera turned around to face Scott. "I told you he was fine. Get back in the truck," she scolded.

Everleigh felt a hand on her back and stepped aside. Sera sighed and allowed Scott to pass her. The two men embraced, foreheads touching, and talked in whispered voices.

Sera nodded to Everleigh and the girls moved away from the door.

"I'm sorry we woke him. Scott got worried when his truck wasn't at the Inn, and he didn't answer his phone." Sera looked back at them. "For a long time they only had each other, and when Scott and I bonded...well, he worries. Not that he would ever admit it of course."

"Are they brothers?" Everleigh asked.

"Not from-the-same-parents kind of brothers. They went through a lot together that I think Jack should tell you about when he's ready. As similar as they are, Scott is a lot more open. Jack keeps things close. Too close sometimes."

They watched them for a moment before speaking again.

"Jack trusts you and he's not one to trust easily," Sera said with a smile. "If you don't believe me, just look how he's dressed. I've never seen him like that, and I've known him since I was eight years old. Jack was always the tough guy. Never let them see you cry kind of guy." She started walking back. "Oh, there's one more thing. The Inn won't open until tomorrow night. After a night like last night, it's best to give everyone time to cool down."

Everleigh followed Sera back to the door where the two men were standing, more leaning on each other than actually standing. Sera smiled and put her arm around Scott. "He's just fine. Can we go home now?"

"Yes, ma'am." Scott smiled and kissed the top of her head. They walked slowly together back to the truck.

Sera closed the door for him and turned back to where Everleigh stood with her arm around Jack. "You mind her, mister! You hear me?" she shouted to them.

"Yes, ma'am." Jack called back and pulled Everleigh closer. They waited at the door for the truck to pull away before Everleigh helped Jack back to the couch.

"What have you been doing all day?" Jack asked. "Every little bump usually wakes me, but I've been out most of the day, it seems."

"Reading mostly, sitting on the floor by that shelf." She smiled looking at the piles of books. "Some I want to take a closer look at. There's writing on the pages but it's not Lilli's."

"What are you doing now?" he asked, watching her pull a large pot from cupboard.

"I'm going to make chicken soup. Would you like to help? You can cut vegetables at the table," Everleigh said as she started gathering items from the fridge.

Jack made his way to the table. Everleigh piled up the vegetables for him to cut and a bowl to put them in. While he was cutting, she went out to the garden and collected some fresh herbs. Once the broth was warm and ready, she added all the other ingredients and put the lid on to allow it cook.

Jack returned to the couch and Everleigh tidied up and joined him.

"How are you feeling?" she asked.

"Stiff," he replied. "Tomorrow, I need to get moving again. How long before we can eat?"

"Are you that hungry? I can get you something now if you like?" Everleigh laughed, turning back toward the kitchen.

"No, I was just wondering." He looked away. "I heard what Sera said about not being open about things. I don't want to be that way with you. I feel closer to you in five days then I do most people I've known for years."

Everleigh sat next to him and took his hand. "I feel the same way. Trusting people isn't easy for me, but I trust you, and I can't explain why. It's just a feeling."

They sat on the couch for a time fingers entwined, her head on his shoulder and his resting on hers. Each waited for the other to speak, but it was Jack who broke the silence.

"Do you remember your vision of the valley on fire?" He felt her nod against his shoulder. "It happened where I lived before I came here. It was nothing like this valley. We had a Hall like Eldaguard, but there was no magical protection. We lived mixed into a city."

"Hidden in plain sight," Everleigh offered.

"Exactly. My parents saw it on the news. Our Hall was burning. Scott lived down the street from us and our parents were friends. We knew they were worried, but we didn't understand why. I was six and Scott was five and we had only been to the Hall a handful of times." He stifled a laugh. "Looking back now, I know our dads were preparing us for what we would become. They bought us foam swords and would fight with us. At the time we thought it was just fun. My dad told me about the Warriors, and what it meant to be one, but I never grasped the true depth of it.

"The morning after the Hall burnt, they made me pack my backpack with clothes and a few things that were really important to me. Mom would only say it's just in case we needed it. A few nights later on the news, at dinner time, I saw a picture of someone I knew. I pointed it out and was sent to my room." Jack's voice grew quieter. "He and his family had been killed in their home. That night we left with Scott's family. All we were told was we needed to do whatever we were told without question and, if anything did happen, Scott and I had to stay together, no matter what.

"We were just out of the city and had to stop at a police checkpoint. My dad turned to me and told me to put on my backpack and be ready to run if I needed to. He gave me his ring. I knew how important it was to him, so I zipped it in my pocket. He told me it would be proof that I am who I say I am. We were stuck there for a while. The police kept asking questions walking back and forth between both our trucks. The cop walked away from Scott's family and mom saw Scott slip out of the back passenger door. She told me to do the same before the cop got too close to our truck. Be quick and be quiet. Stay close to her door."

Jack had started to slowly rock, and he was holding Everleigh's hand tighter. "She told me she would knock on the lower part of the door, and I was to run and not look back. We weren't far from a thick forest. There would be lots of places to hide if we could get to the trees. I heard the knock, and I started running as fast as I could to make it to those trees. We made it, Scott and me. We found an old tree with a spot we both could get into, and we hid there for the night.

"We fell asleep at some point and when we woke up, we were careful and went back to where we could see the road. There was nothing there. No trace of anything. We were alone. Scott knew we were looking for a man named

Carl Villon and I knew we would find him in a city called Langford. We each had a piece so we could remember it. I don't know what would have happened if we had been separated."

"Is that near here? Langford?" Everleigh asked as Jack let go of her hand and put his arm around her.

"No, it's actually about two days' drive from here," he answered. "We were much closer to it at the time. We had nothing but what was in our bags. It was a lot of walking, wondering, and worrying but we got there. We found a campground with an open shower room, so we washed up and put on clean clothes before we went into town. We knew would draw less attention if we were clean kids."

"Even so young, you two were clever." Everleigh cuddled up close to him. She had a feeling this story was going to get a lot sadder.

"It took a couple of days, but we found who we were looking for. Carl told us he left when our families didn't arrive when we were supposed to. He came back when the news reported finding the bodies of our parents in a burned-out car. There was no mention of children with them."

Everleigh could feel his chest struggling to keep it together and she reached for the hand not gripping her shoulder. There were so many things she wanted to say, but she didn't trust her voice.

"Carl took care of us and brought us here. We were given a room to share in the Travelers Inn. All that was asked of us was that we find ways to help out. We were enrolled in a school in Strawsburg and we learned everything else in the Hall. We're trained as mercenaries.

Get in, get out, without being noticed, but fight our way if necessary. Instead of working for ourselves, we work for the Darkvale Brotherhood," he said giving her a squeeze, grateful for her closeness. "You're the first person I've told this story to in a long time."

"Thank you for telling me." She looked up at him and smiled.

"It's starting to smell good in here." He smiled back at her.

She sat up but didn't move away from him. "I need to check on the soup."

He slowly let her go and followed her to the kitchen. The soup was ready, and she put it in bowls while Jack set the rest of the table. Grayling sat perched on the far edge of the counter watching her every move. She put the soup bowls on the table along with a bowl of buns and went to pick up his dish. She filled it with dry cat food and topped it off with a bit of tuna.

"What do you think, Gray?" She showed the little cat his dinner. "Do you forgive me?"

Grayling ran across the counter, put his paws on her arm and rubbed his face to her chin, purring happily. She carried him and his dish over to his mat and set them down before joining Jack at the table.

"I hope you don't think you can win me over with food," Jack joked when she sat down.

"We'll find out soon enough. How's the soup?" she asked sitting next to him.

Jack laughed, causing his ribs to hurt. He coughed. "I'm ok," he said when he saw the concern on her face.

Everleigh waited for his breathing to settle before starting to eat.

"This morning, Justin asked you something and you told him you had to talk to me about it first. What is it?" Everleigh asked to break the silence.

"I asked the guys if they would be willing to help you move, but after last night we're all going to need a few days to recover." Jack smiled. "They all agreed to help, and last night won't change that. What's wrong?"

"I need time to sell my shop, find a realtor, get it listed, and show it. All that stuff takes time. Maybe a lot of time." Everleigh sighed. "I want to tell Bess and Jen first. I owe them that much."

The two ate slowly. As soft as the chicken and vegetables were, it was still hard for Jack to chew with his aching jaw.

"What about the soup?" Jack asked when Everleigh had finished cleaned up.

"It needs to cool before I can put it in the fridge."

Jack got up and took her hand. He left her at the couch and went to set a fire in the hearth. The sun had set behind the hill leaving it dark in the cottage. With the fire crackling warmly, he returned to the couch and sat with her. As he hoped, she curled up against his side again.

"There is something I need to tell you, but I don't know if I can." Everleigh's voice was soft.

"Not tonight then. Tonight, we sit here and enjoy the fire light," Jack whispered. "We have plenty of time."

They spent hours curled together on the couch in front of the fire. It was a cool night, so the heat wasn't unwelcome. They talked about the books she had been reading and the things he had been building in the training yard, carefully avoiding any talk about the Balordran, though it continued to be a burning question in her mind.

"I will show you. We should have the yard done tomorrow." Jack looked down at her in time to see her yawn. "It's late and you're tired. I should go."

"Or you could stay." She hadn't meant to say it out loud and was suddenly feeling her face heat up.

Jack stroked her cheek and smiled to himself. "If you would like me to, I will stay."

Everleigh nodded against his chest. "I would like you to stay." She knew he needed to hear her say it.

Everleigh went to the kitchen and put the soup in the fridge while Jack put out the fire. Her heart felt like it was going to pound out of her chest. She turned on the bedside light and took her PJs to the bathroom to wash up and change. When she walked into her bedroom the bed was turned down and Jack was sitting on the edge.

"You first. A lady never has her back to the door."

Everleigh crawled in and Jack covered her up. He laid down next to her on top of her blankets, allowing her arms out the top, and pulled another blanket over himself.

Everleigh lay there feeling warm and safe in his arms, but she was quickly losing control. Her tears came fast, and she was helpless to hold them back.

Jack tossed his blanket to the floor and crawled under hers. He wrapped her in his arms holding her as tightly as he dared, not wanting to hurt her. He felt her hands gripping his shirt.

"About three years ago, did you see a news report about a woman who was beaten by her boyfriend? Her neighbor found her. She was in hospital for months." Everleigh was struggling to keep her voice steady.

"Yes, I remember that. Scott and I talked about what we would do to that guy every time they updated the story." Jack's heart was racing knowing what was coming next. He had heard whispers that a witch had been found beaten in London, but no one had said it was her.

"Donald wasn't always like that. When my mother introduced us, he was amazing. We did everything together. For two years everything was great. Then he met a guy at work who got him into the gym, and he discovered a passion for weightlifting. He started competing and everything was fine until he started traveling to bigger competitions."

The more she talked the more Jack could feel her calming.

"A year later and he wasn't the man I had known. I know we all change but everything about him changed. He became short tempered and cruel. I asked him if I could go with him. He had a big competition, and he was training long hours. I hardly saw him at all, and I thought it would be a way of being part of his new world. He called me stupid and said I would only be in his way.

"While he was away, someone got hold of his phone and sent me a text, 'This is why Don doesn't want you here,' and attached videos of him..." She left the sentence hanging and curled her head in against Jack's chest. "I sent back 'tell him we're through.' I was hurt and angry. I wasn't thinking. When he got back, he came to my apartment and that's when it happened. If Sam hadn't found me, I wouldn't be alive right now."

Jack was running his fingers through her hair.

"I don't remember anything. Just that he was yelling that I was his and he would decide when we were through. I woke up in the hospital. I was restrained but everything hurt so much I didn't try to move. I looked like a train wreck. Most of me was black and blue with shades of purple and green. I had so many broken bones it took months before I could even get out of bed. But what was worse than all of that, worse than anything possible, I had been pregnant."

Jack could feel her starting to tremble in his arms.

"I can't give you a child, Jack."

There was nothing he could do until she cried it out and he knew it. He held her tight to his chest and waited. Her breathing began to slow, and he moved away from her. He took off his tear-soaked shirt and dried her eyes with it before tossing it to the floor.

He wasn't sure what to say. Having a child had never been something he wanted for himself. He wasn't sure if she would believe him, or think he was just trying to make her feel better, so he said nothing.

Everleigh rolled over and faced the wall, her hands tucked up under her chin. He hadn't said anything, and she didn't want to see him leave.

Jack curled his body around her. His strong arms crossed hers pulling her so tight to him she couldn't move.

"You're not running for the door?" Her voice, while soft, sounded frightened.

"I will love you if you'll let me," he whispered his lips against her ear.

Everleigh couldn't stop her tears though this time they were tears of joy and relief.

After a moment he felt her body relax and knew she would be asleep soon. He held her close to him for the rest of the night.

CHAPTER 7

It was late in the morning when knocking on the door woke her. Jack was pulling on his jeans when she rolled over.

"I was hoping to get to the door before the knocking woke you." Jack was still moving a little slower than usual, but he had his energy back.

"It's alright. What time is it?" she asked as she stretched.

"I'm not sure, but I'm guessing I'm late and this is the search party." He laughed and went to the door.

Jack returned for his shirt. "Do you know where my keys are?" he asked.

"They're on the table by the door," she answered sitting on the edge of the bed.

Jack turned to her and dropped to his knees. He took her hands in his. "I was hoping we would have time together this morning. I don't like leaving like this. I will see you tonight at the Inn?" It came out as more of a statement than a question. When she smiled and nodded, he kissed her hands and left.

Everleigh was more determined than ever to get things sorted in the cottage. An hour after Jack left, she had all the bookshelves cleared and the contents were in three piles. A pile for things she knew she wanted to keep, a pile for things she wasn't sure about, and the smallest pile were the things she knew she didn't want to keep. She had moved all the herbs to the shop but was having trouble finding places for them all. She guessed Lilli had the same problem and that was why they were everywhere.

Some of the newer books she recognized from her own collection. She remembered recommending the one she was holding and started flipping through its pages. There were notes here and there marking passages that read 'Talk to Everleigh about this'. She read the passage and remembered talking about it during one of Lilli's visits to the flower shop.

Her phone rang. When she looked at the screen, it said her name, so she answered it.

"Hi, it's me. I grabbed the wrong phone when I left. I took a call. I wasn't paying attention when I answered it. It was Bess. She sounded upset. Said she really has to talk to you. There are a bunch of missed calls and texts from her. I told her I'd call you and you can call her from my phone."

"I'll do that. Did she say why? Did her texts?" Everleigh was starting to get a little worried. It wasn't like Bess to panic or stress about things.

Jack flipped through the texts from Bess. "There's nothing here but 'please call me'."

"Thanks, Jack. I'll call her. And I'll bring your phone with me tonight."

Everleigh stretched her back and dialed the number.

"Hello. Eve?" Jack had been right. Bess sounded upset.

"Bess, what's wrong?"

"Your mother has been coming in asking about you. Where are you? Have I heard from you? Yesterday she came in with someone. She was showing him around. She wouldn't tell me why. Eve, it just didn't sit right, you know." Bess was sounding more and more stressed.

"Ok, don't say anything to her but I'm coming back. I'll get to the bottom of it. Please try not to worry." Everleigh was almost begging.

The two talked for a little longer about happier things. The shop was doing well. There was no trouble with any of the orders and they had picked up a new wedding order. Bess had gained a new belt in karate and started taking a drawing class at the Community Center.

Everleigh sat holding the phone close to her chest. 'I can't wait.' She went to the bedroom and found Grayling had stretched out on the bed. She sat next to him.

"I guess I don't have to pack any clothes, do I, Gray? I have to find someone to look after you." She patted him on the head, and he happily rolled over for a belly rub. "Would you like Justin to look after you, Gray?"

It was getting late in the afternoon and the shadows were growing long. Everleigh gathered a few things in a bag, locked up, and went in search of the Millstone house to talk to Justin.

She started walking through the village, truly taking in the sights. Whenever she had gone out, it was always because she was looking for something described in one of her grandmother's journals and she hadn't taken the time to look around.

This truly was nothing like London at all. Each house she passed was unique in some way, not like the cookie-cutter houses in the city. The construction was the same, stone foundation with plaster and beams above, lots of big windows, but each home was a different size or shape. Some were two story, others one. The gardens had bountiful vegetable patches and beautiful flowers according to the preferences of the family living there.

The only thing missing, she thought, was a way of knowing who lived there. This was a place where everyone knew everyone, and they all looked out for each other. Jack had told her as much. The way he spoke of Lilli, it made sense that they all knew who lived where. It would take time, but she would get there eventually.

She remembered Mia saying they lived near the Hall, so she decided to take the road to her left. The road led her passed a blacksmith forge. A little farther on, she saw a seamstress shop with a lovely summer dress in the window. As she was admiring the dress, she heard someone call to her.

"I thought it was you." Tom smiled as he joined her. "Maria does lovely work." He stood next to her looking at the dress. "Have you met her yet?"

"I think I have at the Inn. Quiz night," Everleigh answered.

"Oh yes. I imagine you met a lot of people that night. It would be hard to remember everything about all of them after one night." Tom turned to her. "I was going to stop by the cottage and invite you to come to the Hall for a chat before you leave. There are a few things we need to clear up. Jack told us you were planning to leave this weekend, so there is plenty of time."

"Actually, my plans have changed," Everleigh interrupted. "I need to go tomorrow. My mom is up to something at my shop and my store manager is stressed. If I'm honest, I want it all to be over."

"Why don't you come with me to the Hall? We can talk more freely there. If you like, we can invite Jack to join us. Would you be more comfortable with him there?" Tom smiled. "It is important we talk before you go."

Everleigh declined to pull Jack away from his work at the training yard and went to the Hall with Tom. He made a quick call to Carl telling him they were on their way.

The Hall was much larger than Everleigh had realized. Her first visit having been late at night, most of the building had been hidden in darkness. The size, coupled with the intricate carvings in the wood beams, made this the most impressive building in the valley.

The heavy doors were also carved. Great trees reached up the sides, their leafy branches meeting across the top. Lower branches were carved to spell 'Eldaguard' across the center, giving each door half the name.

Tom allowed her a moment to take it in before opening one of the huge doors. He led the way down the same corridor to the alcove at the end. Everleigh walked slowly, looking at each item displayed on the walls. Axes, swords, a mace, each had a small plaque beneath with a name and date.

"Each item you see here on our walls has a story. It was used by someone who did a great service in aid of the

Brotherhood," Tom explained when she joined him, and each took a seat at the small table. "It is important we honor those who give themselves to our cause and this is our way of keeping them forever in our thoughts."

"Sorry it took so long. I wasn't expecting this to be today," Carl said as he joined the other two at the table. "Welcome back, Everleigh. Always nice to see you."

"It's getting late so let's get to it. What do you know of Amelia's, I mean your mother's, affiliations?" Tom asked, getting straight to the point. "We've had people in London looking into her a lot closer since you've been here, and we have uncovered some things. We want to know how much, if anything, you know about them."

Suddenly Everleigh was feeling very uncomfortable, and regretting having declined Jack's presence.

"What Tom is so bluntly saying is how much do you know about who your mother's associates are? What they do together, the groups or clubs she belongs to?" Carl took some of the sting from Tom's question, but the tension remained.

"When I applied for the Botany programs at a couple of universities, I didn't tell her. I knew she would be mad. I have a major in Botany and a minor in Business. The business program was my attempt at keeping her happy while I studied what I really wanted." Everleigh's head dropped and she was wringing her hands. "A few months in, I got a job closer to the school and applied for a housing grant to get away from her. I wasn't doing what she wanted, so she was making it almost impossible for me to study or sleep. We never really talked much after that, and we've never been close. To answer your question, she's worked for the same company for as long as I can remember. Mostly office work, filing, accounting, calls, stuff like that. She was in a book club and a knitting circle that made baby hats for the local hospital. I don't know if she still is or not."

Tom and Carl looked at each other but said nothing.

"I don't really know what else I can tell you. I don't really know her, or her friends. I hadn't seen her in weeks until I called and told her I was going away."

"She knows you're here?" Tom asked. There was an edge to his voice. "Does she know how you got here?"

"Can you tell us what you remember of the conversations you had with her before you left?" Carl still had a softer tone, but the same edge was creeping into his voice.

"I told her that Grandma Lilli had passed, and she had left me her cottage. I asked her if she knew how to get here, and she said no, and there was no reason for me to go. She was dead set against me leaving at all. She poked a bit of fun at the name Mallard Pond and—"

Everleigh stopped when the door opened and a group of laughing men entered the foyer. Carl called Jack to bring a chair and join them.

"Do you have my phone?" Everleigh asked when Jack sat down. He pulled it out of his pocket, and she opened it to the messages her mother had been sending and handed it to Tom. Then she gave Jack his phone.

Carl handed Everleigh a couple of sheets of paper and asked her to read them over while he brought Jack up to speed on the conversation and Tom read through the messages.

"They're not very motherly," he said before handing her phone to Carl. "How do I word this? Do you think Amelia could find us if she wanted to?"

Everleigh sat for a moment, looking at the floor, before going over the papers a second time. They could tell she was trying to work it out.

"In one of the books, I found the draught that Lilli gave Mom the day she left. It's a nasty mix of highly toxic plants." Everleigh shook her head. "If I'm reading this right, I'm surprised she remembered anything at all. It would have had to have been absolutely perfect for it to work without being harmful."

"What did she do exactly?" Tom asked.

"I can't be a hundred percent sure, but I think this is a combination spell." By the looks she was getting from the three men, she knew she was going to have to keep it simple. "Think of it like baking. Sugar, chocolate chips, butter, flour, eggs: you can eat them all separately, but if you measure and bake it right, you get cookies."

"The individual spells are stronger in combination than they are apart," Tom said and the other two smiled in agreement.

Everleigh looked at Jack. "Can't win a man over with food, huh?"

Jack rolled his eyes and shook his head with a smile.

"I think we missed an interesting conversation at some point." Carl elbowed Tom and the two men laughed.

"Separate spells combined to form one. If I'm reading this right, it should have altered her memory permanently. It actually makes sense. All the crazy things she said about this place. Her memory wasn't completely wiped. See here." She was talking more to herself then to the men. "Some memories were altered so as not to leave a memory gap of her entire childhood. It wasn't all bad here as a kid. She just remembers it that way, so she has no desire to come back."

"Lilli was one smart cookie," Jack said, causing Everleigh to laugh. "What's so funny?"

"Still stuck on the cookies, are you?"

Jack shook his head again. "I haven't eaten all day. Give me a break."

"That explains some of what we've found out." Tom looked at Carl but continued himself. "Several of the ladies she is close to have ties to the Balordran. They seem to have been keeping tabs on her. If I may guess, you told your mother you were leaving around the beginning of the month?" Everleigh nodded. "I thought so. That's when the activity around her picked up and our people took notice. Your mother started going for coffee more often, lunches and things like that with these women, but they never approached you."

"How can you know that?" Everleigh was starting to see the Darkvale Brotherhood's reach far exceeded what she had imagined.

"That might be left for another time," Tom suggested.

"She deserves to know. We can't keep her in the dark forever," Carl said as kindly as he could.

"This isn't another thing that will start a disagreement like the other night?" Everleigh was a little nervous.

"No, no, my dear, that has been put to rest and Carl is right. You do deserve to know." Tom's voice took on a tone Everleigh had not heard before.

"Maybe this is something we should talk about privately?" Carl suggested.

"Just tell me, whatever it is." Everleigh was desperate to know. It was starting to feel like she hadn't had control of her life like she thought she had.

"Four years ago, you got a new neighbor. Sam wanted to be close to the hospital so his commute would be shorter. I have waited a long time to say this to you." Carl moved close to her, his knees touching hers, and he took her hands in his. "I am so sorry. Sam was right there, and we had no idea Lilli's granddaughter was in danger. We should have been protecting you and I regret every day that we didn't."

"Carl's right. Lilli wanted you left alone, but we knew better. As soon as she started visiting you, we should have assigned someone to watch over you," Tom agreed.

"Donald? Is he a Balordran?" Everleigh was fighting hard to keep control of her emotions, but something inside her wanted desperately to know.

"We didn't look into the people around you as closely as we should have, but we can if you would like. We just need his first and last name." Carl was still holding her hands.

"Donald Pullman," she answered.

"I'll run it right now." Carl got up almost knocking the chair over. Jack saw the expression on his face change as he hurried away and slid into Carl's seat to hold Everleigh.

"Mom introduced us," Everleigh whispered. "What if she knew? Any memories she had of them wouldn't have been altered."

"If there is a connection, Carl will find it. There is also the chance that Amelia had no idea who these people were. She still may not know," Tom said, trying to add some form of comfort to the situation.

Everleigh told Tom about the conversation with Bess and that she wanted to get back before anything happened. She was starting to see that her world had been changing in ways she couldn't imagine for much long than she realized.

"You're going to need a realtor. It just so happens I can help you out there." Tom made a note to himself before he finished. "There is a law firm, Adams and Adams. Paul Adams' specialty is real-estate law. I can call him for you, and he can set you up with someone you can trust. I will do it now before I head to the Inn for dinner. I'll see you there?"

"That would be a huge help. I've met Mark, and he was really nice." Everleigh smiled. "I was sort of worried about where to start."

Tom got up and took his papers and files with him.

"We should go. I'm starving and there are still things to do before I can open." Jack picked up the chair he had brought and replaced it on the way to the main door.

"What's behind those doors?" Everleigh stood looking at a second set of carved wooden doors just as lovely and large as the front doors.

"That is the main hall of Eldaguard. Nothing that happens behind those doors is spoken of to anyone but other Warriors, including the other night's disagreement." Jack rubbed his jaw. Just thinking about it made it ache.

Everleigh climbed up into Jack's truck and they drove to the Inn. Working together, they got the place ready, the chairs off the tables (having been put up to mop the floors the night before), the tables and bar wiped down, and the fire set in the hearth.

When Jack had served the first group, Everleigh retreated to the kitchen.

"Can I help in here?" she asked Sera.

"There isn't a whole lot to do at the moment," Sera said over her shoulder as she filled bowls with chili.

Everleigh said nothing. She didn't feel like trying to pretend to be happy. The chili, as lovely as it smelled, wasn't enticing her to eat. She slipped upstairs and didn't hear what Sera said next.

"If you like, you could cut the bread," Sera offered.

"Sure can. It's just the boys from the farms so far," Jack answered.

"Oh, I'm sorry. I didn't mean for you to do it." She took the knife from Jack and looked around. "Everleigh was just here asking if she could help. I guess she left before I remembered the bread."

"She must have gone upstairs. I didn't see her."

Sera added a slice of fresh bread to each plate and Jack took it out to the boys. His intention to make sure she was alright was put on hold, as more and more people piled in.

Sera was widely known as an excellent cook and her chili normally drew a large crowd. Being a weeknight, they wouldn't stay late, but it made for a busy few hours.

When the Millstones arrived, Jack asked them if they would stay until Everleigh had a chance to talk to Justin about a little job she had for him. He was excited and agreed to wait, but as the night wore on, there was no sign of Everleigh. The Inn had almost emptied when Justin approached Jack.

"Mr. Jack, are you sure Miss Everleigh wanted to see me tonight? It's just that she doesn't seem to be here." Justin always seemed nervous when talking to people he held in high regard.

"I know she's here. She must be doing something in the kitchen. I'll go track her down." Jack tossed his towel on the bar and gave the bell a pull to signify closing time to all who were still there. He headed to the kitchen first and then upstairs.

"Have you been up here all night?" he asked sitting on the bed next to her.

"I just couldn't sit there with all those happy people. I can't stop thinking about everything Tom said." Everleigh felt tired and was hoping her face didn't show it.

"Well, I talked to Scott, and he agreed to cover for me while we're gone. I told him I'd call when we were ready for the guys to come and move everything. He's also headed into town tomorrow and said he would come to the pet store with us and take cat food back to Justin." He let the hint hang for her.

"Oh, I forgot to talk to Justin, and I meant to go into town and get the food." Everleigh buried her face in the pillow. It wasn't like her to be so forgetful.

"Scott doesn't mind, and Justin is waiting for you. I told him you were busy in the kitchen." Jack rubbed her back.

"Thank you." Everleigh sat up and hugged him.

They went down and she thanked them for waiting. Justin, as Jack had said, was thrilled to be asked and agreed immediately. She could tell by how closely he paid attention to everything she told him that Grayling was in the best hands.

Jack walked them to the door and locked it behind them. He turned back to Everleigh and took her hands.

"Would you start putting the chairs up? I'll get the mop and we'll be done in no time," he asked before looking towards the kitchen door. "Not that it isn't always a pleasure to see you, Tom, but what is it now?"

"Nothing you're going to want to hear, but you should know," Tom answered.

The three of them took seats at one of the round tables.

"We did some digging with our brothers in London on the name you gave, and he is a known member of Balordran," Tom said softly. "I can show you everything we managed to find and now that we connect him to you, well things are much clearer."

"Just tell me what I need to know," Everleigh said as she closed her eyes preparing herself for what she expected to hear.

Tom raised his hand before Jack could say anything. "You want to know if Amelia knew before she introduced you to him?" Everleigh shoulders sank, and he knew he was right. "There is no direct evidence that she did. She is a friend of his mother. His father, Richard Pullman, is one of the highest-ranking in the Order. He also owns the company she works for. What we think is that the

Balordran wanted someone close to you, and who could get closer than a boyfriend?"

Everleigh sat without moving and stared into the embers of the slowly dying fire. The two men waited for her to say something, but she stood up without a word and walked to the far end of the long room and started putting the chairs up on the tables.

Jack leaned closer to Tom. "Was there anything about his attack on her?"

"She told you," Tom sighed. "As far as we can tell, the Order wasn't happy about it. I think the police had it right: a mix of hormone pills, steroids, and plain old entitled anger." He could tell Jack was getting angry. "I know you're falling for her, and I am happy for you. It's about time you had someone like her, but you need to keep your head. You do her no favors holding anger over something that happened years ago. He's locked up for nine more years and we have her safe with us now and that's where we'll keep her."

"I just don't get it." Jack knew he was right and had to keep his temper in check.

"We know how they operate if they think they have a line on a witch! I think they were hoping a real relationship would grow, but it didn't. He viewed her as an assignment and, when she tried to end it, I think it went south so fast they had no time to rein him in and he almost killed her. He's probably lucky the police got him before his Order could."

"He's sure lucky I can't get to him now," Jack said through gritted teeth.

The two men hadn't realized Everleigh was listening to every word. A chair fell down and they both looked up to see her leaning heavily on a table.

Scott came running in from the kitchen where he had been helping Sera with the clean up before walking home with her. "I'll finish up in here. You take her upstairs."

Tom let himself out, knowing nothing he could say was going to make the situation better. Scott locked the door behind him.

Jack collected the shaking bundle in his arms. "Meet you here around 9:00am?" Jack asked, as he passed Scott heading for the stairs.

"I'll be here. Sera and I will finish up down here," Scott said again and ran a comforting hand over her head. He didn't need to know the details. He knew pain when he saw it.

Jack laid her down and held her until she cried herself to sleep. He carefully extracted himself from her, pulled out his rucksack, and started packing. With everything he wanted to take stacked neatly by the door, he went back to the bed and gently woke her.

"Let's go to the washroom. You can change and wash up. You'll sleep better." He offered handing her one of his t-shirts and an extra pair of his PJ pants.

He walked her to the bathroom, quickly returned to his room, and changed himself. He turned down the bed and returned to the hallway to wait for her. From where he was standing, he could see most of the main room of the Inn below. He leaned on the railing and watched as the lights went out. The last light was the kitchen, and Scott and Sera were gone.

Everleigh came out holding up long pant legs. While she waited for him to finish, she rolled the bottoms up so she could walk.

Everleigh lay wide awake, Jack's arms keeping her close to him. "Who are the Balordran?" she asked feeling his soft steady breathing on the back of her neck.

"They are sort of like us, except where we protect magic, they use it to gain power and influence," Jack told her as gently as he could.

"Is that why you're worried they may come after me?" she asked snuggling closer to him.

He held her tighter to him and kissed her neck. "I won't let that happen."

* * *

Morning came with bright sunshine, but Jack let her sleep as late as possible. He wasn't sure which one of them had gone to sleep first, which likely meant it had been him. Breakfast was almost ready, so he went up and woke her.

Everleigh was dressed and ready to leave when she joined him at the little table in the kitchen. There was just enough time to eat and clean up before Scott would be there.

"I was thinking," Everleigh said has they headed back upstairs to get his bags. "Maybe we should take my car. It would be easier to get around and find parking in the city with a smaller vehicle."

Jack was clearly not thrilled by the idea, but he agreed she had a good point. They left the bags at the back door and hopped in the truck. By the time they got back from the cottage, Scott was waiting with Sera.

"We thought you left without us until we saw your bags," Scott called from his truck window looking down with a grin. "How did you get in there? You know you can put the seat back," he joked.

"As far back as it goes, smart guy," Jack quipped back and Scott drove off, laughing, toward the only road out of the valley.

Everleigh hopped out, grabbed the bags, and tossed them onto the back seat. She knew Jack would have done it, but she could get out and back in faster and easier than he could.

Jack followed Scott in what felt like a very small car. The ride out of the valley was much bumpier than he was used to, and he found he had to drive more carefully to avoid the larger potholes. Everleigh had offered several times to drive, but Jack told her to rest and she could drive after they stopped for lunch. She knew how to get to her apartment once they were in the city.

They made their way to the pet store and Everleigh bought enough food to last for two weeks. She couldn't imagine it would take longer than that, but just in case it did, Sera had joined her inside and Everleigh showed her where to find his food and treats.

The two returned outside to see Scott with his hands on the ground falling, or crawling, out of Everleigh's car and both men laughing.

Sera hugged Everleigh and Jack, wished them a safe trip, and took the bags of cat food. As she walked to

Scott's truck, she called over her shoulder, "When you're done playing, dear."

Scott jumped to his feet and scooped Everleigh off hers and hugged her. He carried her to the car where Jack had opened the door. "We'll be ready when you need us."

She thanked him and got back in the car. The two men spoke for a moment and with a quick hug got into their separate vehicles.

The drive to London was going to be a long one and, at about the second hour, Everleigh nodded off.

CHAPTER 8

Everleigh pulled into her parking spot in front of her building, like she had done for the past five years. Sam's spot was empty, and she assumed he was at the hospital. The building hadn't changed, and she wasn't sure why she was surprised by that. She had been gone a little less than a week. So much had happened in that time that it seemed like more time had passed. Who would have thought visiting such a small place so removed from the big city would have been anything but quiet and relaxing?

"This is it," she said aloud.

"I can see why you like it here," Jack replied. "I'm guessing yours is the one with the flower boxes hanging off the balcony."

"Yup, they're empty. I only use them to put the inside plants out in the sun." Everleigh smiled. "I guess that would be a bit of a giveaway. Are you ready to go in?"

Jack nodded and they got out of the car. It was quiet for late afternoon on a Friday. In another hour, the street would be full of cars as people returned home from work.

They passed the front doors, and the smell of cleaning products assaulted them. She checked the mail and pulled out a few flyers. That Sam had kept up with the mail wasn't a surprise.

They went up to her door. She unlocked and opened it, watching Jack's face.

"Wow, it's so bright," he said smiling. "The cottage is so dark compared to this!"

She hadn't really thought about it, but he was right. Her apartment was a lot brighter. While Jack looked around, she took a quick look at the pile of mail on her kitchen table.

"You have no plants?" he asked setting his bag on a chair in the living room.

"Of course I do. I moved them to my office at the shop so Bess could look after them for me." Everleigh laughed at the look he gave her. "We should go. We're meeting Bess and Jen for dinner soon. I bet you would like to see the shop?"

"I would. I've never seen the inside before," Jack said.

The two got back in her car and she drove to the Little Flower Shop. Everleigh parked the car behind the building and sat for a moment with her eyes closed.

"Are you alright?" Jack asked softly.

"Yes," she answered, taking off her seatbelt. "How am I going to tell them, Jack? Bess loves this shop as much as I do."

They got out of the car and Jack hugged her tight. "It won't be easy, but they'll understand."

They walked around to the front of the building. Bess had the stand next to the door full of cut flower bouquets. Jack reached in, pulled out one of the bright daisy bouquets, and held it next to Everleigh's face.

"Nope, not that one." He smiled, replaced it, and took out another. This one had yellow and orange flowers. He held it next to her and shook his head.

When he pulled out a third and held it up, Everleigh laughed. A voice from behind her said, "Can I help you find something?"

"No," Jack answered. "None of these are as lovely as my Everleigh."

Everleigh shook her head and turned to face Bess. Immediately the two hugged and Bess pulled her away from the big store window.

"I am so glad to see you," Bess said as she took a quick look into the shop. "Remember I told you your mom brought someone in? Showed him around and left without a word? He's here now. I don't know who he is. He's just looking around."

"We should wait until he's gone," Jack said, watching him carefully.

"We could go in through the back. Is Jen here? I wouldn't want to surprise her." Everleigh moved a little farther from the door.

"Ok, if he asks, I'll tell him it's a delivery. Jen is at school for another half hour," Bess said and went back inside.

Everleigh led Jack around the building to the back door. They went in quietly and Everleigh sat down at her desk and pulled up the security camera's live feed on her computer. She let Jack have her chair so he could watch the man wander the store.

When the man left, and the store was empty again, it was time for proper introductions. The two girls walked around the store pointing out things they liked with Bess pointing out things that had arrived after Everleigh had left.

Jack happily followed the two giggling girls but wasn't strictly paying attention to them. He was looking for whether or not there had been a pattern to the man's movements around the shop.

"That's what you were doing!" Jack said out loud. The two girls stared at him. "He wasn't just wandering. Can you play back the camera to when he first came in?"

Everleigh did as he asked through the app on her phone and handed it to him. Jack went to the door and followed the man's movements. Pausing the playback to look in the direction the man had looked at each point he stopped, confirming what he guessed.

"I thought you said this guy runs an Inn? What is he doing?" Bess asked watching him with a confused look.

"Everleigh, come look at this," Jack called. "Stand here and look up in that direction, then over that way. What can you see?"

"The security camera?" she replied and followed Jack to the next point. "The camera again! Why would he keep looking up at the cameras?"

"My guess is he was trying to find the blind spots." He handed her phone back. "Why is he looking for blind spots is the better question."

"Bess, are there any orders being picked up in the next couple days?" Everleigh asked.

Bess shook her head. "There is nothing ordered until next Saturday. It's the big wedding order." Bess was getting worried again and the door chime made her jump.

"Bess, I'm here," Jen called.

"Jen, we have a guest," Bess called back.

The three girls laughed and hugged while Jack watched, amused. Eventually he was introduced, and the giggling and whispering started again. He could tell they were teasing Everleigh about him because her face was red when she looked at him.

The phone rang and, while Bess handled it, Everleigh told Jen about the strange man and that she thought it best to close the shop for a couple days. It would give her a chance to try finding out what was going on and who this guy was.

* * *

When they got to the restaurant, they were seated at a table near the back. Their server had suggested that, since they were not there to watch the game, the back tables would be quieter for them to talk.

Jack sat quietly for most of the conversation, allowing the three girls time to catch up on the past week's events. There weren't a lot of changes in the city and most of the questions centered on what Everleigh had been doing all week. Eventually, they turned to Jack and grilled him on everything they could think of. He answered most of their questions honestly while carefully dancing around others by asking questions of them.

When dessert was brought to the table, and the evening neared its end, Everleigh knew it was time to tell them. The longer she waited, the harder it became. Jack saw the growing tension in her posture and took her hand under the table.

"There is something I have to tell you." The table fell silent, and she looked at each of them sitting across from her. "I know it's sudden, but I've decided to move permanently to my grandmother's cottage."

The silence at the table was heavy and Everleigh couldn't bring herself to look at them.

"You're sure about this? What about the shop?" Jen asked, her voice a little shaky.

"I can't run it from so far away." Everleigh forced herself to look Bess in the eyes. "I have to sell it."

Silent tears ran down three faces. Jack saw the server coming but waved her off and, seeing the girls' faces, she nodded and turned back to the packed front room.

"Can I have a moment with Eve please?" Bess asked.

"Of course," Jen answered. "You can walk me to my car, cutie." She smiled at Jack.

"Take the keys," Everleigh told him. "I'll see you in the car."

Jack leaned over and kissed the top of Everleigh's head and left with Jen.

"You're seriously moving? And selling the shop?" Bess asked when they were out of ear shot.

"I know it sounds crazy, but it feels right. It's hard to explain but I feel like I belong there. Like I've always belonged there." Everleigh hoped she understood. "I can't run the shop from so far away."

Bess nodded. "You know, watching the two of you, if I didn't know any better, I would think you'd been together for years." Bess looked up. "Eve, would you let me buy the shop? I would have to talk to my hubby of course but would you give me a chance before it goes on the market?"

"What? Yes of course!" Everleigh had not considered that possibility and it took a second to sink in. "I have a meeting with a real-estate lawyer tomorrow morning. I can call you after?"

Jack had paid the bill on his way out so the two thanked the server and walked to their cars, arms around each other. Jen was gone and Jack was sitting in the car smiling at them. They parted at Bess's car and Everleigh continued to her car where Jack now had the door open for her.

Everleigh put her arms around him. "You don't have to open every door for me."

"No, but when I can, I will."

They made one stop at a corner store for some munchies before going back to her apartment. Sam's car was in its usual spot and the light was on his side of the second floor. By the time they got up Sam's lights were out. Everleigh was a little relieved. She liked Sam a lot, but it had been a long day, and she was looking forward to curling up on the couch with Jack and watching a movie.

Ten minutes later they were doing just that. Jack put on an action movie. Everleigh put the popcorn in a bowl, grabbed two pops and put them on the coffee table. By the time the movie started, they were both changed and curled up on the couch together.

"Bess asked if she could buy the shop," Everleigh said.
"Really!"
"I hadn't considered that. I guess it makes sense. She knows as much as I do about it. She has done everything

at one point or another." Everleigh sighed. "I agreed to talk to her about it before it goes on the market."

"Sounds like it will go to someone who will love it as much as you do," Jack said and hugged her.

* * *

The sun was shining, and Everleigh sat up with a groan. The two had fallen asleep watching the movie and spent the whole night on the couch. Her back and neck ached as she tried to stretch out.

Jack pulled himself up straighter with an equal groan and looked at his watch. "We've got to get a move on, or we'll be late. It's almost 9:00am. You take the bedroom." He stood up and grabbed his bag and headed for the bathroom.

Everleigh drove because she knew the way, giving Jack the chance to have a good look around. He had been to London many times but was always the driver. He never felt comfortable here and not because of the number of people. It was the tall buildings downtown. They had a way of making him feel small, and he didn't like it.

Everleigh pulled into the parking lot at the same time as Mark Adams. He remembered her as soon as she stepped out of her car and waited for her.

"I didn't think I'd be seeing you again so soon, Miss Roberts," he greeted with a smile. "I would shake your hand, but I would likely drop something."

"It's ok. Can I help you with something?" she asked.

"If you could get the door, that would be a great help. You're meeting with my father today, right?" he asked.

"Yes, he was recommended to help me find a realtor to sell my flower shop," Everleigh said and scooped up a fallen file for him.

Jack got the door and followed them inside. The receptionist was on the phone but offered a friendly wave.

"I'll pop into his office to see if he's ready." Mark set down the boxes and took back the folder. He went to an office in the back corner and waved for them to follow. "Dad, this is Everleigh and... I'm so sorry I just realized I didn't introduce myself," he said looking at Jack a little embarrassed.

"Jack Killian." He offered his hand to Mark.

"Good to meet you," Mark said with a slight bow. "This is Paul, senior partner of the firm, and my father. I'll leave you to it then."

"Mark, would you stay for a moment? Things have changed and we may need your expertise," Paul said before welcoming the other two.

Mark closed the door and took a seat in one of the chairs. Everleigh and Jack took the couch.

"I don't know how much you know about our firm, so I'll start there. My father did legal work for the Darkvale Brotherhood and when I took over, I continued, as I am hopeful my son will do also." He was gathering papers from his desk as he spoke. "I received a call from Tom this morning and he told me there has been a fair bit of commotion being stirred up the last few weeks. Let me get him on the line."

When Tom answered, Everleigh and Jack recounted what Bess had been worried about as well as what they had seen the day before with the strange man in the shop.

"If you're right, Jack, and I don't mean to scare you Everleigh, they may be planning to take her when they find out she's back." Tom's voice was serious, giving it a cold tone. "We have seen no indication that they are aware of her return, and I would aim to keep it that way as long as possible."

"Everleigh, try not to think about it too much. You focus on what you need to do and let Jack do what he does best." Tom's voice lightened somewhat, but the warning was still there. "Paul, I would suggest going ahead with the measures we talked about. It may be helpful if the sale does not drag on too long."

They said their good-byes and Paul joined them, taking a seat in the empty chair.

"Tom and I spoke this morning, so I know time is not on our side. Just to be safe, I would suggest filing a Power of Attorney. This would give a selected person the power to act on your behalf. If, for instance, if you have to return to Mallard Pond before the sale is complete, and it's not safe for you to return, the person you select can complete the sale, sign the documents, and look after anything outstanding." Paul extended his hand toward Mark. "That is why I asked him to stay. This is Mark's expertise."

"I can choose anyone?" Everleigh asked.

"The only thing I would suggest is that you choose someone you trust, but yes it can be anyone," Mark answered.

"Can it be challenged? I mean, if my proxy makes a decision for me, can someone else challenge it?" Everleigh was squeezing Jack's hand.

"They can try, but courts rarely overturn POAs unless they are filed while the individual is taking substances, medical or recreational. They would need to prove your state of mind at the time of filing or prove mental impairment of some kind. You seem coherent to me, if I may say so." Mark tilted his head. "Do you foresee someone creating a problem?"

"There may be someone. My mother didn't want me leaving to visit, let alone moving there permanently." Everleigh looked at Jack. "I would rather she didn't know about the sale, or the move, until it's over."

"I dealt with a similar family situation not too long ago. It was siblings fighting over a parent's care, but I think I can rework it to fit you. Do you want to go ahead with it?" Mark asked, pulling out a notebook from his pocket. Everleigh agreed. "I just need some info on your chosen proxy."

"Jack, would you do it for me?" Everleigh looked pleadingly at him.

"You're sure you wouldn't want to ask Bess?" Jack asked.

"I can't if she's going to be the buyer. You're better suited if it comes to dealing with Balordran." Everleigh looked into his eyes. "Please, Jack."

Jack nodded. "What do you need from me?"

"Your driver's license would be all the info I need." Mark started making notes. "Everleigh, there are different types of POA that give different powers. I can keep it to the sale, or I can include financial, medical—"

"Cover everything," Everleigh interrupted. "I want Jack to be able to make any choice in my stead with no exceptions and no loopholes."

"Ok. I have my marching orders." Mark took Jack's license. "I'll get on this right now. If I can meet you before you leave, I can file it before the courthouse closes today."

Everleigh nodded and Mark left for his office.

"With that out of the way, let's talk about the sale." Paul pulled out a note pad.

They talked for an hour about every aspect of the business. Everleigh told him that Bess wanted a chance to buy it and she wanted to do everything she could to help her.

"That changes things a little, but I know the perfect man to make it happen." Paul went to his desk and pulled out a business card. "I work with Josh on lots of business sales. He is not in the know, but he is good at what he does, and he is discreet when I've asked him to be. I'll call him and get him up to speed. If I may give him your number, I'll have him call you?"

Everleigh agreed and the meeting concluded. On their way out, Mark met them in the waiting room.

"If I can get you two to sign this, I can have it filed this afternoon." Mark pointed out where they each needed to sign.

"That was fast," Jack commented.

"She gave you complete Power of Attorney without exception. Makes my job pretty easy." Mark shook their hands and returned Jack's license. "It is my sincerest hope you do not need this."

On that, they both agreed.

Everleigh was very quiet on the drive back to the shop. She wanted to get a start on the paperwork and a full inventory was going to take time. The one thing she didn't have to spare was time.

Everleigh settled herself at her desk and started going through all the papers scattered around while Jack watched from a chair on the other side.

"I was just thinking," Jack said absently. "How long have you had your car?"

"About three or four years, I guess. Why?"

"Are you attached to it?" Jack was staring up at the ceiling.

"I like it, if that's what you mean." Everleigh put her papers down. "What are you getting at?"

"I was just thinking. The people who know you know that car. What if, while you work on this, I go see about getting something else?" He sat up and looked at her. "Something that can better handle the field road to the Pond?"

"You want me to get a new car now?" Car shopping was the last thing she wanted to do at that moment.

"I'll look after it while you toil away here. All you have to do is test drive whatever I bring and, if you like it, sign the papers." Jack smiled and Everleigh nodded. "Have anything in mind? Something you've always wanted?"

"I don't want a big truck like yours. I like it but it's too big for me to drive all the time." She thought for a moment. "Something comfortable for you and small enough for me. I don't have a clue, Jack."

"Let me try and find something. You can drive it and if you don't like it, I'll find something else." Jack looked around. "The only thing is, I don't want to leave you here alone."

Everleigh smiled and called Bess, as she promised she would the day before. She asked her if she would help with the inventory and, as expected, Bess agreed. Jack waited until the two were busy laughing and working away before he left.

It took most of the afternoon, but the two of them got the entire shop counted down to the last petal. Everleigh made two copies of the inventory list along with the price sheets.

"You count up one and I'll do the other. Hopefully our numbers will match, and we can put them on the master tomorrow," Everleigh said with a sigh as they were finally able to sit down. "Still sure you want all this?"

"I'm sure, Eve." Bess smiled back. "Brad said if I was sure, he would support it, and I am sure. I hate to do this, but I have to go."

"It's ok. It's well after our usual closing and I'm sure Jack will be back soon." Everleigh walked Bess to the back door where they hugged and said goodbye.

Before she had a chance to close the door, Jack pulled up driving a steel blue Jeep that loosely resembled a small pickup truck. It was bigger than her car and he was able to get out easily.

"Well, what do you think?" he asked with a smile. "It's two years old, low mileage, mechanically sound, and yours if you like it."

Everleigh walked around it without a word, which made Jack a little nervous. When she got back to him, she threw her arms around him. "I love it!"

"My buddy at the car lot said he could have the paperwork done for tomorrow. Provided you like driving it." He handed her the keys.

"I just have to get some stuff I need to finish tonight, and we can go." She ran back inside, excited. She checked the front door was locked and grabbed the file box full of papers she was going to work on and locked the back door.

Jack took the box and put it on the back seat. Everleigh got in behind the wheel. Jack showed her how to adjust the seat and mirrors and she settled in quickly.

He got in the other side and off they went. Everleigh was surprised how comfortable she felt driving it. It was bigger than her car, with a full-size back seat and short, pick-up style bed, but she could see more than she could in Jack's truck. She had to admit Jack had done a good job picking out her new vehicle.

After driving around for a while, they made a quick stop to pick up some dinner and they were on their way home.

It didn't take long for Everleigh to have papers covering the kitchen table. Jack sat on the couch watching TV, occasionally looking over his shoulder to see her working away. Hours went by before she was able to stack it all neatly back into the box. She hoped with all her heart her numbers would match what Bess got, so they wouldn't have to do it again.

Jack waited a few minutes to allow her time to get ready for bed. He checked the door and turned out the lights before getting ready himself. The bedroom light was bright enough for her to get a drink in the kitchen while she waited for him.

As she stood at the sink, she heard a familiar sound. She set down the glass with a shaking hand and walked to where she could just see the road over the balcony rail. She watched in silence as her mother got out of her car and walked up to the blue Jeep parked in her spot. She really hoped she hadn't left anything sitting in it her mother would recognize as hers.

"Jack," she called as loud as she dared, while keeping an eye on her mother. "She's here."

"Who's here?" he asked as he joined her at the balcony door.

"That's my mother. That's Amelia." Everleigh was starting to worry.

"Does she have a key? Can she get in?" he asked. Everleigh said no. "Then we wait and see what she does. There's no reason to think she knows you're here."

The two watched until Amelia started walking toward the building. Jack led Everleigh to the bedroom, where he turned out the light and again they waited, not daring to speak.

"Everleigh!" There was a loud bang on the door. "Come on, Everleigh. I don't have the patience for games," Amelia shouted.

Then more banging, but it was softer this time. When she didn't get the answer she wanted, she turned her attention to the door across the hall.

"How can I help stop your pounding and yelling at this late hour, Mrs. Roberts?" Sam asked.

"You have a key to my daughter's apartment, and I want it," Amelia demanded.

"I am certain you understand why I have NO intention of doing that," Sam replied calmly. "If Everleigh wanted you to have access to her apartment while she's gone, she would have given you a key. Now if you don't mind, I have an early rotation at the hospital in the morning and I don't think the folks on the ground floor would appreciate you waking their baby with all your yelling and banging."

Jack went to the door so he could hear Sam's side of the conversation better, but there wasn't much more to it. She asked who was parked in Everleigh's space and Sam said he didn't know, but as she didn't need it at the moment, there was no harm.

Amelia, realizing she wasn't going to get anywhere, stomped back outside. Jack went back to the balcony door and Everleigh stepped up next to him. They watched her walk around the Jeep again before getting back in her car and leaving.

There was a softer knock at the door and Jack went to answer it. He opened the door and welcomed Sam inside. The two men spoke for a moment before Sam turned his attention to Everleigh.

"Hi, Eve. I knew you were home, but I left so early this morning, I didn't want to wake you." He smiled. "I did want to invite you both over for pizza tomorrow. Dom is home and I know he would love to see you before you go again. He has some news I think you're really going to like."

"I would love that!" she answered. "It's been so long since I saw him last."

"I'll be back in a minute," Jack said as he stepped out and closed the door behind.

Everleigh went to bed to wait for him. She had almost drifted off when she felt Jack lay down behind her and pulled her close.

"I haven't seen Sam in a long time," he whispered. "I told him you know about the Brotherhood among other things."

"Do you think we're safe?" Everleigh asked. She hadn't really thought about it until now, but the possibility seemed to have been growing in her mind unnoticed.

"I think you need to get some sleep and let me worry about that." He kissed her neck.

"That's not an answer." She said it so softly he almost missed it.

"No, Everleigh, I can't promise we're safe." His voice was soft. "What I can promise is that I will do everything in my power to protect you from whatever comes."

His promise was good enough.

CHAPTER 9

Everleigh woke early and was going through her inventory list for the third time when Jack joined her at the table.

"I bet it's still the same as it was last night." He smiled.

"It is. Are you ready to go?" she asked, stacking it all back into the box. "We can pick up something to eat on the way."

Jack agreed. He carried the box out to the Jeep so he could take a good look around before waving for her to join him. With last night's visit from Amelia, he wanted to make sure she hadn't returned.

Everleigh hopped in the passenger seat and Jack drove. They stopped for a cheap drive-thru breakfast and stopped again at the park to eat it. It was too early to head to the shop so they went to a moving store and got what they hoped would be enough boxes to add to what they brought with them. They looped back around to the car dealership where Everleigh signed the papers for her new Jeep and collected her things from the car.

By the time they got to the shop, Bess was getting out of her car with a box of papers that looked very much like the one Everleigh was carrying. Jack opened the back door of the shop, taking a careful look around before following the girls inside.

"I'll leave the two of you to do whatever it is you're doing, and I'll be back soon." Jack kissed her cheek. "Keep the doors locked and try to avoid that huge window if at all possible."

Everleigh smiled and agreed.

"What? No kiss for me?" Bess joked as Jack headed for the door.

Everleigh laughed at the shocked look on Bess' face when Jack turned back and kissed her cheek too.

With Jack out the door, they settled into working on the numbers and completing the master inventory sheet. Their numbers were a match, which made the whole process go much faster than either had expected.

By the time Jack returned, it was time for lunch. They walked down to the cafe at the end of the block. Both Bess and Everleigh were glad to get out of the shop for a bit. As much as they loved flowers, that kind of paperwork was draining.

It was a nice day, but Jack gently requested they eat inside, to which both girls sighed but agreed. They took their time, listening to the stories Jack told about the lovely places he'd been over the years. They, in turn, told him about fun they had in the city. This was a side of Everleigh he hadn't seen. He enjoyed seeing her so happy and having fun. Her time at Mallard Pond had been so unsettled. He had never heard her laugh like this.

On the walk back, Jack followed the girls giving them as much time as they wanted to look in the other shop windows and enjoy the sunshine.

He noticed a man peering in the window of their shop and asked them, "Wait here."

"He's protective, isn't he?" Bess asked with a sly smile.

"Yes, he can be." Everleigh smiled back.

"Hi, can I help you?" Jack asked, approaching the stranger.

"Hi, I hope so. My name's Josh and I'm supposed to meet the owner of this shop, Miss Roberts. I'm a little early I know. I was hoping it would be alright, but it seems she's not here at the moment," he replied, handing Jack a business card.

"This is Everleigh Roberts, and Bess is the shop manager." Jack extended his arm for the girls to join him.

"It's nice to meet you." Everleigh shook his hand and Bess did the same, with a smile.

Jack held the door and locked it again when they were inside. The conversation turned from friendly to business quickly. Jack took Everleigh's arm and pulled her aside.

"I'll leave you two for a while. There are a couple more errands I need to see to for our Hall. They shouldn't take more than an hour. If Bess leaves, you call me! I don't want you here alone." The warning in his voice was clear.

"I'll call you," she agreed. "Goodbye," she said and kissed his cheek.

Jack walked to the door pulled out his phone and took a quick picture of Josh and left. When he got back to the Jeep he sent the picture to Carl in a text along with the details from his business card, and asked Carl to check him out. He was recommended by Paul Adams, so Jack didn't expect anything to come up.

* * *

Jack was at his last stop before heading back to the shop. "Hi, Tom. How is everything?" he asked as he answered his phone.

"Where is Everleigh?" came the sharp reply.

"She's at the shop with the realtor guy and her friend Bess. Why, what's wrong?" He started walking faster back to the Jeep.

"I don't know who you think you left them with, but the guy in the picture you sent is Kenneth Monto. He's been on our radar for a while." Tom sounded worried. "I printed copies of everything we have on him. I'll give them to Scott and send him to you. They're moving fast, Jack and we now have proof her mother's involved. She knew everything, just as Everleigh feared."

Jack raced back to the shop. Everything looked as he had left it. He tried the back door, but it was still locked. Taking a deep breath, he forced himself to walk calmly around to the front door. He had to use the key to open it and hoped that was a good sign.

Everything was silent. His heart started racing. "Everleigh?" he called to no response.

He kept moving slowly, careful not to touch anything. When he walked to the back room, Bess was lying on the floor with a nasty-looking cut on her head and there was no sign of Everleigh.

He dialed 911. "Hi. My name is Jack. I need an ambulance to the Little Flower Shop corner of East and Main. Bess is on the floor with head injuries."

"Ok, sir, help is on the way. Is Bess breathing?"

"Yes, steady pulse, but she is unconscious. We're going to need police too. The owner is missing. She should be here and she's not." Jack's temper was rising more with himself than anything else.

"How do you know she's missing, sir?"

"If you could see the mess in here, you wouldn't be asking that." Jack hung up the call.

"Jack?"

"Tom, she's gone." Jack's voice cracked but he recovered quickly.

"Tell us what you know, Jack." Tom sounded farther away, indicating the phone was now on speaker, so others in the room could also hear.

"Her friend Bess was knocked out. She's alive. I have help coming for her." Jack slid easily into his role as the observant Warrior. "It looks like she put up a fight. There are papers all over her office. Her chair is flipped, broken pots and plants on the floor. Her phone is here. They left it so we can't track it. Police have arrived."

"Jack, take the phone. Don't let the police have it," Tom said. "Call us when you can."

"I'll meet you at her apartment. I have the address and I'm leaving now," Scott said.

Jack hung up, tucked his phone in one pocket, set hers to silent, and tucked it into the other before going to the door.

"Are you Jack?" the officer asked. "The one that called?"

"I am." He led the EMS workers to where Bess was and rejoined the officers at the door.

"I'm Detective Mitchell. Can you tell me how it is you found this scene?" he asked.

"The owner, Everleigh Roberts, is my girlfriend. I left her here with Bess, her store manager, and this guy." He handed the detective the card the 'not Josh' guy had given him. He explained she was in the process of selling the shop and that Bess was helping her and she was the intended buyer.

Jack told them how he went in and found Bess on the floor, the office a mess and Everleigh gone.

"She would never just walk away from Bess like that," Jack said as the EMS workers wheeled her past them and out of the shop to the ambulance.

"Can you describe the man you left the ladies with?" Detective Mitchell asked. The officer taking notes over his shoulder stepped up closer.

"I can do one better." Jack pointed to the security camera but noticed it wasn't facing the same way.

The two men went into Everleigh's office. Jack set her chair upright and sat down. Detective Mitchell excused the officer following them and closed the door.

"Now let's cut the crap and tell me everything." He put his hands on the desk tapping the ring finger of his right hand against the wood. Jack looked down and saw the blue sparkling stone of his Brotherhood ring. "Let's start with where you're from."

"Eldaguard Hall." Jack waited for him to pick up a chair on the other side of the desk and sit down. He handed him his phone with the picture of the man open. "This is who I left her with. He said his name was Josh. We had never met Josh, so we had no reason not to trust him. The real Josh was recommended by a friend of the brotherhood. I sent the picture to Elder Carl and Elder Tom called saying his name is really—"

"Kenneth Monto," Detective Mitchell interrupted. "I've had dealings with this guy before. Nothing I could grab him for, legally speaking, but in a dark alley, it would have been a different story. I'll get someone to track down this Josh guy and make sure they didn't kill him to take his place. I sent that picture to my private phone, so you have my number if you need any off-the-books help."

"I have the security footage." Jack accepted his phone back. "Thank you."

Detective Mitchell moved his chair around beside Jack so the two could watch together.

The four cameras were set up on the screen so all four could be viewed at the same time. One camera showed the group enter and Jack leave. Another showed the girls walking to the back while the first camera showed Kenneth walk back to the door and unlock it before joining them in the back.

The third camera showed the back work area. By the girls' lack of reaction, they hadn't noticed him return to the door. The three entered the same office where Jack and the detective were now sitting.

"Look." Jack pointed to the front door camera.

Another, much larger man had entered the shop wearing a ball cap. He walked toward the camera and suddenly the camera's view was the wall. The same happened to the camera on the other side of the shop.

The camera over the door of the back room could clearly be seen from the office and Jack looked up at it. It, too, had been turned to face a wall.

"Look! He put his finger on the glass. We may be able to pull a print from it or maybe even a clear image from the feed." The detective made a note of the time of the feed.

They continued to watch. The girls were still calm. Everleigh was standing at her desk, with her back to the door, and Bess was standing next to her. Kenneth, who had a clear view of what was happening, made no indication anything was amiss.

There was no sound on the video but something outside the office got their attention. Bess left the office and Everleigh walked around the other side of her desk and sat down to type on her computer.

Jack had to force himself to keep watching, knowing any second all hell was going break loose in that tiny office.

Everleigh's head popped up and he could feel her fear. The new man was walking towards the office door. He wasn't on camera yet, but both men could see her reacting to something.

Suddenly Everleigh jumped to her feet and Kenneth grabbed her arm roughly, yanking her back, knocking over her chair, and forcing her to her knees. The new man's head was now blocking the camera, whether by accident or intent, they didn't know. Two minutes later the two men left the room.

"Where is she?" the detective asked. "Did you see her with them?"

The room on the screen was almost a match for the room they were sitting in. Chairs overturned, papers everywhere, and the laptop was now closed, as it had been when they entered to view the feed.

"Look there." Jack's heart skipped a beat.

Everleigh was pulling herself up from the floor. Cut and bleeding, she lifted her laptop, slid something under it and looked up directly into the camera before falling back to the floor.

The two men entered the room again. One grabbed her arms and the other reached for her feet. Everleigh gave a kick that sent the man at her feet backwards into her bookshelf, knocking the potted plants to the floor.

"That's my girl." Jack smiled with a quick stab of pride.

The man quickly recovered bleeding badly from his nose and hit her hard across her face. Her head rolled and she was still. They carried her out of the office and that was it.

Jack slumped in his chair. Detective Mitchell lifted the laptop and pulled out a torn piece of paper with blood on it. Written in what obviously had been a shaking hand was 'Donald'.

"Mean anything to you?" Detective Mitchell showed the paper to him.

Jack jumped to his feet, turned, and punched the filing cabinet so hard he dented the door and cut his knuckles.

"Sir, are you alright?" An officer, seeing what happened, opened the door hand on his still holstered weapon.

"We're fine thank you," Detective Mitchell said as he pushed the chair over to Jack. "Could you toss that first aid kit over?"

The officer did and closed the door behind him.

"I'm going to guess this little note has a larger meaning," he commented as he bandaged Jack's bleeding hand.

"Check your files. Three years ago. Donald Pullman." Jack was breathing deeply trying to get his anger back under control. "He should be in prison, but she would know him better than anyone."

"I will help you in any way I can, but if you're going to make a move, I need to know. It can't look like police interference. The last thing I want to have to do is arrest you." There was no threat in his tone as he spoke. "I'm a detective, Jack. I can only draw attention away from you if I know what you're doing."

Jack understood what he was saying and thanked him.

"Where are you staying?"

"Everleigh's apartment." Jack leaned forward in the chair and saw blood on the floor, Everleigh's blood, and sat back again. "The Elders have already sent my partner and contacted your Hall."

"I have no problem with that, but I want an officer to go with you. Have a look around the apartment and if you don't see anything out of place, he'll leave." Detective Mitchell put his hand on Jack's shoulder. "We'll find her."

"There is something else," Jack offered. "This was planned. There was a man in here the other day. He was looking at the cameras. He was also here with a woman a few days before that. It's all recorded."

"Do you know who she was?" He had the feeling there was more coming.

"I'm going to trust you with this because I have to find her. It's not just any woman we're looking for. She's a witch." Jack sighed and pulled Everleigh's phone from his pocket and held it to his chest. He told the detective about the arguments between Everleigh and her mother and that it went back even further into Brotherhood business.

"I get what you mean," Detective Mitchell sighed. "This life has divided more than one family. If I need to know more, I'll go through Brotherhood channels. Keep it off the books."

Jack showed him the messages from her mother and the ones from Bess, as well as the voice messages from both.

"The woman who brought that guy here was her mother!" Detective Mitchell sat on the desktop. "You don't think she was trying to draw her back here? She set up her own daughter?"

"Her name is Amelia Roberts. It's a long story, but the point is her magic was taken somehow. They didn't know about Everleigh until she came to us," Jack said coldly. "We're not assuming anything but it's starting to look that way." Jack sighed and picked up the photo from her desk of the three girls together in front of the shop. "Our Hall found proof linking Amelia to the Balordran Order."

"Ok, this is...I don't really know what this is. We have a couple of names to start with. Why don't you go home and wait for your partner? Take her phone with you. If I need it, I'll get it from you later. I can say it was found tucked under something." He looked around. "It really could be found anywhere. You may want to upload everything on her phone just in case. Here, take this too. It's a copy of the footage from today. I recorded it while we watched. I'll be taking the computer with me."

"I'll send it to my Hall," Jack said accepting the drive with a shaking hand. "The Elders may see something we don't."

Detective Mitchell agreed. "Let them know it's coming. Wouldn't want them to see it cold, if you know what I mean."

The two men parted company and Jack went to wait by the Jeep for the officer who was following him home.

It was a long, lonely drive back to the apartment. Everything looked good from the outside. Part of him hoped he would find her inside. He opened the door and, with the officer, took a quick look around. Nothing was out of place. Everything was just as they had left it that morning.

Jack walked the officer to the door and thanked him for coming to check. Sam was coming up the stairs with, who Jack assumed must be Dom, their arms full of pizza and laughing. That ended as the officer passed them and they looked up and saw Jack's face.

"Not now." Jack was quickly falling apart.

He walked back into the apartment, her apartment. He kicked off his shoes and walked into the bathroom. He stood for a long while with his head against the shower wall. The hot water beating on his back, and he cried.

Time had no meaning. Five minutes, or ten minutes, it all felt empty. He got out of the shower, dressed, and went into the kitchen but wasn't hungry.

"Jack, come sit with me, my boy."

He turned around and there sitting on the couch was Lilli. Jack did as she requested and sat at her feet, leaning on the couch like he had when he was child and she told him stories.

"If you lose hope, then she is lost," Lilli said softly stroking his hair.

"I don't know how to find her, Lilli. I've never felt like this." Jack's voice was pleading. "Tell me what to do."

"You're a Warrior, Jack, you know what to do. Don't shut out those who can help you. Accept their help, but know it is you who will find her. If you lose yourself in your grief, you will lose her forever."

A knock on the door drew his attention away from Lilli and, when he looked back, she was gone, just the way Everleigh had described when she saw her. A quick look around and he realized he had no memory of leaving the shower, getting dressed, or sitting on the floor, but here he was with Lilli's words echoing in his mind.

Jack went to the door. Scott stood there with the dossier Tom had made and his rucksack on his back. Sam and Dom stood behind him.

Scott stepped inside and embraced him. "We'll find her," he whispered as both men parted with tears in their eyes.

Sam and Dom took the pizza to the kitchen and busied themselves so the two could have a moment. Scott had arrived while Jack was in the shower. Sam, hearing the knocking, went to see who it was, greeted him, and invited him in to wait. Scott had used the time to tell them what he knew, and they completely understood Jack's reaction to them earlier on the stairs.

While they ate, they carefully went over everything in the files, putting pieces together like a puzzle. When they had gone through everything in the file, and everything that had happened that afternoon, Jack walked to the coffee table and picked up the drive.

"Jack, what's that?" Scott asked.

"It's the security footage from the shop," he answered coldly turning it over in his hands.

"Have you watched it?" Scott was speaking carefully unsure what he was about to do with it.

"I have and I don't want to see it again." He reached out and Scott took the drive.

"Why don't you two go across the hall? That way you don't have to see it, Jack," Dom suggested.

After a time, Scott came back alone with the drive in his shaking hand.

"Dom, you best go," he suggested. "Sam needs you."

"Try and sleep, Jack," Dom said as he stood up from the table. "If you want something to help, I can give you something of mine. They're pretty strong but you need to rest."

Jack understood his kindness but declined.

With the door closed and locked, Scott turned in time to see Jack fall to the floor. He was on his knees sobbing. Scott sat down at his side.

"It's my fault. I shouldn't have left her. I have to get her back, Scott." Jack coughed. "You know what they'll do to her."

"We'll get her back. Jack, I promise we'll get her back." Scott helped him up and took him to the bedroom.

Jack lay down and pulled her pillow tight to his chest. Her PJs had been folded under it and he tucked her t-shirt under his face and cried himself to sleep for the first time since he was a child.

CHAPTER 10

It was late in the morning and Scott had been up for hours. He had his laptop out on the table poring over everything the Hall was sending him that had come in from their unnamed sources in the city, as well as the Brotherhood's Hall. Most of it was not helpful at the moment but might be useful later on.

Sam and Dom were also up early and had gone out for coffee. Sam went to work at the hospital and Dom brought back breakfast for Scott and Jack.

"I sent the footage to the Hall this morning. I called Carl and told him about it first." Scott looked down at the drive. "It's not easy to watch."

Everleigh's phone buzzed on the counter and Jack picked it up.

"It's been going off all morning. Maybe we should just turn it off?" Scott suggested.

"Jen, it's Jack." Jack answered her phone when he saw the name.

"Oh my God. Where's Eve? I can't reach Bess and you have Eve's phone. What's going on?" Jen's panic was rising but Jack let her go on. "The police just left. They were asking all kinds of questions about Bess and Eve and that strange guy that kept showing up. Jack? Jack, are you there?"

"I'm here," he said calmly. "Is there somewhere we could meet? I would rather tell you face to face."

"Is the park ok? By the picnic tables?" She was starting to breathe heavily, and he could tell she was worried.

"I know where that is. I can be there in ten minutes. Is there someone you can bring with you?" He knew this wasn't going to be easy for either of them.

* * *

Scott followed Jack's directions to the park and waited by his truck. As they expected, Jen had arrived early and, as Jack had requested, she wasn't alone. As soon as she saw him, she jumped from the bench and waved. He could tell, as her smile faded, she was looking for Everleigh.

"Jack, this is my boyfriend Connor." Jen gave them time for a quick greeting before diving in. "Where is Eve?"

"Before I tell you, I need to know what you said to the police." Jack could see panic rising and he walked her gently back to the bench to sit down. "You may have a detail I don't have, and I need every bit I can get. It's very important, Jen." He was kneeling in front of her.

She told him everything the police asked and repeated her answers.

"Is that everything? Is there anything you remember now that you didn't tell them?" he asked when she stopped.

"What's going on? Where are Eve and Bess?" She was begging now, and Jack knew he had to tell her.

"This isn't going to be easy to hear, ok? I need you to listen to everything." He glanced over at Conner, who moved closer and put his arm around her. "Bess is in the hospital. She took a blow to her head yesterday afternoon. She has a concussion, so they are keeping her for a day or two."

Jen was staring into his eyes and rocking, common, he thought, for someone so upset.

"Everleigh is missing." He was talking slowly allowing her time to digest what he was saying. "They were attacked in the shop. It looks like they were only after Everleigh."

"Eve?" Jen cried and doubled over. Jack caught her and helped her back up on the bench where Conner took her in his arms.

"We are going to find her, Jen, that I promise you." He looked at Conner. "Try to keep her focused on Bess. Maybe together the two of them might come up with something. If not, they will at least be a comfort for each other."

Conner agreed and helped Jen back to the car, promising to take her to the hospital to see Bess before going home.

Jack and Scott waited until they left before leaving themselves.

"Where is she?" Jack asked, looking around at all the tall buildings through the trees. "Is she even still in the city?"

Scott put his hand on Jack's shoulder. "We'll find her, brother. Why don't we look into the realtor? The real Josh what's-his-name. Maybe there is something there," Scott suggested.

* * *

They spent the next few days in Scott's truck running down every lead no matter how remote it seemed, but found no trace.

"Hello?" Jack answered his phone. "I can be there in a few minutes. We're not far."

"Make a left up here. We have to go see Everleigh's lawyer." Jack's face may have been unreadable to most people, but a quick glance told Scott he was on edge.

"Jack, thank you for coming so quickly," Mark greeted him. It was clear he had been waiting at the front desk. "Come with me. I'm sorry. You are?" he asked seeing Scott for the first time.

"This is Scott Mason. He's my partner," Jack said as Mark picked up his case and started for the door.

"I am sorry for the rush, but we are going to be late for a hearing I found out about just before I called you. We'll take my car. Get in," Mark said unlocking a shiny black BMW.

Jack and Scott got in the passenger side. Mark put his case on the back seat next to Scott and got in behind the wheel.

"The courthouse isn't far, so you had better start telling me anything I may need to know before we get there. I can explain what's happening later, but for now I need to know what happened from the day Everleigh went missing through today." Mark was speaking quickly.

Jack summed up the events the news had not included in their report and was able to finish as they reached the courthouse parking lot.

"Ok, we need to get through security fast. Leave anything electronic in the car." Mark opened the console and put in his own cell phone as well. "Any loose change, jewelry, anything metallic, the less we have, the faster we can get through."

They made it to the courtroom door and Mark stopped and faced them. "You're going to stand on my left side. You're not going to say anything. You're not going to react to anything. That's what they want. If the judge asks you a question, answer it with a direct answer, nothing more. If he asks, 'what colour is the sky?' you answer 'blue' not blue with clouds, not blue but sometimes gray, just 'blue, your honor.' Understand?"

Both men agreed and followed Mark into the courtroom. Glancing at the people on the right-hand side, Jack thought he recognized the woman as Amelia, but he wasn't sure.

The judge took his seat, shuffled a few papers, and looked to the petitioner side. "Mrs. Roberts, you have come to court today to request guardianship of your daughter's, a Miss Everleigh Roberts, home and business. For ease and clarity, we will refer to her as Miss Everleigh." Both sides nodded in agreement. "You claim she is a missing person. What I find confusing is that you dispute the claim, Mr. Adams, so please would you enlighten the court as to why?"

"Yes, thank you, Your Honor. In the interest of clarity, we do not dispute that Miss Everleigh is missing at this time. However, at the time this request was filed on the 27th of August, she was in fact in my office that morning, at her business Little Flower Shop in the afternoon, and seen by neighbors that evening at her apartment."

"You have evidence to prove this?" the judge asked.

"I do, Your Honor. I can actually do better than that. There is a surveillance video in police evidence that shows on the 28th of August Miss Everleigh was abducted while working in her office. The detective on the case is—"

"Stop, stop, stop." The judge looked up from his papers and looked directly at Mark. "Mr. Adams, correct me if I'm wrong, but did you say abducted?"

"Yes sir, I said abducted." Mark took a quick look at Jack before continuing. "I am told the video is rather graphic and shows a beaten and bleeding Everleigh being removed from her office unconscious by two as yet unidentified men."

The judge sat back in his seat and looked towards Amelia. "This does not seem like the missing person case you're attempting to sell me, Mr. Bly."

"Your Honor, we have no knowledge of any of this being true. Mrs. Roberts is simply looking out for her daughter's best interest as she has had no contact with her for several days," Mr. Bly stated in a matter-of-fact tone.

"If I may approach, Your Honor?" Detective Mitchell stood from his seat in the gallery holding his badge up for the judge to see.

"You may," the judge said, looking very unimpressed by all the surprises so far.

"I am Detective Mitchell, the lead on Miss Everleigh's case. I am in possession of the surveillance video mentioned. There is also evidence that this was a highly planned and well executed abduction, resulting in the severe injury of the store's manager as well."

"Mr. Adams, can you account for the lack of communication in the days leading up to this unfortunate event?" The judge was leaning forward making notes.

"I can, sir. Detective Mitchell has provided transcripts of the text conversation between mother and daughter. They are not very civil exchanges. I would suggest Miss Everleigh simply decided to stop engaging." Mark picked up a pile of papers and held them up. "Further to the point, the day before this petition was filed, Miss Everleigh came to my office and requested Power of Attorney to be filed with the court, which was subsequently approved by the court."

"I would like to see that." The court officer retrieved the document and they all waited for the judge to read it.

"Jack Killian, am I pronouncing that correctly?" the judge asked looking for someone to answer.

Mark motioned for Jack to stand. "Yes, sir. You are," he answered.

"Good. We don't have to waste time looking for you." The judge continued reading. "So, you, Mr. Killian, have control of her assets until the time she is found safe and sound."

"Yes, sir," Jack offered.

"Then this court has no choice, in light of the evidence presented today and the open investigation into what happened, but to uphold Miss Everleigh's wishes." The judge closed the file folder and leaned forward looking at Jack. "Mr. Killian, my most sincere hope for her safe return goes with you. Until that time, this court is entrusting you, as she has, to act in her best interest." Jack inclined his head and the judge turned to the other side of the room. "Mrs. Roberts, it is clear from the little I read of these texts that she had not responded to many of your demands for the last couple weeks. That makes this request even more suspect. Instead of reaching out in a pleasant manner, you resort to using the courts to force her to deal with you. I hope that when she is found, you will make an effort to apologize for some of the things you sent her." He sat back in his chair. "The ruling of the court denies the request of Mrs. Amelia Roberts and upholds the Power of Attorney issued to Miss Everleigh Roberts, naming Mr. Jack Killian her proxy. Count is adjourned."

"Where is my daughter? What have you done with her?" Amelia was on her feet and yelling across the courtroom.

"Do not respond. Just follow me back to the car," Mark said, calmly looking at the two men.

Jack and Scott looked at each other but said nothing. They followed Mark back through the courthouse and out to the car. Jack noticed Mark nod at someone in a car several spaces away before reaching the BMW.

The three were silent while Mark unlocked the console, and they collected their phones.

"What was that about?" Scott asked, still trying to put it together. "Imagine if you had a child and you heard they went from missing to violently abducted. Wouldn't you react? That woman didn't flinch. Not even a tear."

"That's because she knows where Everleigh is." Jack's voice was unnervingly steady. He was staring straight ahead taking long deep breaths.

"She could have made this kind of request through her lawyer, but I had a feeling she would be here." He opened the small door to the charging port on his dash and pulled out a small slip of torn paper and handed it to Jack.

"What's this?" he asked looking at the series of letters and numbers.

"The man you saw me nod to. He's a PI friend of mine. I sent him Amelia's picture and asked him to watch for her to show up here." Mark paused as he pulled the car out into traffic and headed back to his office. "He calls himself a 'Technogeek'. Basically, he has lots of handy gadgets and knows what he's doing. I asked him if she showed up, could he place a GPS tracker on her car. In your hand is the access code to follow the tracker."

"That's great!" Scott said, hoping it would lighten Jack's temper, which seemed to be growing shorter by the minute, but he said nothing.

When they got back to the office, Jack handed back the paper and walked towards Scott's truck. Mark went inside to get started and to give the two a minute. Jack stopped at the bed of the truck and leaned over the side, resting his head on the cold metal. Scott stood beside him with his back to the truck and watched the cars passing on the road.

"I want her back, Scott," Jack said after awhile. "I want her back in my arms, NOW!" He punched the tire so hard his arm ached all the way to his shoulder.

Scott jumped. There had never been any doubt that Jack was much stronger than he looked, but he moved so quickly and with a ferocity Scott had never seen or thought him capable of.

"She has her." Jack was pacing next to the truck. "She has her. I know she has her." He was shaking and breathing heavy.

"Jack, you wait here. I can get the website and—"

"No, I'm fine. I'm sorry." He sighed and leaned back over the truck.

"Last night I tried to imagine how I would feel if it were Sera." Scott stood beside him staring blankly into the truck bed. "Jack, I just couldn't."

"Trust me you don't ever want to feel this." Jack started walking towards the building.

* * *

Days turned into weeks and the only thing they were sure about was the places she wasn't.

Thanks to the GPS tracker, they knew where Amelia was at all times and, with the help of Detective Mitchell and the Brotherhood's members in the city, there was someone watching her from the moment she parked to the time she drove away again.

Jack was getting restless following up on leads that lead nowhere. Lilli's words began haunting his thoughts. 'If you lose hope, you will lose her forever'.

Thunder crashed and the rain started anew. It had been raining off and on for two days and Jack and Scott had agreed being out in the cold, late September rain was not a good idea. The TV was on, but they weren't paying much attention to it.

"Jack, I think we should try and sleep." Scott stretched. "There isn't anything we can do right now anyway, and we've been chasing our tails in here."

"No, I get it. We should try and rest," Jack agreed.

Scott nodded, turned the TV off and curled up on the couch.

Jack took a quick look at Scott and went to bed. He pulled Everleigh's phone from the bedside table and looked through the photos again.

He knew them all and every detail. There were pictures of her with Bess and Jen, the three together, some of her with people he hadn't met. When he got to the one with Sam and Dom, he stopped. He knew the next one. The last picture she had taken was of the two of them together with the pond behind them.

"Wake up, my boy. It's time." A soft voice woke him, and he was surprised to see Lilli sitting on the bed with Everleigh's phone in her hands. "I like this one of the two of you. Why don't you look at it anymore?"

"It hurts too much to see me smiling with her head on my shoulder." Jack pulled himself up and his hand went to his jaw where her lips had been seconds after she took the picture.

"Do you remember what I told you about pictures?" she asked, still looking down at it.

"They are a special kind of magic," he answered.

"They allow us to remember people long after they have left this world, whether they are in frames or in these little boxes." She turned and shook the phone at him.

"Are you telling me I'm too late? I've lost her?" Jack's voice cracked as his breath caught.

"No, but it is time now. This time, you will find her." Lilli set the phone down on the table and stood up. Jack followed the ghostly figure to the kitchen table and watched as she touched the laptop. "That is where you will find her. Keep your head my boy. Be the Warrior she needs you to be."

"Jack." Scott woke up rubbing his eyes and looking around. "Who are you talking to?"

"I know where she is." The loading screen changed as the GPS relocated to show a heavily wooded area with no icons for any type of buildings.

"What? How?" Scott scrambled to his feet to look at the screen. "There? You're sure?"

"Yes, she's there." Jack picked up his phone. Staring back at him was the picture of him with Everleigh at the pond. He paused to look at it, wondering how it got from her phone to his. Then he smiled to himself. "Lilli," he whispered.

"What was that?" Scott looked at the picture. "That's cute."

"I want to tell you how I know, and I need you to believe me," Jack said as he realized how it might sound.

Scott listened carefully. He wasn't sure if it was as real as Jack said it was, or just a vivid dream, but if it meant Everleigh was where Jack said she was, it was worth the trip out to have a look.

Jack called Tom and set the phone on the table.

"Jack, how are you doing?" Tom asked when he answered.

"Are you still watching the tracker?" Jack asked. "Can you tell us where Amelia is right now?"

"May take a second, but we should be able to tell you," Tom answered. "The tracker shows her car is at her home and the Warrior watching her confirms she's there."

"Can you check a set of coordinates for us and get a satellite look at what's at that location?" Jack read off the longitude and latitude and they waited.

"How is this tracker giving us a different location?" Scott whispered.

"Lilli gave us the location, not the tracker," Jack confirmed softly so Tom wouldn't hear. He didn't want to have to explain it to Tom.

The only sound was the clicking of the keyboard as Tom set his phone down to work the keys. "I got it. Whatever it is, it's well hidden. From what I can make out, there are a few buildings, maybe four. Two large ones and what looks like a vehicle shed maybe. There is something off to the side, but I can't really tell what."

Jack could feel himself growing impatient.

"Hang on." Tom was typing as fast as he could. "There could be another building. I can't be certain with all the trees in the way and, the closer I get, the more distorted the picture gets. Check your email."

"Got it," Scott answered and showed the picture to Jack.

"That first image is of the compound. Looks like chain link and barbed wire." Tom also sent the best images he could of the individual buildings and told them where they were located so they had a solid layout. "This last one I'm not sure. There could be a building there, but it's set away from the rest and there too many trees around it."

Scott printed the image of the compound. It would be the only map they were going to have when they found it, and Jack circled the building set away from the others.

"Jack, I have to ask. Your interest in this place. You think she's there?" Tom had been avoiding the question opting to focus on getting them the information first. "Do you need any help?"

"She's there. I know it." Jack was lost in the last image to print. It was hard to see, but there was a shape there that looked too rectangular to be natural.

"I think we'll go have a look at it first," Scott answered. "We'll let you know if we need anything."

Jack ran his fingers over the building he knew was there. "Hold on Leigh, just a little longer."

"Leigh?" Scott smiled.

"Oh, hush up." Jack felt his face heat up and turned away. "We need to get ready."

Scott knew Jack had only taken his knives when he left so he stopped by the Inn before leaving and got the rest of Jack's gear. A leather jacket and a set of sharp twin blades fit perfectly in sheathes sewn into the back of the jacket. When they were dressed, Jack sent a message to Detective Mitchell that they had a location to check.

As they walked out to the truck, he opened the tracking app on his phone and loaded the location, and they were ready to go.

"Guess I picked a good time to come by," Detective Mitchell said as he walked over to the truck. "You're not dressed to go out for dinner, so where are you headed?"

"Jack feels good about this one," Scott said smiling.

"We're going to check out a compound in the woods." Jack showed him the printed map and the detective smiled.

"Follow me. I have something you may need," he said and went back to his car.

Scott and Jack exchanged a look but did as he requested. They followed him to a large building on the opposite side of the city from where they wanted to be. The large door opened, and they drove inside.

"This is part of our Hall's buildings. We keep odds and ends here, things that may come in handy someday." They walked down a row of vehicles and stopped in front of a small pickup truck.

It was an odd green colour that was obviously custom painted. No electronics of any kind, not even windows or door locks. It had a bench seat across the back, but it was far too narrow for even children to sit on.

"I know the place you're talking about. We raided it a few years ago. There hasn't been anything out there since, but that's not to say there can't be now. This is one of the vehicles we took. You're welcome to take it, but there is something you should know. When I got your message, I was coming by to tell you I just got word from the prison and you're right. Donald should be there but he's not."

Jack and Scott shared a look.

"Turns out he met someone in the holding center while waiting for his transport. This guy had a shorter sentence, and he talked the guy into trading shirts with him. They each took the other's place. When they got to the prison, an extremely lazy and, as of a couple days ago, former intake guard was convinced by some half-baked story that their mug shots got mixed up on the files." Detective Mitchell was flexing his fists.

"So, Donald served the other guy's shorter sentence and was released?" Scott asked. "Without Everleigh's note, there's a good chance no one would have ever found out."

"That is a very real possibility," the detective had to admit.

"Have you been to this compound?" Jack asked.

"I wasn't there as a cop, but yes. I can give you a bit of the layout. It's a long drive into the woods as I recall." Jack handed him the printed overhead view that Tom had sent. "These two buildings are barracks and training. That's where you'll find most of them. That is nothing more than a carport, no walls, just beams holding up a roof."

"What is this building?" Jack pointed to the one he had circled.

"I remember going in there. I don't know what it was when it was built, but there was nothing in it when I went through it. It's a long hallway with lots of little rooms and some cages. Might have been for small animals and storage at one point I guess." Detective Mitchell looked up from the paper. "You think she's there, don't you?"

"I know she's there." Jack picked up the paper from the truck's hood and folded it back into his pocket.

"Keys are in it, and you've got a full tank of gas." Scott shook his hand. "You need help out there, call me. I won't be coming with cops, if you get my meaning."

Scott moved his truck into a parking spot, so it was out of the way and got in the green truck with Jack. They pulled out onto the road and started back across the city.

As they neared the edge of the city, Scott took Jack's phone and set the navigation. A robotic woman's voice began giving directions.

"You have reached your destination on the right," she said and both men looked at each other. It was the entrance to a conservation area. A closed sign hung in the center of a chain reaching across the entrance.

A young man popped out of a small shack, approached the truck and Jack rolled the window down.

"Hi," the young man greeted them with a smile. "Is this your first time here?"

"Yes it is. Not really sure where we're going," Jack said with a well-practiced tone.

"It's about three miles back. Just stay on this road and you'll find it." The young man moved the chain and Jack drove through with a wave of thanks.

"That was far too easy," Scott said, and Jack agreed.

The conservation area was not just a front to hide the Balordran compound; it was actually an operational conservation area. They passed roads with signs in the shape of arrows saying picnic area, swimming, family camping and bike/hiking trails.

"Everleigh told me about this place," Jack said looking around as they passed the lake. "She said she used to come here to day camp when she was a kid."

Large trees, groomed trails, and picnic areas made the two men begin to wonder if they really were in the right place until a large chain link fence appeared in front of them with a guard standing on each side of a sliding gate.

"What's the plan, Jack?" Scott asked.

"We can't turn around. They've seen us." Jack looked over. "We go in blind. It's not like it's the first time we've done it."

Both men slid into their Warrior mindset. Instinct and training would take over now.

As they slowly neared the gate, it opened, and they rolled past the guards with a nod. Looking around, they saw several trucks similar to the one they were driving and gave a silent thanks to Detective Mitchell.

Jack took a quick look and steered the truck toward the building that had become his sole focus. The closer they got to it, the fewer people seemed to be around. Jack backed the truck in next to the building, out of sight from the rest of the compound.

He waited for Scott to join him, and they walked to the door like they were supposed to be going inside. To their great relief, it was unlocked. They went inside and the door slammed closed behind them. They waited, frozen in place, listening for the sound of an alarm being raised but heard nothing.

"Jack, this place is huge. It's going to take forever to search it in the dark," Scott said. The faint light through the dirty windows wasn't going to help.

"A phone light is better than nothing, but we need to move. That truck will be noticed eventually, and I'd rather not have to fight my way out of here," Jack replied, pulling out his phone and turning on its flashlight.

Scott did the same and their search of the building began.

CHAPTER 11

Everleigh woke in a soft bed. The sun was up and shining through leaves. There was a light breeze bringing the smell of forest into the room.

She tried to sit up and realized, beyond her splitting headache, there was a tight collar around her neck. She reached up to touch it and was thrown back down onto the bed by a sharp shock that took her breath away.

"I'm sorry. I was hoping I would be here when you woke up." Amelia walked into the room with pitcher of water. "Here, take this. It will help with the headache."

"I'm not taking anything from you," Everleigh said as she watched her mother set the pills on a table next to a glass of water. "Where is Bess? What have you done?"

"Bess is fine. She'll have a bump on the head that's all." Amelia sat in a chair across from the bed. "I bet you're wondering what's around your neck. It's a silver collar. There are rules here that must be followed or, well, you felt the collar's power."

Everleigh sat up slowly, but the room started spinning.

"They are just Tylenol, nothing you haven't had before. There really is no need to suffer." She offered them again and this time Everleigh took them. "The collar is simple. You cannot touch it. In fact, no one can. The more you touch it, the more painful the shocks become. There is a single key and, as long as you stay close to it, nothing will happen. Right now, you are free to move around this room as you wish, though you may not leave it without punishment. The farther you get from the key, the worse the pain the collar sends into your body."

"So, I am a prisoner in a fancy cell," Everleigh said looking around. The room was very nice. The bed was next to a large window facing the forest. A table and two chairs, bookshelf, paper and pens rounded out the room. There was a soft carpet, and the walls were white with nothing on them. "Captors usually have something they want from their prisoners. Why else would they keep them alive? What do you want from me?" Her voice was cold and steady, not at all how she was feeling.

"I must apologize to you, Everleigh. I didn't see the potential in you, and I should have. For that, I am sorry." Amelia waited for a reaction but when she didn't get one changed her tact. "What I want, what we want, is for you to be a part of our organization."

"To what end?" Everleigh kept pushing.

"Everleigh, you can help bring magic back to the world." Amelia was starting to sound excited. "Witches shouldn't have to hide. They shouldn't have to be afraid use their gifts. We want to create a world where witches are free, not feared. Your magic can help us create the tools we need to make that world a reality."

"Tools or weapons?" she asked coldly. "Seems to me if you were giving me a choice, I would have been asked instead of beaten and dragged off."

"Your wounds were all healed as soon as you arrived." Amelia smiled, ignoring Everleigh's question.

"Not the point, mother," Everleigh said coldly.

"The point is you can help us, and we will take care of you." Amelia's tone softened again. "You can give up that flower shop and join us here. We have everything you could want and there are witches here who can teach and guide you."

"And when I decline your offer?" Everleigh did her best not to betray the growing fear as she remembered the story Marcus had told her about how he met Lilli.

"Decline? Why would you decline?" Amelia smiled sweetly. "This is a chance for us to get to know each other again, for us to reconnect with a common purpose."

"I have a purpose, mother. You have never understood that." Everleigh's fear was turning to anger. "Nothing I ever did was worthy of your praise or even garnered your acceptance."

"That's going a little far don't you think?" Amelia was losing patience. She hadn't expected Everleigh to be so strong-willed.

"Amelia, can I speak to you for a moment?" The voice came from a man outside the room, and it didn't sound happy. Everleigh carefully moved closer to the door to try and hear what they were saying.

"You said she would be easy to break. The only thing broken is my son's nose."

She knew instantly who the speaker was. Donald's father. What she had feared became very real. The Balordran had her. She wished she had pushed Jack harder to tell her about them.

"Again, sir, I am so sorry for that. She was scared and if—"

"If nothing. I am going speed this up." He turned to Everleigh. "I will give you one final chance when I return with her." His voice was angry, and Everleigh decided not to push this man too far.

When he entered the room, Everleigh was sitting on the bed again. He walked to the center of the room, took out a strange-looking object and put it into the floor. A little door popped open, and he retrieved something, holding it up for her to see. It looked like some kind of green stone about the size of a large marble.

Looking past him, she saw her mother standing next to the door. Her head was down, eyes to the floor, hands at her side. Everleigh couldn't be sure, but she seemed frightened.

"Do you remember me?" he asked in the same cold tone, to which Everleigh didn't answer. "You will learn I do not repeat myself."

With a slight turn of the green object he was holding, a sharp pain tore its way down her spine. Everleigh was again thrown down, this time to the floor at his feet.

"Richard Pullman," she panted. "You're Donald's father."

"Better. Now maybe you'll answer when spoken to." He took a step back. "Get on your feet and keep up."

He walked at a pace that almost made her have to jog and didn't let her look around. They stopped in what seemed to be the center of the compound. She could see the fence surrounding it and the armed guards at the gate.

"You are at least a day's hike through heavy brush in every direction from where you now stand. That is assuming you can survive the pain of the collar long enough to get out of the key's range. Let me assure you. No one who has tried got more than five or six steps into the pain before they died an agonizing death." He smiled a menacing smile that chilled Everleigh's blood. "Now walk back the way we came!" he ordered.

She hesitated for a moment before turning and taking three steps. There were people watching from all over and she knew what was coming. On her fifth step the collar sent her to the ground, to the amusement of those watching.

He walked up and knelt beside her. "We both know what you are. Your mother doesn't believe it, but we know better. Why else would Darkvale want you? You will serve me, or I will hand you over to my son to do with as he pleases. The choice is yours. Keep up."

Everleigh scrambled to her feet and kept up. He returned the green key to the box in the floor and locked it up again. He stopped at the door, looked at Amelia, who hadn't moved, and walked out.

Everleigh collapsed on the bed. Her heart was racing, and her body ached.

"Eve, are you alright?" her mother asked.

"Don't call me that," she moaned. "Go away."

Amelia left her there and that was the last time she saw her.

Day after day was the same routine. When she woke, there would be fresh fruit, milk for her cereal and a glass of juice. Then the key was removed from the floor, it was off to a room with all kinds of objects. She was asked over and over if she knew what each one was. She always answered no, and for the most part it was true. Now and then they would show her a simple thing, like a candle or a knife, to make sure she was paying attention, and those she would name.

Back in her room around mid-day she would find soup, a sandwich, a pitcher of water, and a glass. She would be left alone for a couple of hours before another round of trying to find out what she knew. Dinner was something different every night. She was given an hour or so to eat before her dishes were collected and a new pitcher of water was left for her.

On the first day, she used one of the papers to start tracking how long she had been there. This time, when she pulled it out from under the mattress, there was a note written on the bottom. 'If you would like a calendar, you need only to ask,' but of course she had no intention of asking these people for anything.

After the fourth day, she started noticing things were missing from her room. Every morning, more books were gone. When the books ran out, the paper and pens were gone. The next morning her food was on the floor because her table and chairs were gone. At the same time, she noticed she was being given less and less to eat each day.

On the morning she woke with nothing left in her room but her bed, she found a single apple sitting on a plate on the floor.

A young girl brought in a phone and handed it to her. "Hello?" she asked hesitantly.

"Everleigh dear, they are not giving me long, so just listen. You're being difficult and there is no need to be. If you don't start helping them, things are going to start getting worse very quickly. You need to—"

The call was cut off and her mother was gone. The phone was taken away and, without a word, the young woman left her alone.

No one came for her that morning. With nothing to do, she drifted off to sleep watching the first of the autumn leaves turn.

Everleigh woke to the now familiar click of the floor box opening and a few seconds later, a sharp pain tore through her body, this time lasting longer than ever before. Panting and struggling to breathe, she sat up.

"Good. You're awake," Richard said. "Keep up." Everleigh jumped to her feet and jogged after him.

The room he took her to had a single chair. He sat down and motioned for her to do the same, so she sat on the floor at his feet.

"You have decided to be uncooperative," he said in his cold toneless voice. "So, I have decided to personally take over. Now you will answer me, or there will be consequences greater than the loss of a few books."

Kenneth came in carrying a small box, which he handed to Richard, and stepped back.

"You've met Kenneth already. He's going to be helping me today." Richard reached into the box and pulled a card with a bind rune on it. "What is this?" he asked.

"I don't know," Everligh answered and instantly doubled over in pain.

"I told you. I don't ask twice," he warned. He pulled a second card with a picture of a basil plant. "What is it?"

"I can't tell you what I don't know." She looked up at him, breathing hard.

He pulled card after card until Everleigh was no longer able to sit up. She lay on the floor shaking.

Richard's anger had reached its limits. He rolled the marble in his fingers until Everleigh's body was limp and unconscious.

"Don," Richard yelled and waited for him to appear. "I'm done with her. Do you want her?"

Donald looked at her for a moment. He used his foot to roll her to her back and shook his head before walking away.

"Ungrateful little brat," Richard huffed and stood from his chair. "Kenneth, pick her up and follow me."

Richard led the way across the compound to the rundown building on the far side. He opened the door and walked through the dark hall until he found a spot so far back that light from the small dirty windows could not reach.

"Drop her in there and leave us," he ordered and waited until he heard the door close before rolling the marble in his fingers again.

The pain woke her suddenly with a cry and again she was shaking and struggling to breathe.

"I guess I shouldn't be surprised. My father had to keep your grandmother in line with a collar. Hers was made of iron and chained to a wall so, you see, we've upgraded. Not all witches are so defiant."

Everleigh had pulled herself up to her knees, so he kicked the iron-barred door closed. She used the bars, and the last of her strength, to pull herself to her feet and look him in the eye.

"Then when your mother came to her senses and tried to escape with you, your grandmother wiped out her magic and made her useless." Richard was pacing in front of her. "You I still wonder about. You're either the stupidest witch I've ever met or the most defiant. Anyway, it's no matter now. If you're not a witch you're as good as dead." He rolled the marble in his fingers.

This time the pain was so fast and strong Everleigh was unconscious before her body hit the floor. Richard found a small shelf, halfway up the wall across from her cell, to put the green marble on and left.

When Everleigh woke, she was alone in complete darkness. She had no idea how long she had been there. The floor was cold stone beneath her. She felt around and found a box. She opened it and lay on top of it. It wasn't great, but it was better than the floor.

Time had no meaning in the soundless darkness. Of all her thoughts, the one that kept forcing its way to the front was a simple one. *Jack will find me.*

"Wake up, little one."

"Lilli, is that you?" Everleigh's voice was hoarse. The lack of food and water was beginning to take its toll.

"I'm here with you, little one," Lilli cooed.

"Can I see you?" Everleigh wanted desperately to see something.

"Would you like to? Would you like to see in the dark?" Lilli offered.

"Yes. Oh yes please," Everleigh begged.

"Say it with me, little one. *Vision, sight, and deep perception. Mystic light and meditation. In consciousness my eyes shall see. The other side will come to me.*"

Everleigh spoke the words with her grandmother, and after the third time Lilli stopped.

"Open your eyes, little one," Lilli cooed again.

Slowly they opened and there before her sat Lilli in her blue dress and gray shawl. Everleigh looked around her. She could see the small room with its iron bars. It was as if there was a light in her eyes making everything visible.

"I can see you, Lilli." Everleigh reached for her, and Lilli gathered her up in her lap and wrapped her shawl around her.

Lilli sat there humming, and Everleigh drifted off to sleep.

There was no way to count the hours, days, or weeks. The only constant was her growing weakness. She couldn't remember the last thing she ate or drank. When the pain began to take hold, Lilli would appear to gather her in her arms and hum her back to sleep.

The only noise Everleigh had heard in a long time woke her with a start, and she wondered if it had been real or if she had imagined it. She laid there on her cardboard bed next to the bars listening and hoping for anything other than silence.

There were voices from somewhere far away, but she was sure she could hear them.

"Jack, this place is huge. It's going to take forever to search it in the dark."

Everleigh closed her eyes and waited for the response.

"A phone light is better than nothing, but we need to move. That truck will be noticed eventually, and I'd rather not have to fight my way out of here."

It was him! Jack was here and he was looking for her! Everleigh's heart jumped and she tried to call out to him. Little more than air passed her dry cracked lips, but her mind was screaming to him.

She tried to sit up, but there was nothing left. So much time without food and water had taken its toll on her body and she couldn't make it do what she so desperately wanted it to do.

The voices were getting closer, louder. A blinding light filled the dark hall forcing her to close her eyes. Then it was gone, and their voices moved farther away.

Her mind screamed to him. "Please, Jack. I'm here. Please come back."

There was one thing she could try, one thing that might draw their attention back. Everleigh wiggled as close to the bars as she could and, with a shaking hand, grabbed the collar around her neck.

The jolt of pain threw her body hard against the bars and tore a scream from her that was little more than a strangled cough. She collapsed back to the floor, struggling to stay conscious.

Both men froze and looked at each other. The echo made it hard to pinpoint where the strange sound had come from.

"Look at this. These look like animal pens," Jack said walking back down one of the side corridors off the main hall. He turned to face Scott. "We need to check every one of them." His voice caught in his throat and his eyes widened.

Scott turned to see what he was looking at.

At the very edge of the light the phone cast, there was a hand on the ground sticking out from between the bars.

Jack's heart was pounding the closer he got to it. He didn't dare look in the cage. He gently touched his fingers to the upturned palm and jumped when her fingers tightened around his.

"She's here!" Jack yelled. "Scott, she's here."

Scott ran down to where Jack was on his knees and started picking the lock.

"It's ok. We're coming." Jack pushed her arm back through the bars so the door could slide open. It felt like an eternity waiting for Scott to get the rusty lock to open.

Finally, the door slid open, and Jack crawled to Everleigh and scooped her up. His arm around her neck touched the collar and pain ripped through them both.

Everleigh's racking cough tore at her chest like claws. Jack caught his breath quickly but dared not touch her again.

She closed her eyes tight as Scott's light lit up her face. He turned it away quickly. "There's something around her neck," he said, carefully raising the light just high enough for them to see it.

"It looks like a collar," Jack said leaning closer.

"Jack." Everleigh fought for every word from her dry throat. "Jack."

He lowered his ear to her lips careful not to touch the silver collar.

"Green marble." She coughed and he repeated so she knew he understood. "Touch collar."

"The green marble controls the collar?" he asked and she closed her eyes. "Ok, so if we touch the marble to the collar, it will come off?" Everleigh again closed her eyes.

The two men returned to the corridor and searched the table and shelves along the wall. "Is this it?" Scott said holding it up for Jack to see.

"It has to be." Jack took it and Everleigh's body began violently shaking. He dropped to his knees, hit the marble to the collar and it snapped open. He dropped the marble and gathered her fragile body into his arms. "We have to get her to the hospital, to Sam."

Jack started walking with his phone lighting the floor. Scott scooped up the marble and jammed it into his pocket, grabbed the collar, and followed.

When they got to the door Scott stopped him. "Let me go first. I'll get the truck open and come back for you," Scott said, and Jack agreed. "We can lay her on the bench behind the seat and use our jackets to cover her. Drive out of here the same way we drove in."

Jack waited with Everleigh in his arms, kissing her forehead, with every one of her racking breaths until the door popped open.

Scott draped his jacket over her head to protect her eyes and Jack followed him to the truck.

They slid her in. Jack pulled his blades out of his jacket and set them on the floor so he could hide her legs. Scott got in behind the wheel this time. Jack took the passenger side so he could turn in his seat and reach her.

"I'm right here, Everleigh. We're almost out." Jack tried to be comforting but his heart was pounding. They still had to pass the guards.

It was as easy getting out as it was getting in. The young man that had to move the chain even wished them a good evening as they passed.

As soon as they were back on the highway headed for the city, Jack reached back and took her hand. He was relieved to feel her fingers tighten just enough so he could feel it.

"Hi, Jack. I'm just leaving work. What's up?" Sam asked.

"We have her, and she needs help." It was all he was able to say.

"I'll meet you at Dom's clinic," Sam answered in a clear doctor in charge tone.

"Sam!" Jack called to get his attention. "What are you talking about? Where is that?"

"Dom opened his own clinic to deal with patients with complex health issues. That's why he travels all the time. He goes to see them before they spend the money to come to him. Trust me, he'll want her there. I've texted you the address. I'll meet you there."

"I got it. She's going to need a dark room. Her eyes can't stand the light," he replied and hung up the phone.

"You should call the Hall. I know Marcus is worried," Scott suggested.

"I'll call the Hall when Sam is seeing to her. I'll have more time." Jack dialed the phone again with one hand.

"Detective Mitchell."

"It's Jack. We've got her."

"What? Where are you?" he asked with a combination of surprise and relief.

"We're taking her to the Core Medical Clinic. We're going to draw attention," Jack told him.

"I'm on my way." The call disconnected and Jack put his phone in his pocket.

They pulled up at the clinic's front doors, where Sam and Dom were waiting. A police car pulled up right behind them. Jack got out and pulled his seat as far forward as he could. He pulled his coat away so they could see her lower body.

The clothes she had been wearing were torn to almost nothing. Her skin was a dull gray that hung on her like a wet blanket covered with dark purple bruises. This was the first good look Jack had of her in the light. He knew it wasn't going to be good, but he was not prepared for this.

"We have a room ready for her," Dom said, clearly concerned by what he was seeing.

"I'll stay with the truck, Jack. We don't want our jackets to go missing," Scott said indicating the set of razor-sharp blades and sword tucked under the seat.

Detective Mitchell had arrived and stepped up to the patrol officer as he was getting out of his car. "I'll look after this and be right with you Scott. Jack, you see to her."

Both men nodded, grateful he had arrived when he did. Neither of them had any idea how they would explain any of this. Sam climbed into the driver's side and quickly pulled the jacket off Everleigh's head. He slid a soft, thick blindfold over her eyes, exposing her long hair matted to her head and all the cuts and bruises to her sunken face.

"Can you bring her in, or should we use the gurney?" Dom asked, knowing full well what the answer would be.

With more care than Jack had ever shown in his life, he reached into the truck and lifted her out. They watched as she curled into his chest, and he kissed the top of her head.

"This way, Jack," Dom said softly and walked into the clinic past the crowd of whispering onlookers. The speeding truck had drawn more attention than Jack liked, but Scott would have to deal with that.

Jack carried her all the way to the room Sam and Dom had set up for her. It was a large room with no windows, two beds, and a pair of chairs. The light was on in the washroom, but everything else was off.

Jack deposited her into the center of one of the beds and slowly backed away to allow the two doctors to get closer. He sat next to her legs and held her hand. The nurse closed the door halfway to keep the bright florescent hall lights off her and Sam removed the blindfold.

Sam and Dom looked at each other and walked over to the nurse, who quickly left the room.

"Please don't cry." Everleigh's voice was no more than a whisper and caused her to cough.

Jack sat up a little straighter. "How can you see my tears?" he asked as he wiped away the single tear that had escaped.

"Everleigh, please don't talk, not until we get some fluids into you. It could scar your throat. Right now, I want to get you cleaned up." Sam knelt down at her bedside so she didn't have to move. "Nurse Millie is getting some warm water and she's going to clean you up and get you into a gown. It's going to hurt, but you'll feel so much better. Then Dom is going to start an IV to get you hydrated. Then you can get some sleep, ok?"

Everleigh knew he was right and smiled in agreement. She already felt better than she had an hour earlier.

Sam and Jack waited for Nurse Millie to arrive before they left.

"Come with me." Sam led the way down a long hall to a room with large windows that looked out over a garden with a small fountain on one side and the parking lot on the other.

"This is the Physical Therapy room." Sam smiled and closed the door. The room had all kinds of equipment, bikes, small weights, and bars, but Sam knew where he was going. "It's just you, me, and this heavy bag. It's not a truck tire but it might hurt less."

Jack circled the bag once before giving it a mighty blow that made Sam look away.

"Feel better?" Sam offered him a set of boxing gloves, but Jack turned them down. "Tell me, where did you find her?"

Jack circled the bag and told Sam everything except the part about talking to Lilli, alternating punches according to the pain in his wrists.

Eventually he sat down on the bench next to where Sam had been sitting and asked, "How do we help her?"

"They had to have been slowly starving her from the time they took her, and that's going to take time to reverse. The same with her eyes. We must move slowly and carefully or there's a chance she could lose her sight for good. She's a witch. She'll heal fast once we get her stable." Sam hoped he didn't look as defeated as he felt. He checked his phone. "That's Dom. He said we can come back."

Jack gave the heavy bag another hit and followed Sam back to Everleigh's room.

CHAPTER 12

As the two men approached Dom met them outside her room. "She's asleep," he said and directed them to a brightly lit room full of comfortable chairs. He passed Sam her chart. "Millie bathed her and put her in one of our gowns. That chart shows all the bruises she found on her."

Sam angled the picture of the little person so Jack could see it.

"What happens now?" Jack asked taking only a quick look at the picture covered in circles.

"For the next couple days, there isn't a lot we can do. I have her on an IV to get her fluids up. She'll be more alert tomorrow, but we have to take our time. I'm going to call a colleague to come and look at her eyes, hopefully tomorrow afternoon." Dom took the chart back and handed Jack a paper. "There are a few items I would like you to bring here for her. When you go home, I want you to take a shower and get some sleep. I gave her a sedative, so she should sleep for at least the next twelve hours."

"He's right Jack." Sam could see Jack wasn't happy about leaving her. "You did your job. Now we need to do ours. There isn't anything you can do for her while she sleeps."

There was a knock on the door frame. Detective Mitchell stepped into the room. "The lady at the front desk said you were back here. How is she?"

"I need to see her before I go," Jack said, standing up and heading for the door. No one tried to stop him.

While Jack was gone, Dom told him about her condition and Sam filled in what Jack told him about finding her.

When Jack came back, he looked even more tired than he had when he left them.

"Jack, I'm going to stay until I can get a Warrior or two from my Hall to come and spend the night. I doubt the Balordran will try anything, but I'd rather not chance it. Give you and Scott a chance to rest," Detective Mitchell offered, and Jack realized it was not an offer open for discussion.

"I was able to smooth everything over with the patrol officer, and Scott's taking the truck back. He'll get his and come back here to get you. We won't leave this place unguarded until you're back and rested," the detective assured him.

"We'll call if anything changes, but I don't expect it will," Sam said trying to be as reassuring as he could be.

When Scott pulled up, Jack was sitting on the bench outside the front doors. This was the perfect part of town for a clinic like this. It was quiet and away from the rush of downtown. On the way to the apartment, they stopped at a department store. Jack took the list Dom had given him and bought the softest pants and t-shirts he could find and picked out a pair for himself. He also found the battery candles Dom said would light the room without being too harsh on her eyes.

Scott stopped one more time for a drive-thru dinner and they headed back to her apartment.

A news van was parked out front of the building, doing what they assumed must be a follow up story about the missing woman. The anchor tried asking them questions as they walked into the building, but the two men said nothing.

The evening passed quietly. Jack cut the tags off the new clothes and took them down to the building's laundry before joining Scott for their cheeseburger and fries.

"We should call Tom. He'll be waiting for news," Scott suggested again. "Do you want me to call?"

"Hi, Sam. We just got home," Scott answered his phone. "The news? Why?"

He hung up, hurried to the TV, and turned on the news. They had been wrong about the reporter. Her story hadn't been about Everleigh being missing, but that she had been found.

The two men listened to the story, wondering how they had found out so fast. Some of the facts were completely wrong, like that she was in hospital with life-threatening injuries. They were grateful to Detective Mitchell for guarding the clinic overnight.

"I think we should call Tom now. Someone will have seen this." Jack pulled his phone from his pocket and dialed.

* * *

It had just passed 6:30pm. Sera looked up from her sink of dishes and out her kitchen window. The village had been unusually quiet since they heard the news about Everleigh. Scott had called her every night with little to say except he loved her and missed her. But something had the village riled up now.

She went outside and joined the crowd of people headed straight for Eldaguard Hall whispering about whether the news could be true.

"What news?" she asked Mia. "What's going on?"

"Did you not watch the news tonight? They said Everleigh's been found," Mia replied, a mix of excitement and fear in her voice. "They said she has life threatening injuries. Have you heard from Scott?"

Sera shook her head and checked her phone just to be sure.

The crowd gathered around the huge carved front doors and waited.

"Everyone, please calm down. We saw the news report, too," Carl called from the doors. "We are waiting for Jack and Scott to call. As soon they do, we will ring the meeting bell and tell you what they said. Go on home. We don't know how long this could take."

Carl went back inside. Some people sat down on the grass while others milled around talking in groups. Not one person left. Their fear grew as they waited guessing about what was happening.

Sera couldn't take it. She walked a little distance away and sent Scott a text. He replied simply with 'Jack is calling now. We have her.' Her heart skipped a beat, but she knew she had to wait.

It seemed to take hours before Carl came back out. He waited until the crowd had gathered close and quieted, so everyone could hear.

"Everleigh has been found alive!" A cheer erupted form the crowed and Carl allowed their celebration. "The news did not get the facts right." He waited for them to quiet down. "Her injuries are not life threatening, though they are severe, and it will be some time before she can be brought home. She is not in hospital, but at a private clinic owned by someone with ties to our Brotherhood. Warriors from the Hall in the city will be guarding the clinic. We will welcome her home soon my friends."

Another deafening cheer went up from the crowd and slowly they started to leave.

"Sera, a moment, if you would?" Carl called to her. She made her way over. "Scott asked if you would pack a bag and come with us to London tomorrow. There are things they need to attend to and would like you to sit with Everleigh so she's not alone."

"Of course. I'll pack now and be ready first thing in the morning."

* * *

Jack hung up the phone just as there was a hard knock at the door. They both stayed sitting at the table hoping whoever it was would simply go away.

"I know you're in there!" Amelia yelled. "I'm not going away this time, Everleigh. Open this door!"

Jack got up and Scott followed. Jack opened the door but had no intention of letting her in.

"What do you want now?" Jack asked in a cold measured tone.

"Where is Everleigh? Get out of my way, you ox!" she shouted, trying to push her way past him.

"She isn't here," he said, without budging and crossed his arms. "Why don't you tell me where she is?"

"I saw the news. The hospital said she's not there and they don't know what prompted that story. The news people say they stand by their sources." Amelia was yelling again. "If anyone knows where she is, it's you and your brainwashing Brotherhood."

To Scott's surprise, Jack stepped aside and allowed her into the apartment. She stormed around checking every room while Jack slowly closed the door and locked it.

"What are you doing?" Amelia asked shocked they were now blocking her only way out.

"You're right. I lied. I do know where she is." Jack's voice was low, cold, and calculating. "What makes you think I would tell you?"

"I'm her mother." Amelia was starting to realize pushing these men may not have been a good idea.

"Really? What have you done to her? You conspired with the men who took her. You tried to steal her home and business. You left her with the Order knowing what they would do to her. YOU LEFT HER!" Jack raised his voice for the first time and Amelia took a step back, but he recovered quickly. "But the worst thing you did was set her up with a man who you knew would never love her, who beat her and left her to die right where you're standing."

Amelia looked at the floor. "I...I didn't know he would do that."

"Didn't know or didn't care?" Jack was eerily calm again. His voice had taken on a new threatening tone, but he still hadn't moved.

"Of course I care. She's my daughter." Amelia's voice cracked but she, too, recovered quickly. "She belongs with me and the Order, where she'd be if you hadn't turned her against me."

"You did that all on your own," Scott said having been silent until now. "She came looking for us. It was her choice. We showed her the life she could have with us. We offered her a home, a community of people who love her. We asked nothing of her she wasn't willing to give. We offered her the choice to stay with us or come back here. She chose to stay. What did the Balordran offer her? A magic collar to keep her in line. To use pain to make her behave as they demanded. When she refused and fought back, they tossed her in an animal pen and left her to die alone in the dark."

Amelia's tears rolled down her cheeks. "You're right. Maybe our ways are cruel, but the order demands loyalty."

"So does the Brotherhood, but we would never use torture and fear to get it." Jack unlocked the door, opened it, and stepped aside. "Everleigh is under my protection until she tells me otherwise, and if that means keeping her from you, so be it."

"You're letting me leave?" she asked surprised.

"There is nothing I want more than for you to leave and never come back," Jack said, and he nodded to Scott. They both moved away from the door to the opposite side of the room from Amelia and watched her run out the door.

Jack slumped to the couch and Scott closed the door.

"Go get that shower, Jack. You need to relax. We did good today." Scott was trying to lighten the mood, but he could tell it wasn't working.

"I'm going." Jack smiled.

Jack was in the shower longer than he intended to be. When he got out, he dressed and went out to the living room where Scott had fallen asleep on the couch. He wrote him a note that he was going back to the clinic and would see him there in the morning and left it on the table.

He took Everleigh's gym bag down, collected her newly laundered clothes, and drove back to the clinic.

"That took longer than I expected." Sam smiled as he looked up from the file he was reading.

"You knew I'd come back?"

"I've seen how you look at her. I had no doubt. Eve's sleeping. I hope you brought something to change into. Jeans will be rough against her skin." Sam got up and walked back to her room with him. "We didn't have time to get everything into her room before you got here."

There was a wardrobe sitting in the hall next to a rolling table that would fit over her bed.

"Why don't you go in and change and I'll hang the rest," Sam offered, and Jack pulled his clothes out and left the bag and walked down the hall to an empty room.

When he came back, Sam was standing next to her bed, brushing hair away from her face.

"See, there he is," Sam said as he moved away from her.

"Be gentle, Jack. Don't hold her too tight," he whispered to Jack as they passed. "Goodnight, you two," he called and closed the door.

Jack lay down next to her and she wasted no time getting as close to him as she could. He rested his chin on top of her head and sighed. She was safe, not sound, not yet, but she was safe.

The two slept late into the afternoon. Dom let them sleep as long as he could, but woke them before the ophthalmologist was due to arrive.

Jack got up, dressed, and pulled one of the chairs as close as he could to her bed.

"Jack." Her voice was quiet. He could tell she was straining and leaned closer. "Bess?"

"Bess is alright. She has a concussion but she's home now. Once you're strong enough she'll be here," Jack assured her.

The door opened a little and Dom came in, followed by another man dressed in a shirt and tie.

"This is Jack, Everleigh's boyfriend," Dom said, and Jack stood and shook his hand. "And this is Everleigh."

"Hello, I'm Dr. Ericks. To put it simply I'm going to look at your eyes and see how we can get you back out enjoying the sunshine." Dr. Ericks looked around the room. "Is there a table we could use?"

"Yes of course. Jack, would you cover her eyes? I need to open the door." Jack put his hand over her eyes and Dom swung the door open and wheeled in the table closing the door behind him again.

"Ok, so if we could get you two out for a moment, I assure you this won't take long." Dr. Ericks was already pulling tools from his bag.

Jack kissed her hand and followed Dom out into the hall to the sitting room with the nice chairs. Scott was waiting for him with Tom, Carl and Sera.

"I need you to sit up a bit," Dr. Ericks said as he reached for the bed's remote. "Dom told me you're having trouble talking so if you need something, tap on the table, and I'll move closer, ok?"

"I see your ring. I know you are Balordran," Everleigh said before he had a chance to move away.

He sat down on the edge of Jack's chair. "You're Darkvale." He sounded surprised. "If you're not comfortable with me, I will leave, but I have no intention to hurt you. I may be Balordran, but that does not mean I agree with their methods. I am a healer. I just want to help you if you'll let me."

Everleigh agreed and he got to work. He was kind and careful when he had to touch her head. When he was done, he picked up one of the battery candles and turned it on. He went to the washroom, turned off the light then sat back down in the chair.

The room was almost completely dark, with just the pale flicker of the little candle he was holding between them.

"You have a neat trick, don't you?" he said with a smile and turned off the candle. "Do they know you can see in the dark?" He held his hand out in front of her.

"How do you know?" She reached her hand out and each of her fingers met his perfectly.

"I've read about this before. Your eyes shine in reflected light." She saw him lean back in the chair and reach for his phone. "Here. I'll try and show you."

For an instant, his phone light lit up his face and he turned on the camera and it was dark again. He handed it to her and held the candle so the light made her eyes shine. She moved the phone around looking at her eyes.

"They are beautiful, those eyes," he commented.

She gave him his phone back. "Will they stay like this?"

"The short answer is, I don't know. As I said before, I believe in the Order's cause but not their methods. I was never told what they did to them. I was just told to try and reverse the damage. They experimented on people to see if they could manipulate sight to heighten it. Most of them were blinded to varying degrees. Others died, and it didn't work for anyone. I did read one case that described a woman who had 'night vision' as they called it, but it never gave her name or how it happened. Fortunately, they gave up. I don't suppose you'll tell me how you managed it."

"You're right about that." Everleigh knew he wasn't really asking.

"I'm going to call them back and we'll talk about how we can get you back in the light." He set the candle back on the side table. "Would you like to have some fun with them? Ask for a deck of cards and have them turn off the lights. Sort them in their suits or you could even put them in order. That'll surprise them." He turned on the washroom light and stood back beside the bed. "Just be careful. This is a rare gift you have, and rare gifts bring their own kind of trouble."

She nodded and he left the room, tucking his ring into his pocket as he walked down the hall. Jack came in first and sat on the bed next to her. Tom and Carl took turns giving her gentle hugs. Tom sat in the chair and Carl sat next to her legs. Scott stood next to the door with his arm around Sera and the two doctors stood at the foot of her bed.

"Well, here's the thing," Dr. Ericks started, and Dom prepared to add notes to her chart. "Her eyes are fine. I don't see any damage that can't be reversed if done slowly. You need to introduce more and more light a little bit at a time. I'll send over a formal protocol when I get back to my office. You're going to want her up and moving soon, I assume, Dom?" He waited until Dom agreed. "I'll send over a set of glasses and instructions. They're very dark sunglasses. As you tolerate more light, you use different ones. I have an assistant that lives near here. I'll ask if he'll drop them by on his way home. Any questions?"

"You're saying if we do this right, she will be able to see perfectly again?" Tom asked hopefully.

"I think she'll be able to see even better." Dr. Ericks smiled.

"I'll walk you out." Dom followed Dr. Ericks out.

"Well, that's good news, if not a little cryptic," Tom said, watching them walk away.

"He means I have something to tell you," Everleigh said softly.

"Everleigh, you shouldn't be talking too much yet," Jack said running his hand over her hair.

"I know, but this is important, and since you're all here I'd like to. I need a deck of cards," she said, smiling.

"I'm on it," Scott said and returned quickly. "I saw them in the sitting room." He handed them to Everleigh.

Everleigh took them out of the box and spread them out all over her lap and the bed as far as she could reach and waited for Dom to return.

"Scott, would you turn off the washroom light?" She waited until he had done so and returned to Sera's side. "You can all see the cards. I want each of you to take one and not look at it or show me." They all did as she asked.

"Card tricks, Everleigh. I thought you wanted to tell us something." Carl laughed.

"You'll see in a minute. I'm going to sort the cards and tell you each one that's missing. Sera, could you close the door? It needs to be completely dark, so you don't think I'm cheating."

Everyone had the same puzzled expression. Then it was dark.

When Everleigh finished, she turned on the candle, asked for the door to be opened, and the light turned back on. On the bed were neatly stacked piles of sorted cards. She went through each of the six missing cards and in turn each of them handed back the card they had taken. No one said a word until Everleigh had the cards back in the box.

"Could I have a minute with Jack, please?" Everleigh asked, breaking the silence. The room emptied and the door closed. "I'm sorry. I should have told you first, but there is something I want you to see. Could you turn off the washroom light please?" She waited until he returned. "Could I have a candle?" He placed it in her hand, and she quickly laced her fingers with his, allowing the LED candle to fall. "I want you to see my eyes." She opened her eyes and looked up at him as she picked up the candle, bringing it closer to her face.

She knew he saw the shine because his eyes opened wider, and he slowly moved his head from side to side. She let go of his hand and he went and turned on the light again.

"They are beautiful." He smiled when he lay back on the bed. "I wonder if that's why Lilli had no lights or lamps in the cottage."

"Who do you think taught me?" she said laying her head on his shoulder. She told him about her time alone in the dark with Lilli.

"It seems she's been guiding us both." Jack told her about the GPS and picture on his phones, wallpaper.

"It would seem that way," Everleigh agreed as someone knocked on the door.

CHAPTER 13

After hours of conversation that Everleigh only half paid attention to, she found herself being hugged by Tom and Carl, who both wished her a speedy recovery.

Dom walked them out and Scott and Sera moved closer to her.

"Scott, she's so tired. Maybe we should go too." Sera smiled down at her. "We'll see you tomorrow. I'll stay with you, and we can let the boys go play."

"If Jack is staying here, you can use my bed." Everleigh tried to smile, but she was starting to feel weak.

Sera thanked her and gave her a hug. Scott kissed her hand and winked.

"I'll walk them out and be right back." The three left the room.

It was quiet and she could feel herself drifting off. For a moment, she idly wondered what time it was, or even what day. There were so many questions popping into her head she wished she had asked.

She woke with Jack's arm around her and her head on his shoulder. She couldn't remember him coming back but was glad he was there.

"Jack, do you feel like we were meant to be together?" she asked a little timidly.

"I do," he answered and kissed her temple.

"Do you think Lilli knew?" she asked.

"If she did, why would she have kept us apart?" he asked, pulling her closer. "I drove her to see you. She could have introduced us."

"You weren't ready for each other then." The answer was simple, and they both saw Lilli standing at the end of the bed. "If I had introduced you in the shop, you would not have seen in each other what you saw the day you met."

In an odd way it made sense to them.

"You must listen to me, little one. I know what's been weighing on your mind, but you must let it go for now." Lilli sat on the edge of the bed and took her hand. "You have to put all your focus and energy into getting well enough to go home. When you do that, you will find your natural magical abilities will speed your healing. When you go home, the book will be on the table waiting for you.

"Jack, my dear boy, the plan you have with Scott and Sera must be put into action. There is no time to delay. Keep only what you need." Lilli took his hand in hers. "There is still one last hardship to face before this is over, and the two of you must face it together." She placed Jack's hand on Everleigh's and held them both in hers. "Together you are stronger than you could ever be apart. The same love that binds you together will aid and protect you both. Teach her the ways of the Darkvale Brotherhood so she can fight at your side."

"Are you up for a late dinner?" Sam pushed the door and it opened more than he meant it to.

Jack covered her eyes with his hand before the light got to her, and when the door was closed Lilli was gone.

"Are you alright? I am so sorry. I didn't mean for it to go so far." Sam had set the food down and was standing over her.

"I'm fine, Sam. You brought food?" Everleigh felt excited and suddenly very hungry.

"It may be a little soon, but I think you'll be ok. Yours is chicken soup with nothing in it. Jack's is chicken soup with double the chicken and veg." Sam set it out on the little table and moved it closer. "Little sips at a time. If the flavor is too much, there's water here you can add. I don't expect you to eat it all. Just a little is good enough for now."

"Thank you, Sam." Everleigh smiled.

"I'm going to eat with Dom in the dining room. If you need anything, Mille is at the nurses' station," Sam said as he left. "Enjoy!"

"It smells so good." Everleigh was breathing deeply as she put the spoon into the bowl.

Jack turned on a few more of the candles. As she lifted the spoon, he saw her hand start to shake.

"Let me help you," he said taking the spoon and moving it to her lips.

It was warm and soothing on her dry throat, and she closed her eyes, enjoying the feeling. Jack was smiling when she opened her eyes.

"This must be good stuff," he said, getting her another spoonful.

Half the soup was gone when she finally said she was full. Jack finished his bowl and took the tray out to Millie, who said she would put the rest in the fridge for tomorrow.

"It seems everything makes me tired," Everleigh said when he returned.

"That will soon pass now that you're eating," Jack said and picked up his PJs. "Back in a minute and we can put the bed back down."

"Jack, what time is it?" she called. Her voice was feeling stronger having been soothed by the warm broth.

"It's almost 9:30 at night," he answered as he returned. "It was a long afternoon with a room full of people. You dozed off a couple times, but I doubt it was very restful. We should have left the room and let you sleep. Carl mentioned reading something about witches healing while they sleep."

"No, I'm tired of being alone." Everleigh waited until Jack had the bed back down flat and curled in next to her. "Can I ask about the plans Lilli spoke of?"

"Of course, you can. Scott and I talked about packing up your apartment for you. We have the boxes already and I thought it would be one less thing for you to worry about. What do you think?" Jack asked.

"I don't want to go back there," she confessed.

"I get that. We can pack it all up and call the guys. It will all be done by the time you can go home, and I'll take you straight back to Mallard Pond." Jack sighed, relieved that she was okay with them packing her stuff. "Now it's your turn. What is it that's been weighing on your mind?"

"The barrier spell. I was thinking today that I have no idea what time it is, let alone the date. There wasn't a lot of time when we first got here, and now I just don't know." She was starting to talk too fast, and she knew it. It happened when she was worried.

"Today is the second of October." Jack could feel her beginning to tense up and gently rocked her in his arms. "If Lilli says there's time, then I would believe her."

"October? I was with them for a month?" Everleigh sounded more panicked then she should.

"Almost a month." Jack untangled his fingers from her hair and smoothed it back down. "You're back now and that's what matters."

"How is it we keep seeing Lilli?" Everleigh asked.

"I don't know how magic works. I simply know that it does. I learned very quickly to trust the witch. Lilli never led us astray and she never let us down." Jack gave her a squeeze. "And neither will you, my Witch."

"Not as long as I have my Warrior beside me." She turned her head up to look at him and they kissed.

"What do you think she meant by 'train her in the ways of the Darkvale Brotherhood'?" she asked when they were cuddled up tight together.

"Let's not jump too far ahead of ourselves. Let's get your strength back and get you home." Jack wasn't about to tell her, but he had been wondering the same thing.

Everleigh drifted off to sleep quickly but Jack lay there wide awake. There was something else Lilli said that had him worried. One more hardship they would have to face together. He fell asleep thinking about the possibilities of her warning.

* * *

Days seemed to pass quickly. The glasses had been delivered and worked well at filtering the light, allowing her to move around the building. The IV had done its job and had been removed. She was eating soft food for now, but that was soon to change. Jack would leave in the morning when Sera arrived and would return with Scott in time for the four of them to have dinner together in the dining room.

Sera would help her dress and get into her wheelchair. Mornings were spent playing games to build her coordination. After lunch, they would meet with the therapist to start building the strength in her legs.

She had been at the clinic for almost three weeks and was progressing much faster than anyone had expected. She was eating and gaining strength. Her eyes were better, and she wasn't using the glasses anymore. The only thing left was for her to walk.

Today was that day. Everleigh sat at the edge of her wheelchair, her hands on the parallel bars. Sera was on one side, Dom on the other, and her therapist behind her to help her position her legs.

"1, 2, 3, up." She was on her feet, a little wobbly at first, but she took a step and another and another. When she reached the end of the bars and looked up, she saw Jack and Scott watching from the door.

Jack crossed the distance between them, scooped her up into his arms, and swung her around. Everleigh was smiling and laughing and for a moment they forgot where they were. He pulled her into him and kissed her.

Dom brought the wheelchair around and Jack set her down in it. The room was quiet except for Scott, who walked past him with a punch to the arm. "About time," he whispered as he walked over to Sera, took her face in his hands, and kissed her.

The room erupted with laughter. Through one of the large windows, they saw a black BMW pull up and park by the doors.

"I'll go," Jack said as Paul Adams made his way into the building.

They spoke for a few minutes before Jack showed him into the sitting room. Everleigh waited impatiently for him to come back.

"Everleigh, he needs to talk to us," Jack said moving behind her chair. Glancing over his shoulder at Scott, he added, "The Order is up to something."

Jack pushed the chair down the hall, watching Everleigh wringing her hands. He knew she was worried, and he could feel his anger begin to simmer. Every time they were able to find a moment of happiness, the Order seemed to find a way to kill it.

Paul stood when they entered the room, greeting her with a smile he was putting a lot of effort into.

"As happy as I am to see you're getting better, I'll get right to the point. Your mother has filed a competency petition with the court. Mark is going before the judge now to see if he can represent you without needing you in court, but I doubt they will allow it."

"What is she contesting?" Jack asked. Everleigh was holding his hand so tightly it was almost painful.

"She is contesting that you have turned Everleigh against her and that you are refusing to allow her to see her daughter." Paul held up his hand. "I know it's not the case, but you have to admit it does look that way."

"Can she do that? What happens if she does?" Everleigh was starting to panic.

"Mark and I don't believe she can. Not for a second. But if she did win her petition, it would call into question all the decisions Jack has made for you." Paul looked at Jack. "The only decision he's made without your direct consent is bringing you here for care and not the hospital. That in my opinion, was the best choice. You're of sound mind and that's what counts. Excuse me a moment." He pulled out his phone and stepped away from them.

"Everleigh, I don't want you to worry about this. Even if she wins and gets what she wants, it becomes your choice as it always was. You're not a child and she can't force her will on another adult." Jack had his hand on the back of her neck, their foreheads touching.

"Well, the Judge wants to see you. He's given us an hour to get you there," Paul said as he put his phone back into his pocket. "The court is a fifteen-minute drive from here, plus maybe ten minutes to get through security. We need to move."

Sera helped her get dressed into the most court-appropriate clothes she could find from what Jack had put in her wardrobe, while Dom gave Jack and Paul a crash course on folding and unfolding the wheelchair.

It was a sunny day and, in the interest of time, Jack put the folded chair in the bed of Jeep after helping Everleigh into the front seat. They followed Paul through the winding side streets to avoid as many streetlights as possible. They parked near the back of the lot. Jack got her chair out and helped her into it. They got to the courthouse with little time to spare.

"I can't go in with you, but Mark will be at the front waiting. Go straight to him and unless the judge addresses you, don't say a word and don't react to anything that is said." Paul knelt down in front of Everleigh. "You'll do fine."

The security guard opened the door and Jack wheeled her in. About halfway up the aisle, Amelia turned to look at her and Everleigh's heart started to race. At her mother's side sat Richard Pullman.

Jack locked the chair behind the table between his chair and Marks and took his seat and then her hand.

"All rise."

Everleigh tried to stand but, between her nervousness and still weak muscles, started to fall. Jack and Mark each caught an arm and helped her back down to her chair, which caught the attention of the judge.

"Is everything alright over there, Mr. Adams?" he asked.

"Yes, Your Honor. Miss Everleigh tried to stand for you, but her legs wouldn't cooperate. We apologize for the disturbance," Mark said very officially.

"Miss Everleigh, from what I have read, you've come a long way in a short time. Have you been walking yet?" Judge Birch asked looking over the top of his glasses at her.

"Yes, I took my first steps this morning, Your Honor. I had help but I did it." Everleigh smiled brightly.

"That certainly makes my old heart happy to hear. If you would be so kind as to stay in your chair for the time being, I'm sure the young man beside you would be very appreciative." The judge smiled.

"I will, Your Honor." Everleigh looked at Jack, who smiled back and shook his head.

"Now to the matter at hand. Miss Everleigh, has counsel explained why you're here?"

"Only that my mother has filed a competency petition," Everleigh answered. "But I don't really understand what that is."

"Your Honor, if I may? My client has just arrived. I've not been able to go over the details of it with her. I, myself, only received notice of the hearing this morning while I was in court on another matter. It seems Mr. Bly is making a habit of offering short notice, and I would hate to think he is trying to catch us unprepared." Mark spoke to the judge, but the comment was directed to the other side of the room.

"I am tempted to agree with you. I caution you, Mr. Bly, I have read the last emergency petition you filed on behalf of Mrs. Roberts. There are notes in the findings that I find highly suspect." The judge was looking at Amelia over his glasses. "I suggest you tread carefully. I will not be as tolerant as my colleague."

"Your Honor, with respect, that case has no bearing on this one. My client is simply seeking access to her daughter that Mr. Killian has repeatedly denied her." Mr. Bly continued with his attempt to make Amelia look like a loving mother worried for her child.

"Are you alright?" Jack asked looking over at Everleigh.

"I think I am going to be sick," she answered trying hard to keep her breathing steady.

"Your Honor, I'm sorry to interrupt, but we may need a trash can," Jack said, half-standing, not wanting to make Everleigh let go of his arm.

Judge Birch passed his trash can to the security guard. Jack was rubbing her back as she slowly rocked with the can between her knees.

After a minute, Everleigh started to feel a little better and sat up, still holding tight to Jack's arm.

"Miss Everleigh, I would like to see you in chambers please." The Judge got up and left the court room.

"It's alright. I'm sure he wants to talk to you away from all the distractions," Mark assured her as the security guard wheeled her out a side door and back to chambers.

Jack didn't like the idea any more than Everleigh did, but there was no choice. Jack sat, refusing to look at Amelia and Richard on the other side of the room, grateful for the security guard keeping them all from talking.

"Miss Everleigh, are you feeling better?" Judge Birch asked with genuine concern as she gave him back his trash can. "I know you've been through a lot."

"I do feel better. One of my doctors taught me breathing exercises to help make the feeling stop. It happened a lot when I first started eating again. I think maybe it was the ride over and all the moving around." She was talking softly and gratefully accepted the glass of water the judge offered her.

"There is a camera just over there and the video feed will be showing in the courtroom so they can all see and hear the conversation we have in here. I want to do it this way because I think it will be easier for you. You're still recovering, and I want to respect that. Ok?"

Everleigh nodded. "You heard what your mother's counsel had to say. I want your say. How do you feel about your relationship with your mother?"

She talked about everything. How hard her mother made it for her to get her degree, how she constantly told her the flower shop was a hobby and she needed to grow up. She talked about the text messages she sent her when she left for her trip. Everleigh held very little back but stopped short of talking about her abduction.

It tore at Jack's heart to listen to her, seeing her cry and not be able to comfort her.

"What about Mr. Killian? How do you feel about him?" the judge asked.

"Jack is wonderful. I got lost on my way to my grandmother's cottage and he came to get me. He showed me the way there, he gave me a tour of the village where she lived, introduced me to so many really nice people. He came back to the city with me when I decided to move. He was going to help me pack..." Everleigh took a deep breath. "He's my hero. He and Scott found me and brought me back. He didn't leave my side for the first few days. He saved my life."

"Is he preventing you from seeing your mother?" The judge's tone became more serious.

"No. I told him I don't want to see her." Everleigh's voice was clear and strong. "It was my choice and Jack honored it."

"You have a flower store called Little Flower Shop. I understand you're selling it. Is Jack looking after the sale for you?" His questions were getting more serious along with his tone.

"I do own Little Flower Shop. Yes, I was in the process of selling it. My store manager, when I told her I was selling, asked if I would allow her time to buy it. I agreed. It was when we met with the realtor, who turned out to be a fake, that I was abducted, and she was knocked out and left with a concussion. I haven't been able to talk to her yet. We have to wait until her doctor says she's ready."

"Do you know what's happening at the store now?" he asked.

"My other employee, Jen, is filling orders for our funeral home clients, but she's in university, so she can't be there to keep it open for walk-ins until the weekend." Everleigh wiped her eyes again. "I am going to sell it, hopefully to Bess when she's ready. I am going to move to my grandmother's cottage. I am leaving London, Your Honor."

"I think that's all I need to hear. We will join you in the courtroom momentarily." The camera turned off and the screen in the courtroom went black.

"She spoke well. I would bet he is going to want to talk to you next so be ready. He won't make it easy," Mark warned, and he was right.

"Mr. Killian, if you would take the lectern." The judge waited for him. "Miss Everleigh made you her Power of Attorney. Can you tell me why?" Judge Birch asked with a colder tone than he had used with Everleigh.

"I was with her when she set it up. At the time, we had no reason to think anything would happen that would require it to come into play. I think we both saw it as a formality," Jack answered.

"Have you had to make any decisions on her behalf? By that, I mean while she was missing or since she has been in care?" the judge asked carefully watching for Everleigh's reaction.

"There is only one decision I made on her behalf without her consent. After we found her, I called her friend who works in the hospital, and he recommended we take her to the clinic. He met us there and assessed her injuries. He and the clinic director agreed she would do well there, and I decided to defer to their recommendation and leave her in the clinic's care."

"There is a question here regarding the sale of Little Flower Shop and Miss Everleigh's car being traded for a Jeep? Can you shed some light on those items?" He was reading from the petition.

"I can, Your Honor. The car was something we talked about because the roads around where I live, and where she is intending to move to, are not well maintained and I suggested she may want to get something a little higher because of the potholes. She agreed to let me pick something I thought she would like, and I got lucky with the first thing I chose. She liked the look and how it drove, so she signed the papers for her Jeep." Jack took a quick glance at Everleigh who was looking straight ahead and wringing her hands again under the table.

"The sale of her business has been put on hold and I guess that was a decision I made. The intended buyer is the shop's current manager. She was in the shop when Everleigh was abducted. Bess suffered a severe blow to her head resulting in a concussion from which she is still suffering the effects. I know Everleigh wanted to help her buy the shop in any way she could, so the sale was put on hold."

Judge Birch told Jack to take his seat and Everleigh immediately reached for his hand. The room was quiet for some time, neither side wanting to rush the Judge.

"I have my decision." He waited until both sides were standing. "I am denying the petition. I'll start with the easy stuff. The sale of the shop is not yet final. Therefore, it cannot be disputed. Regarding the vehicle, I find that Everleigh signed the papers and, dare I ask, do you like the Jeep, Miss Everleigh?" he asked again looking over his glasses at her.

"I do, Your Honor, very much," she answered with a smile.

"Good enough for me. As for her medical care, I see no fault in Mr. Killian's decision. His decision was made with the consultation of two very highly respected doctors. Yes, they are her friends, but they also had her best interest in mind. Reading over the medical report of her condition when she arrived, the fact that she is starting to walk already is nothing short of magical."

"Mr. Bly." Judge Birch took off his glasses. "I am going to issue a no contact order against your clients. Further to that, I am going to request the three of you remain here until you receive your copy, as it will be signed, or I will place your clients in contempt of court. I expect you will explain to them what that means momentarily."

"Miss Everleigh and Mr. Killian." Everleigh pulled on Jack's arm, and he turned and helped her to her feet to the genuine pleasure of the judge who smiled back at her. "The no contact order is in your favor and will last, until you, Miss Everleigh, are released from the care of your supervising physician. It is the court's wish that you continue to recover in as stress-free an environment as possible. That is my ruling."

"Your Honor, I am sorry to interrupt." Mark jumped in. "Mr. Killian drove Miss Everleigh here. Would it be alright if they returned to the clinic? I am more than happy to wait here for the paperwork."

"Yes, I would agree to that." He glared over his glasses. "Mr. Bly, do you see a problem with that?"

"I do!" Amelia almost shouted. "She is my daughter and I want to talk to her. These people have been actively keeping her from me for no reason and I want to speak to her."

"Judge Birch," Everleigh was shaking, and Jack wrapped his arm around her to keep her steady. "If it's alright, I will speak to her privately while you write the order, but as soon as it's written, we're done."

"I will allow it, under strict conditions to which you both will agree. You will speak in a holding room with large windows and a security guard watching. You each will stay on opposite sides of the table. There will be no physical contact of any kind and no raised voices. If one of you wants to leave the room, raise your hand and the guard will bring you back here one at a time. Miss Everleigh will be taken out first. Understood?"

Everleigh and Amelia both agreed. Jack, however, was not impressed but kept his opinion to himself.

He helped her back down into the chair and kissed her before the security guard took her to the room the judge had directed him to.

CHAPTER 14

Everleigh waited on pins and needles wondering what her mother would say.

"Oh, Everleigh!" She tried to hug her, but the security guard was ready and stepped in front of her. She sat down on her side of the table. "It's so good to see you. I was so worried. They wouldn't tell me where you were."

"You know very well where I was." Everleigh was not going to listen to her excuses.

"No. After Richard took you away, I was sent back to the city." Amelia was almost believable.

"What did you do to come back for me?" Everleigh asked amused by the quizzical look on her mother's face. "You knew where I was. You could have fought to come back. To save me. But you didn't. You left me alone to die in the dark trapped in an animal pen with a shock collar around my neck."

"You were not left to die." Amelia sounded surprised. "Haven't you figured it out yet? You, my daughter, are a witch. Richard was trying to force you to use your magic to escape. It was your choice to sit there as long as you did. Once you got out of your cell, the stone was on the shelf and the building door was open."

"How was I to know how to do that?" Everleigh sighed. "You never taught me anything. You never even told me who I am or how to use the magic I have."

"I was trying to protect you from this world. My mother stole my magic. How was I to know she didn't take yours too?" Amelia was getting angry. "I don't know what those people told you, but they took me from my home, my friends. I had a good life until Warriors showed up and took it all away."

"Do you know how they treated grandma when you weren't there?" Everleigh's voice softened. "While you were off playing with your friends, she was chained to a wall by an iron collar and forced to create whatever the Order demanded. Just as you would have let them do to me."

"Who told you that? Darkvale would say anything to keep you with them. Do you think Jack is any different than Donald?" The look of pure anger on Everleigh's face made Amelia sit back in her seat. "Eve, I didn't—"

"Don't call me that!" Everleigh almost shouted. "You sat there and tried to get a court to do what? Order me back into your care? What care, mother? You're sitting next to the man who tortured me until I was unconscious from the pain. The man whose son beat me and left me to die in my apartment."

"Everleigh, that isn't fair." Her voice was eerily calm.

"You knew!" The realization hit her hard and she felt her anger turn to hatred. "You were working with the Order all along. Donald was only to find out if I was a witch or not. I was nothing to him." Her voice was almost a whisper as she continued. "He was my first and you knew that too. He was the father of the child I was carrying when he beat me. Donald knew and he didn't care. Did you know that?"

"You were pregnant?" Amelia was genuinely surprised, and Everleigh knew it.

"I guess that's how much you care. He killed our child and left me barren. That's who you choose to side with. I will die fighting before you and your Order take me again."

With that, she raised her hand, and the guard came in and took her back to the court room.

Jack moved his chair closer to her so he could put his arm around her. "Should I ask?"

"She knew, Jack." She was too angry to cry. "She knew about Donald." Jack stood and picked her up out of the chair and sat back down with her on his lap.

When Amelia returned, she saw Jack slowly rocking Everleigh and forced herself not to look.

The room was silent until the judge returned. He walked over to the table and had Amelia sign a copy of his order. He took that to Everleigh and placed all three copies in front of her. When she signed the first one, he took it and signed it himself and had the court officer stamp it while she signed the other two.

"This is your copy. I want you to leave while I have your mother sign the other two." Judge Birch took her hand. "I know you're strong. I can see it in your eyes. Don't let this weigh on once you leave here."

They thanked the judge and left the room. There wasn't much more to say. Jack wheeled her back to the Jeep, set her in her seat and put her wheelchair in the back.

"We'll talk soon about the sale once Everleigh and Bess are up to it." Paul shook Jack's hand and Mark did the same.

Jack thanked them and climbed in the Jeep. He looked at Everleigh sitting with her head down. He stopped at a drive-thru and got strawberry milk shakes before heading back to the clinic.

They went straight through to the clinic's back garden, where there was a small fountain and flower garden. Jack set the drinks down, picked Everleigh out of the chair and placed her on the ground. He slid in between her and the tree and pulled her close.

"Everything go alright?" Dom asked, bringing them a warm blanket.

"Yes," Jack answered. "I left some paperwork at the front desk for you. It's an interesting read."

Everleigh didn't say anything for a long time. She curled into Jack and closed her eyes.

"Jack, I'm cold. Can we go inside?" she asked as it began to get dark.

"Of course." Jack stood up and lifted her back into the chair and covered her with the blanket. He grabbed the empty cups and tossed them in the trash by the door.

"Could we ask Millie if she can help me change clothes, please?" she asked as they neared the nurses' station and he agreed.

"Oh, you're back. Did Dom tell you about the surprise?" Millie was almost bursting to tell them. "Come with me."

They followed her to a room further down the hall. The room had a lovely big window that looked out over the garden with the setting sun behind.

"This is your new room. Since your eyes are better, Dr. Dom thought it was time you have a room with a view." Millie was excitedly waiting for her reaction.

"It's lovely. Thank you, Millie." It was the first time Jack had seen her smile since Paul had arrived that afternoon, but it wasn't the reaction Millie was expecting.

Jack stepped away and motioned for Millie to follow. "I know she loves it. It's just been a rough afternoon. I think she just needs to rest. Could you help her change?"

Millie agreed and Jack took his clothes to another room. He knew he had time, so he called Scott and told him what happened.

"I called home, and the guys are ready to leave tomorrow. They'll be here before dark, and we'll load up in the morning." Scott sounded tired. "Sera and I were talking, Jack. What if tomorrow night Sera stays with Everleigh and you come here with us? Sam is coming and the guys will get to meet Dom. We'll have pizza and beer. We can get the girls whatever they want, and they can have a good old girly night."

"I'll talk to Everleigh, but I'm sure she'll agree." Jack was starting to feel a little better, knowing the end of this ordeal was in sight.

He went back to her new room and Everleigh was curled up on the bed looking out the window. Jack told her what Scott had planned and she agreed.

"Do you think I could come and watch them pack the trucks?" Everleigh asked.

"I think the guys would love to see you. We can ask Dom to help you get in the truck and get the chair in the back. Sera can drive. It will be nice to get you out again for a while and I'll be there to help you..."

Jack looked down at her and she was sound asleep. He carefully slipped out of the room and found Dom reading the paperwork he had left for him.

"Really?" Dom said shaking the papers at Jack. "Is she nuts?"

"You have to remember there's a fair bit of what we know that can't be said in a courtroom. They were hoping to use that against us and spin it so it looks like I'm keeping them apart," Jack said sitting at the table across from him. "I think she knows when Everleigh is better, we'll be gone."

Jack leaned back in his chair and looked around making sure they were alone. "I haven't told Everleigh this, but they didn't leave her in that pen strictly to die. That collar she had on is too valuable a piece of magic to leave behind."

"You're saying they were going back for her at some point?" Dom was confused.

"I'm saying, you know Everleigh, and there wasn't a speck of fat on that woman. How long could she go without food and water?"

"Not as long as she did," Dom answered. "I would really like to know exactly what happened. See if we can build a more solid timeline."

The two men walked back to her room. Everleigh had the bed propped up and she was watching a couple birds fight over the feeder. "I keep drifting off. I thought if I sat up, I could stay awake."

"Everleigh, we would like to ask you about what you remember of your time with the Order," Jack said as he sat on the bed and took her hand. "I know you would rather not, but we need to know anything you remember."

Everleigh agreed and Dom pulled her table over. He lowered it for the chair so he could make notes. She recounted everything she could remember, from the time she woke up in the white room, to hearing Jack and Scott talking while they searched for her.

"They had been giving her less and less food every day and then nothing for at least two weeks, given her body at the time." Dom looked at Jack. "The best case I can come up with still has her starving to death before you get there."

"Anyone else would have died. Your magic kept you alive," Jack said fighting back the growing lump in his throat. "Only a witch could survive those conditions. They left the collar on because they were coming back for you," he said softly, looking into her eyes.

"It was a test of endurance?" Dom asked.

"No. It was show of their power. They wanted to show me what happens when you fight back." The sad tone returned to Everleigh's voice, but there was no mistaking the pride that was also there. She had fought back and, in a way, she had won.

Dom excused himself when his phone rang. "I'll see you in the morning." He said as he left the two alone.

"What did your mother say that had you so angry?" Jack asked sitting closer to her.

Everleigh knew what he meant and laid her head on his chest so she could see outside. "She compared you to Donald. She said you're no different." She felt Jack's chest tightened under her and she could feel his anger. Everleigh watched out the window as the birds fluttered around the feeder looking for a spot to land. "You are different, you know. You're nothing like him."

"It still frightens you, knowing he's out there," Jack said and felt her tremble. "I'm going to change. I'll be right back." He took his PJs from the wardrobe and went back to her. "When I get back, we'll try to forget all this and get some sleep." He kissed her softly and left.

It had been hours since they curled up together and Everleigh felt more homesick than ever after their conversation. She wanted nothing more than to go home and forget ever leaving Mallard Pond in the first place. She missed her warm cottage and the fantastic herb gardens and green house, but most of all she missed her little gray cat.

"I miss Grayling," She hadn't meant to wake him. Jack was curled around her and gently breathing on the back of her neck. "And there's no one to care for the killer greenhouse."

"Leigh, it's too late to worry about it now. We can spend all the time you want in there when we get home." Jack was still half-asleep and he pulled her tighter to him. "Go back to sleep. In the morning we'll call Justin and check on Grayling."

Everleigh laid there thinking about her sweet little cat. She wondered if he missed her and how mad he would be when she finally showed up. Just as she was drifting off, she smiled. 'He's never called me Leigh before'.

* * *

Jack was up early that morning. He told her there were still things to pack but, in truth, he had a surprise in mind, and he needed to move quickly to get it done in time. Everleigh had been looking forward to talking to Justin but didn't mention it. Jack was in a hurry, and it could wait.

Jack left the room so she could dress and took the time to find Dom and beg a favor. When he returned to her room, Everleigh was dressed and sitting on the side of her bed with Sera.

"I'll be back in time for your therapy," Jack told her kneeling down and taking her hands. "I have to go." He kissed her and was gone.

"He's in a hurry this morning," Sera commented.

"He said there were still a few things to pack before the guys get here," Everleigh told her.

Sera smiled and agreed though she wondered what it could be. The apartment was completely packed and had been for a couple days. Jack had brought her clothes so she could get dressed properly during the day and it had made a huge difference in her energy level. It was getting late in the afternoon and, with her therapist watching closely, she had finished all her muscle building exercises in the therapy room, but Jack had not turned up. She made it to the end of the parallel bars and could feel her legs starting to struggle.

"Don't stop there. Keep going." Jack was standing just out of reach.

Everleigh gritted her teeth and took another step, and another, and another, until she could reach his outstretched hands. He picked her up and swung her around. To everyone's surprise he set her on the floor and stepped away.

From somewhere in the hall, a little gray streak leapt into her arms knocking her backwards.

"Grayling! I've missed you too buddy." Everleigh laid there with the little cat standing on her face and licking her nose.

Everyone laughed as she sat up with the little gray ball cradled in her arms.

"I had to leave early so I could call John and get Justin to bring him for you." Jack smiled. He picked up the little cat so she could get back into her chair, but Grayling was having none of that.

He hissed and swatted at Jack, finally getting hold of his finger and biting hard enough to make Jack drop him. His paws hit the floor and he ran back to her using his claws to climb her pant leg and get back into her arms.

Jack tried to pat his head, but Grayling swatted at him and hissed again. "Ok, little guy, I get it."

After a short rest, Everleigh was ready to try again. She pulled herself up with Grayling on her shoulders and walked to the end of the bars. Again, Jack was waiting at the other end, a little farther away than the first time.

This time when she let go, she started to fall, but caught the bars. "No, I got this!" she said before anyone could get to her. She pulled herself up again, took a deep breath, and walked a little shakily all the way to Jack.

This time, Jack was careful when he hugged her. When Grayling jumped to his shoulders, he picked her up again and hugged her tight.

"I think it's time we lose the chair," Dom said from the door. "I'll set chairs in the hall, and you can sit whenever you need to, but I think you're ready to start walking again. I think tomorrow maybe we should talk about you going home."

Everleigh was so excited to hear that she almost tried jumping, but Jack sensed it and picked her up in a hug again instead. Jack walked backwards to let Everleigh hold his hands and they slowly made their way to the dining room, where Scott had set out a lovely dinner for her and Sera, including a bowl of food for Grayling.

"Here are the keys to the Jeep." Jack handed them to Sera. "We'll see you in the morning."

"And you," he said kneeling down in front of Everleigh now seated in a chair. "There is one more surprise coming in about an hour. Do try and behave yourself." Jack was very proud of himself when he kissed her confused smile, and he and Scott left them to enjoy their dinner.

However, they didn't leave the building. They went down the hall to her room, set up the TV from the sitting room, and brought in an extra bed, pushing them together. Dom brought in lots of pillows and the biggest bowl he could find filled with popcorn. There was all kinds of pop on the table and a stack of movies to pick from.

"That should keep them out of trouble for a bit anyway." Scott laughed and slapped Jack on the back. "Let's go. The pizza and beer await."

Everleigh and Sera enjoyed the spaghetti and garlic bread. Spending so much time together, the two found they had more in common than either had expected and they enjoyed each other's company very much.

Dom came into the dining room and scooped up the cat, which immediately wiggled out and jumped from his arms onto Everleigh's back.

"Sorry about that," Dom said, laughing. "He was heading for the door. I didn't think he'd jump on you like that. Are you done with dinner? Your guests have arrived."

Everleigh looked at Sera. "You knew about this, didn't you?"

"I knew about this part." She smiled. "I knew nothing about this little one." She stroked the cat and started picking up the dishes. "I'll meet you in a bit."

Dom held out his arm and Everleigh stood up and very slowly started walking with him down the hall to her room. She could hear people talking but couldn't place the voices.

"Eve!" Bess and Jen shouted together when she walked into the room.

Dom extracted himself from the arms wrapped around Everleigh and waited for it to calm down before helping her to sit down.

"Would you like to change? I can ask Millie to come help," he offered.

"We got this, Doc." Jen laughed. "Remember the time we went skinny dipping in the lake a few years ago?"

The three burst out laughing and Dom left the room. She was in good hands.

Soon all three were in their PJs. Apparently, Jack had been busy planning this night for her. A sleepover in a medical clinic couldn't have been easy to pull off, but someone was missing.

"Where's Sera?" Everleigh asked, but the other two hadn't seen her. "Would you mind finding her for me?"

Bess went out and found her sitting alone in the sitting room. "Everleigh asked me to come find you. Aren't you going to join us?"

"I thought I'd let you guys catch up," Sera offered.

"No way! This night is for Eve and Eve wants you too." Bess took her hand and pulled her up out of the chair. "But it is a sleepover, and, by sleepover rules, you are overdressed."

Sera smiled and went into the party room. She picked up her overnight bag, changed, and crawled up on the bed next to Everleigh.

"About time you got here," Everleigh said with a hug.

Stories went on late into the night. The popcorn was gone and so were the drinks but none of them wanted to sleep.

Sera had Grayling chasing her fingers around under the blanket and the other three watched.

"Good to see your cat is still completely nuts," Jen laughed. "I still say he tried to kill me." Bess laughed and Everleigh shook her head.

"Can I ask how you found him?" Sera asked pinning him on his back and rubbing his belly.

"It was almost a year after Donald attacked me. I didn't want a pet. I mean I wasn't looking for one. I was working and when Bess came in, I offered to go down to the cafe and get us some lunch. There is a pet store next to the shop and on the way back I saw a little poster for kittens that needed a home taped to the door. That store just had food, toys, supplies, and stuff. They never had animals. I don't know why I went in, but I did, and I asked about the kittens, and she said if I was serious, she would ask if there were any left. I said yes," Everleigh smiled lovingly at Grayling.

"She didn't even know if she could have a cat." Bess slapped her leg. "You rebel."

"I thought about it all afternoon. When I got home, I called the building's management company and asked them to get back to me. They called in the morning and said I could have the cat, but they would be tacking on a pet deposit to my rent that month and I agreed. So, when I got to the shop, I went out to the sidewalk to see if the pet store was open, but the sign was gone from the door. I asked her and she said the last one was being picked up that morning," Everleigh sighed. Telling the story reminded her how sad she felt in that moment.

"I went back to the flowers. I was heartbroken. I never even wanted a cat until that day, and I was gutted. About two hours later, I heard the door buzzer and went out to find the girl from next door standing there with something small in her hands. She said the people that were taking him came to pick him but decided they didn't want him. He was mine if I still did." Everleigh was smiling brightly.

"They were the smart ones," Jen said as Grayling swatted at her hand.

"I took him and that was it. I gave her a box and asked her to put in whatever I needed to care for a kitten, and I would pick it up later. I couldn't take him home, so I put a notice on the door 'Please don't let my new kitten out' and I let him roam."

"She let him terrorize the store," Jen corrected.

"He wasn't that bad," Bess added. "Sure, he got into stuff, but he certainly didn't try to kill anyone."

"Ok, let me tell her what happened. I came in after school and was tucking my bag under the back counter and I see these two shining eyes. Then they charge at me. This little thing launches out from under the counter, knocks me on my butt, and runs off into the office." Jen fell back on the bed for dramatic effect. "I think my heart stopped for a minute," she added sitting up.

The other three were laughing and holding their sides.

Sera lifted the little gray cat up and looked into his eyes. "You say you're sorry to Jen." She set the little cat down and he walked over the pillows and sat between Jen's legs looking at her.

"Yeah, ok. You're forgiven." Jen petted his head. "You are a cute little thing."

Everleigh yawned. She had been fighting it for a while, but it was getting really late.

Bess noticed it and the four agreed they should get some sleep. They arranged themselves so that Sera was on the end with Everleigh next to her with Grayling curled between them in one bed. Bess was next to Everleigh and Jen was on the other end as far from the cat as she could get.

* * *

Morning came and Dom knocked on the door. Everleigh woke first and, when she saw Jen, quietly woke the other two, who started giggling. Sera passed Everleigh her phone and she took a picture of Jen sound asleep with a little gray ball of fur sleeping on her chest.

Dom let them have their fun and, when the laughter died down, he said, "Bess, Brad's here."

Dom closed the door allowing them to dress. He walked with Everleigh to the door for a tearful goodbye and took a picture for them that Everleigh sent to the others.

Everleigh walked back to the bed and sat down next to Sera.

"You know I'm leaving too, right?" Sera asked worriedly. "When the men head back to the Pond, I'm going with Scott."

"I know. But let's not think about that until we have to," Everleigh said and held her hand.

"Well, let's get going. I thought we could stop and get coffee and doughnuts for the guys." Sera picked up her bag and they walked out to the Jeep.

Dom was there to help her up into the Jeep. He told Sera to make sure she waited for help getting down, and they were off.

CHAPTER 15

As soon as Sera pulled up to the building and parked on the road, the guys stopped what they were doing and gathered. Everleigh opened the door and started passing trays of coffee and boxes of doughnuts out to them.

Jack waited until everything was laid out and walked up to the Jeep. He picked her up and set her feet on the ground. She took his arm and they all cheered, watching her walk to the blanket Jack had on the ground for her.

Fortunately, for the end of October, the weather had been sunny, warm, and comfortable for sitting outside. Grayling was happy to be on the grass and found lots of hands to jump on while the guys sat gathered around the blanket, grateful for their mid-morning treat.

Everleigh watched as all her stuff was taken out of her apartment and loaded into the trucks. It was a strange feeling realizing her stuff was going to Mallard Pond without her. She had a sudden realization. Where exactly was it going?

"Jack," she called as he walked by. He stopped and sat with her. "Where are they going to put it all? It's a very full cottage already."

"I set a few things aside that will go to the cottage and the rest is going into the storage room at the Inn. There is plenty of room and, no, it won't be in the way. You can take all the time you need to get it all sorted. I can bring it over a bit at a time so you're not too cramped for space."

As one truck was filled, it was moved to the road, and another took its place.

"Dad!" Justin called after loading another box. He was pointing at something Everleigh couldn't see.

"Get Jack, son." John walked around the truck and spoke to someone while Justin ran back inside.

Jack came striding out and smiled at Everleigh as he stopped beside her.

"Officer Brant, this is Everleigh Roberts," John introduced them.

Jack slid his arm around her and helped her to her feet and she shook his hand.

"We've had a complaint that an apartment was being emptied unlawfully." He looked around at all the men standing at a distance watching. "I'm told by this gentleman it's your apartment."

"Yes, it was my apartment, and this is all my stuff." Everleigh looked around at it all. There seemed to be a lot more than she had realized in that tiny apartment.

"I assume you have a driver's license? Something with your picture and address printed on it?" he asked.

"I do but... Jack?" she said looking at him for help.

Jack was looking around the yard. "Guys, where did the boxes go that were going to the Jeep?" he asked to the group.

"They're in the Jeep," Steve called back, and the guys started laughing.

"Her bag is in one of those boxes. I'll find it." Jack lowered her back down and jogged to the Jeep. He dug into the back seat, pulled out her bag, and brought it back.

He set it down next to her on the blanket and she quickly pulled out her wallet and handed him her license.

"Can I ask who made the complaint?" she asked looking up at him.

"I can answer that when I get back. I just have to verify the identity," Officer Brant said with a smile.

Jack went to speak with John and returned to the Jeep. He found what he was looking for and returned to sit with Everleigh.

"What have you got?" Everleigh asked, curious what he had retrieved from the Jeep.

"This is the no contact order." Jack had the same thought Everleigh was having. Somehow this was going to lead back to Amelia and the Order.

"Is it easier if I come down to you, Miss?" the officer asked when he returned and sat down on the grass in front of her. "So, the complaint was that the apartment was being emptied by unknown people who the caller claimed did not have permission, which I can clearly see that they do, especially since you're sitting here watching."

Scott was standing on the balcony watching. He looked around and saw her coming and she wasn't alone. "Jack," he called down. "Incoming."

"Officer, I need you to have a look at this. It's a no contact order against Amelia Roberts, her mother." Jack was speaking quickly, and he could feel Everleigh's hand tightening around his. "This has been ongoing, and she is still under the care of the Core Medical Clinic. Dr. Dominic Noah knows she's here and we will be retuning once we're done."

"I assume you're telling me this because that's who he saw coming from up there?" the officer asked, flipping through the pages.

Everleigh watched as all the guys gathered closer around her. Sera moved tight beside her and the girls linked arms. Looking at their faces, she saw that they had all changed, just like Jack. Each one was now a Darkvale Warrior in protection mode.

Amelia stopped when she saw them all standing together. She knew what these men were capable of even if there were police officers there. When she saw Everleigh sitting on the blanket, she started towards her, but Jack stepped in front of her, and the others closed the circle.

Everleigh and Sera were now completely encircled, looking through their legs to see what was happening, though they were not willing to let go of each other.

The officer that had been approaching with Amelia and Richard stepped forward, as did Officer Brant. They spoke for a few minutes and looked at the court order Jack had given them.

As Officer Brant approached, the men did not move. "Your suspicions were correct. This was prompted by her mother and the other officer is telling them to leave and not to return. I do need to speak to Miss Roberts."

"Guys, let's get the rest of the boxes. We need to get moving," Jack instructed, and they went back to work, leaving Jack with the girls.

"Hello again." Officer Brandt handed her license and the court order back. "There will be a report written on this. I need to hear you say you want these men, clearly your friends, to continue moving you out of here. Do not say anything you don't want written down, like where you're going."

The hint was clear, and Everleigh told him what he wanted to hear. He made a couple notes, took some names, and shook her hand.

Officer Brant stood up and shook Jack's hand. "My car is parked in the alley over there. I'm going to wait until you all leave just to be safe. You're almost done anyway, right?"

"Yes, just a few boxes left," Jack said.

Everleigh watched her mother walk away. She was trying to decide if the tears were real or just part of the act. She saw a friendly face walk past her.

"Ella, over here," Everleigh called, and the two men looked.

A smartly dressed woman approached and Jack helped Everleigh back up to her feet.

"This is Ella. She works for the management company," Everleigh told them.

As the last boxes were being put into the trucks, Jack helped Everleigh up the stairs one last time. Everything was in order with the apartment. The paperwork complete, keys turned over and that was it. They went back down to the trucks where the guys were waiting.

"Thank you all so much for this. I only wish I could have helped." Everleigh smiled and, six hugs later, she watched her stuff drive away.

"Scott, thank you." Jack hugged him while Sera and Everleigh said their goodbyes.

"You know I got your back, no matter what," Scott said to Jack and turned to Everleigh. He scooped her up in a big hug and sat her in the Jeep. "I'll see you when you get home."

For the first time that morning, she laughed. Jack closed the door and walked them to their truck before joining her in the Jeep. A last wave of thanks to Officer Brant, who was waiting in his car for them to leave, and it was truly over.

Jack let Everleigh pick what she wanted for a late lunch, and they went to the park to eat. They sat at a picnic table watching a kids soccer game. Everleigh was unusually quiet.

"What's wrong, Leigh?" Jack asked.

"There's just one thing left to do," she replied.

"Yes. Are you ready for it?" he asked taking her hand.

"I think so. Jen and Bess did another inventory and updated the numbers. I called Paul while you packed the truck and he's working with Bess to get the papers ready." Everleigh looked down at her fries again.

"A little too real, isn't it?" Jack slid closer and put his arm around her. "Just think about how much work is waiting for you at home. That greenhouse is going to take days to clean up."

"Is that supposed to make me feel better?" she asked a little shocked.

Jack laughed and gave her a squeeze. "Did it work?"

"It did." She smiled back.

* * *

It was their last day and Dom got to the clinic early and made a lovely breakfast for the four of them. Jack ate quickly and while Everleigh finished, he put their last bag in the jeep and went to get gas.

"I guess we should tell her." Dom smiled to Sam. "We're not going to see her until we get to our new home."

Everleigh looked from one to the other waiting for one of them to tell her what they were talking about.

"I grew up in Mallard Pond with Jack and Scott." Sam smiled. "I got permission to move so I could go to medical school. I got a job at the hospital and a few weeks ago I got a transfer to the hospital in Strawsburg."

"That's wonderful. You'll be moving back to the Pond then?" Sam nodded but her smile faded. "What about your clinic, Dom?"

"You didn't ask why I requested the transfer." Sam smiled.

"Stop teasing her." Dom elbowed him playfully in the ribs. "I've been talking to the hospital in Strawsburg for awhile and, long story short; the new clinic's building is almost finished, the Elders have agreed I'm not a threat, and we'll be ready to move in June."

"That is great news." Everleigh smiled brightly.

The three cleaned up the dishes and the kitchen. They were happy to let her help but kept a close eye on her and when they saw her wobble suggested she go to the sitting room to wait for Bess and Paul to arrive.

Everleigh sat in a comfy sitting room chair with her head back, her eyes closed, and the sun on her face, Grayling curled up in her lap. Their bags were packed and in the Jeep, which Jack had taken to get gas. He wanted to get as far away from the city as he could before having to stop.

"Eve," Bess called softly wondering if she was asleep.

"Hi, Bess." She sat up and stretched. "You're early."

"Actually, I'm late. Not as late as Paul seems to be, but still," Bess said and pointed to the parking lot.

Everleigh had lost track of time sitting in the sun. The two girls went to meet him and then into the dining room, so they had a table. Paul walked them through the paperwork and they both signed it in all the places he pointed out.

"This was by far the easiest sale I think I've ever worked on," Paul said when it was all done.

The two girls walked out with him and sat on the bench. With Grayling's leash looped around one of the iron flowers on the end, the girls watched him drive away.

"I guess that's it then. You'll be leaving now," Bess said, unable to look at Everleigh.

"I guess so," was the equally sad reply.

They laced fingers, shoulders touching, and sat there. Nether wanted to be the first to say the words. The Little Flower Shop delivery van pulled up and Jen joined them, taking Everleigh's other hand. Grayling jumped up on Jen's lap and she let him stay. The other two smiled.

They still had not said a word when Jack pulled up a few minutes later. He took the little cat and put him in the carrier in the center of the Jeep's back seat and waited at the open door.

"I have to go." Everleigh was the first to speak. "I'll miss you both so much."

The other two agreed and, together they helped her up and wrapped their arms around each other. Everleigh pulled letters out of her pocket and gave one to each of them.

"I knew I wouldn't be able to say it, so I wrote it all down." She was fighting hard not to cry, and she could tell they were too.

Everleigh turned to the Jeep and walked over to Jack, who helped her up and closed the door. The three stared at each other. Bess and Jen were holding hands. As Jack pulled away, Everleigh put her hand to the glass and forced herself to smile at them.

He pulled out onto the road and reached over, taking her hand and, she cried until they reached the first of the now-harvested corn fields.

* * *

After a few hours on the road, Jack turned down a gravel side road.

"Where are we going?" Everleigh asked looking over at him.

"I need to be sure of something." He smiled at her and looked into the rear-view mirror. "Shit," he mumbled under his breath.

"What? What's wrong?" she asked, and realized she wasn't meant to have heard him.

"We're being followed," he said. "Can you reach my leather jacket? It's heavy. It has my blades, so be careful."

Everleigh lifted the jacket from the back seat and laid it across her knees. She could feel the weight of the blades resting there. Only the hilts were visible, poking out through two holes neatly sewn into the back. They were hardened steel, leather-wrapped, and formed for his hands. Each had a blue gem in the pommel that sparkled like the one in his ring.

Jack pulled the Jeep into a short lane to turn around to park facing the SUV that had been following them. He opened his door and took the jacket before getting out. He slipped it on and turned back to her.

"If anything happens, get your head down." Jack was clear and waited until she agreed.

The SUV stopped and the driver got out.

"Donald!" Everleigh inhaled sharply and looked at Jack who showed no indication of hearing her.

The two men stepped away from their vehicles to stand in front facing each other.

"All I want is the collar. Give it to me and you drive away," Donald said coldly.

"I don't have it," Jack replied in an equal tone. It wasn't a lie. Tom had taken it with him when he left the city almost a month ago.

"Maybe I don't believe you. Maybe I kill you, take the collar, and the witch." Donald smiled cruelly at Everleigh sitting in the Jeep trying to keep her heart from pounding out of her chest.

Jack didn't reply. He simply took a step to his right to break Donald's view of her.

Donald walked back to his SUV and opened the back seat. "I gave you an opportunity to hand it over willingly. I will only give you one more." He pulled a sword from its scabbard on the back seat and returned to the front of his vehicle, swinging it in circles at his side.

"Give me the collar." Donald pointed the sword's blade directly at Jack.

"I can't give you what I don't have." Jack's reply gave nothing away. "I suggest you leave."

Donald took a step forward. Jack reached back, crossing his arms and pulled the twin blades from his jacket. They caught the sunlight as he lowered them to his sides and spun them once, preparing for whatever came next.

Everleigh noticed Donald take a step back when he saw them. Grayling meowed. She looked back at him, taking her attention away from what was about to happen.

The clash of steel brought her attention back as the two men met each welding his weapon with well-practiced maneuvers. Everleigh didn't want to watch but couldn't force herself to look away. The advantage went back and forth between them for what felt to her like hours, but it was over in mere minutes. She saw Jack stagger and drop below the front of the Jeep where she couldn't see him, as Donald moved in quickly.

Then everything was quiet.

Everleigh slid from her seat and slowly walked to the front of the Jeep, heart pounding even harder than she thought possible.

Donald was lying on the ground with Jack on one knee, shoulders heaving, both blades covered in blood.

"Leigh, I need you to listen to me and do as I say." He didn't move his body, only tilted his head down and looked at her over his shoulder. "Find me some clean clothes. Put them on the tailgate and get back in the truck. I want you to put your head down and close your eyes until I tell you it's over. I don't want you to see what I must do next. Will you do that for me?"

"Yes, I will," she answered and walked back to the Jeep.

Jack waited until he heard her door close before standing. He glanced back at her. She was doing exactly what he asked.

Jack dragged Donald's body back to his SUV, put it in the driver's seat, and secured the seatbelt. He tossed the scabbard towards the Jeep and closed the back door. Donald had parked so close to the edge of the deep ditch it took little effort to push it off the road and, as he hoped, the air bags deployed. He found some dry wood and lit it on fire before setting it under Donald's seat and closing the door.

Jack walked back to the road, kicking the gravel around, hiding the blood that had been spilled. He picked his blades out of the dirt, along with the sword and scabbard, and walked to the back of the Jeep. Everleigh had laid out clean jeans, a t-shirt, and his zippered hoodie, along with the last two bottles of water they had.

He washed his hands and face before putting on the clothes. Leaving the bloody items in the Jeep's bed, he closed the tailgate and got back in.

"Just a little longer, Leigh, it's almost over," he told her as he started the Jeep and drove back to the main road.

Jack drove a few miles before pulling over. He walked around to her side of the Jeep, opened her door, and pulled her out. Cheek to cheek, he held her tight to him for a few moments before setting her back on the seat.

"Thank you," he said and kissed her. "You did everything I asked, and I am so proud of you."

Everleigh opened her eyes. She wasn't sure what to expect but Jack looked as if nothing happened. "It's over?" she asked.

"For now," Jack replied. "You've seen what I do. This is part of my life and I hope you never have to see it again."

Her arms still around his neck, she pulled him close. "I was scared for you."

"I know, but you were strong enough to allow me to do what I needed to do. It's ok to be scared, as long as you do what I tell you without question." Jack stood in the open door with his arms around her. "I love you and I will protect you." He pushed her back and looked into her eyes. "I am never letting you out of my sight again."

Everleigh smiled back. "I love you too."

Jack got back in the Jeep, and they continued the drive home. It was getting late when Jack pulled the truck into a parking lot. He walked to the back and pulled his jacket out.

"You go get dinner and I'll join you in a minute." He smiled and kissed her hand.

Everleigh walked slowly over to the Burger Bar and waited in line, watching Jack through the big windows of the dry cleaner. She walked over to a picnic table with their food. Jack got Grayling out of the Jeep and gave him the last of wet food Justin had left for them.

"You know what I'm really looking forward to?" she asked him. Jack shook his head. "This being the last burger and fries for a very long time."

"I have to agree," Jack laughed. "I asked Mia if she could make up a list of everything she threw out at the cottage. I'm not sure who, but someone went shopping for you. You'll have fresh food when we get back."

* * *

When they reached the hill surrounding the valley, the sun had reached the treetops. Jack stopped the truck so they could look out over the valley.

"This is a view that will never get old." Everleigh sighed.

Jack smiled, happy she felt the same as he did.

They made a quick stop at the cottage so Everleigh could take Grayling inside, one more at the forge so Jack could leave his blades with Larkin the forge master, before heading up to the Hall where Marcus was anxiously awaiting their arrival.

No sooner were her feet on the ground, Marcus was squeezing her tight. He shook Jack's hand and they all walked into the Hall with Marcus holding tight to her hand.

"I sent everyone off," Marcus said. "They will see you soon enough."

When they entered the Hall, the second set of large carved doors stood open, allowing Everleigh to see into the huge room. There were rows of chairs for their meetings and behind them, a large open floor. Around the sides of the room were racks of every sort of weapon one could imagine.

"Jack, we need to talk." Tom and Carl approached from the big room. Jack kissed her cheek and followed Tom, leaving Carl to welcome her back.

"You'll have to excuse him, Everleigh." Carl smiled. "There was something interesting on the news tonight."

"You mean Donald?" she asked hesitantly. "Jack didn't want me to know what he did with him."

"That couldn't have been easy for you." She smiled but didn't say anything, so Carl continued. "There is something I would like your opinion on while we wait for Jack. If you don't mind, Marcus?" Carl smiled.

Marcus reluctantly let go of her hand and headed off to wait.

Everleigh followed Carl into a work room. Two large worktables sat in the center of the room, with smaller ones on the walls. There were large shelves and toolboxes that held everything you could possibly need.

Sitting on the table in the center was the silver collar. Seeing it made Everleigh take a step back, but Carl caught her hand.

"I promise it is harmless now, but you need not touch it." She relaxed and he let her go. "We've been testing it and, if I may say, you, my dear, are incredibly strong! This thing had Warriors on their knees in seconds begging to take it off."

Everleigh knew too well what he was talking about and slowly moved closer to the table.

"It's only active when it is closed. It's made of almost pure silver, which is why the shock moves so quickly into the body. The magic moves very much like electricity." He picked up the collar and angled it so she could see what he wanted to show her. "Do you know what these are?"

"They look like runes," she said getting as close as she dared. On the inside of the collar there were markings carved into the silver. "I can't read them, but I can write them out and check my books back at the cottage."

"I was hoping you would say that." He smiled handing her a piece of paper. "I drew them out for you. Silver is an excellent conductor, but it is also a very soft metal. It's my hope that these markings can give us a clue as to how the magic works."

"This one." Everleigh pointed to a rune set apart from the others on the paper. "I don't see it on the collar."

"That's because it's not on the collar. That one is carved into this stone." Carl put the collar down, picked up the green stone and passed it to her.

As the stone touched her fingers, Everleigh immediately dropped it, pulling away. The stone, glowing bright green, rolled across the table.

"Everleigh are you alright?" Carl asked, grabbing the stone before it fell to the floor.

Everleigh held out her hand. Where the stone had touched her was a small burn. She reached out to it again with the tip of a finger and again was burned.

"Why can I hold it and you can't?" Carl asked.

"I don't know," Everleigh said, confused herself. "It looks like green calcite, which I have in my own stone collection, but it's never burned me before. It must have something to do with the markings." Everleigh took a closer look. "Can you hold it up the light? There's something else there."

Carl held the stone up to a light on one of the benches but couldn't see anything more than what was there before.

"Do you see it?" Everleigh picked up a pencil and drew the new marking onto the paper.

"I don't see that at all." Carl rolled the stone in his fingers and looked back at the paper. "In fact, I've never seen any marking like that."

"Can I take this?" Everleigh picked up the paper.

"Yes, of course. If anyone is going to make sense of this, it's most likely you." Carl smiled and set the stone back in the box he had taken it from. "Shall we go see if Tom and Jack are done?"

They went back out to the main hall, but the other two had not returned. Carl and Everleigh joined Marcus, who was glad to have her attention back. They talked until Tom and Jack joined them.

"We should let them go, Marcus. It's been a long day and they need to sleep," Tom suggested looking at Everleigh's drained smile. "I'm sure there are many things around the cottage you would like to see to as well. We'll talk later."

"Yes, there are." Everleigh smiled and hugged Tom. "I'm just happy to be home."

It wasn't a long drive from Eldaguard Hall to the cottage, but Everleigh found herself nodding off in the Jeep. She slid out and walked to the cottage door and went inside.

It was dark, almost completely black, but Jack tried to follow her. He made it into the cottage before kicking the table next to the door. "Everleigh, could you help me out?"

Everleigh walked around behind him, trying to sneak up on him, but as silent as she was, his training told him exactly where she was, and he caught her easily.

"I may not have your sight, but you'll have to do better than that," he laughed and tossed her over his shoulder.

"Ok, you win this time." She laughed. "Now put me down."

She turned on the desk lamp and sat down. "What's that on the door?"

Jack turned and pulled the note off the closed door. It had his name, so he took a quick look and shoved it into his pocket.

"What was that?" Everleigh knew he was up to something. She met him halfway across the room and hugged him.

"One last surprise for you." He got hold of the hand sliding down into his pocket. "No peeking. Sera left your PJs in the bathroom. And yes, before you ask, I talked them into setting it up for you."

Everleigh was too tired to keep going so she went and changed in the bathroom. Jack changed quickly, grabbed the remote Sera had left on the table by the door, and used it to turn on the LED candles.

He had just turned off the desk light when she came out. In the faint light he saw her eyes shine and was reminded again of how well she could see in the dark.

She turned to walk into the bedroom and froze. Her grandmother's bed was gone, along with the side table and dresser. In its place was her bedroom set. The bed was made, and candles were placed around the room.

"I hope you like it," Jack said as he gave her a gentle push into the room. "I wanted you to have one room without stuff piled everywhere. We can change it however you like."

"No, it's perfect." She turned around and hugged him. "I love it."

CHAPTER 16

Grayling had waited as long as his stomach would let him before jumping up on the bed and pawing at Everleigh to get up. She topped up his dish with an extra treat for letting her sleep in.

She set the kettle on the stove and went back to the counter. It didn't take long for her attention to be drawn out the window to her garden. There was something odd about the plants. She went out to have a look and she was right. There were no weeds anywhere and the bushes and hedges had been trimmed.

Jack got up when he heard the kettle whistling. Everleigh didn't answer when he called. He took it off the heat and saw her in the garden.

"Still where I should look first whenever I need you." He laughed as he joined her. "What are we looking at?"

"This garden is exactly as I left it," she said putting her arms around him. "There are no weeds, nothing's overgrown. It's as if I never left."

"That may be due to Mia. When I asked her to go through the kitchen, she may have had some of the ladies pop over and help with the garden." Jack smiled. "Come inside before your water gets cold."

They sat at the table together eating toast and jam, Everleigh with her tea and Jack with his coffee.

"How can I thank everyone?" she asked.

"You don't have to. They're as happy to help you as you would be to help them." Jack finished his coffee. "I do have to go." He left the table depositing his cup in the sink on his way by.

While Jack dressed, Everleigh started washing up. When he finished, it was her turn. He unloaded the remaining boxes from the Jeep into the cottage and piled them against the wall out of the way. Everleigh was waiting for him by his truck's door. She hugged him tight and kissed him before he got in.

"I'll let you know later if I'm needed at the Inn tonight," he told her as he started the truck.

"OK," she called back. "Goodbye," she said and turned to go back into the cottage.

As she reached the door, Jack grabbed her wrist roughly and spun her around. "Don't ever say that again." He hugged her tight.

"Say what?" she asked confused. "Goodbye?"

"The last time you said goodbye, I almost lost you." He was looking deep into her eyes.

"Then how about I say 'I love you' instead?" she asked holding his face in her hands.

"That would be much better." He smiled.

"I love you." She smiled back and kissed him.

* * *

Everleigh spent most of her day pulling her things out of boxes and putting things she wanted to get rid of into them. She had just finished going through the pile of books she had left on the floor before they left, when she heard Grayling meowing.

She got up to check on him, but he was fine. She found him sitting on the table with his front paws on a pile of papers tied together, with a leather strip, and the words 'Barrier Spell' on the first page.

"This is it," Everleigh said carrying the pages and the cat to the couch. "Thank you, buddy." She wondered for a moment how it got there as she and Jack had been sitting there a couple hours ago and hadn't seen it.

She spent the rest of the afternoon reading every word contained in the pages, careful not to miss anything. She moved into the shop and started scouring the shelves for the ingredients, most of which she managed to find. Others she knew, or rather hoped she could get, from the killer greenhouse depending on the condition of the plants.

Grayling was pawing at the door. He had never really liked being outside before, but this place was very different. She pulled on her hoodie deciding to go for a walk. It didn't take long for the little cat to disappear into the trees. She walked the path to the killer greenhouse. She had no intention to go inside but she was curious to see what, if anything she could see from outside.

She walked all the way around the outside of the iron fence and, as she came around the far side, Jack was standing at the gate.

"How long have you been following me?" she asked as she walked into his outstretched arms.

"I saw you walk into the trees. Shall we go in?"

Jack opened the gate, then the door. They only took a couple steps in and stopped. The plants had almost doubled in size. Some were so high they would have to be lowered for her to trim them and one had roots that were cracking the pot.

"Wait here," Everleigh said as she moved closer to the worktable, slipping on the apron and face shield. Inching her way slowly down the line of overgrown dangerous plants, she found what she was looking for. Relieved it was alive and healthy she began the walk back. A sweet scent got her attention. Looking around for the source, she began to feel a tickle in her throat.

"Jack, we need to leave right now!" she said pulling off the safety gear. When she spotted the source, she moved quickly back to the door where Jack waited to close and lock it behind them.

"Do you feel a tickle in your throat just there?" she asked placing her fingers on his throat, but he said no. "Did you notice a sweet smell?"

"Yes. I've never noticed that in there before," he said following her back to the cottage.

"That's because it shouldn't be there. The oleander is in bloom. It's deadly if ingested, even the spores." Everleigh started coughing and Jack knew why she was hurrying.

By the time they reached the cottage, Jack had started coughing too. Everleigh made a thick paste with herbs from a bunch of jars in her shop. She dumped the entire mixture into a pitcher and filled it with water. She poured two big glasses full of the most unappetizing muck Jack had ever seen and handed one to him.

It tasted worse than it looked, if that were possible, but they both choked it back. Jack was breathing hard trying to recover but Everleigh took his hand and led him outside to the compost pile.

"Now what?" he asked, fearing what she might say.

"It's not over yet." Everleigh felt it coming and was trying to take long, even breaths while she tied her hair into a bun.

Jack tried to ask what she meant, but it was too late. Everleigh gripped the fence that surrounded the compost and emptied the contents of her stomach onto the pile. Jack wanted to help her but there was no time.

When he finished, Everleigh was on her back in the grass breathing hard. He knew how she felt because he was feeling the same burning in his throat and stomach, not to mention the pounding in his head. He laid his head next to her in the cool grass, so they were looking at each other upside down.

"If we survive the cure, what do we do next?" Jack asked.

"There are plants in there I need in order to complete the barrier spell. I'll find out how much of them I'll need before I go in there again. I also need a mask. I'm not doing this again." Everleigh closed her eyes trying to enjoy the cool grass.

"My goodness, are you alright?"

"We're not dead, so I guess that's something," Jack answered, unable to move.

"What can I do for you, Margi?" Everleigh asked, wondering when she had joined them.

"I know you're just home, but I was hoping you could refill this jar for me. Your grandmother made me a paste for my knees. I've been out of it for a while now and my old knees really hurt." Her voice was full of concern for what she was seeing as much as much as it was for the pain in her knees.

"Grandma wrote it down in your book. I can make it up in no time." Everleigh forced herself to roll to her stomach. "But it may take me a few minutes to get up."

"Steve, can you take Margi home please?" Jack asked, seeing him approaching from behind her. "When Everleigh gets it made, I'll bring it over for you, Margi. Just as soon as I can get up." He tried to sit up but fell back on the grass.

"Is there anything I can do for you first?" Steve asked, with the same concerned tone Margi had.

"We just need to let it pass." Everleigh moaned and rolled into a ball. "Leave the jar on the wall please. I will make it up for you, I promise." And another wave of pain rolled through her stomach.

Steve drove Margi back to her home on the hill and returned to find the two still laying in the grass. The pain was starting to ebb, and they told him what happened in the green house.

"I hate to say it, but Tom has asked to see Everleigh in the Hall right away." Steve felt bad saying it, as they were both in visible pain.

"Jack, you go." Everleigh tried to sit up and rolled back down. "I'm just going to lay here."

"No, you're not. He wants you," Jack said giving her push.

"We should change and wash these clothes. The spores could be in the fabric." Everleigh moaned.

Jack struggled to his feet first, staggering as he reached for her, but Steve stopped him.

"I'll get her up," he offered and took her hands, pulling her to her feet.

Jack followed her inside, noticed her hair had fallen down and that she had some muck matted in it. His had been tied back, so he steered her into the bathroom and started the shower, setting clean clothes on the counter for her.

Steve and Jack were sitting at the table when she came out. She tossed her clothes and towels into the washer with Jack's and started it before heading to the sink for a glass of water.

"How are you feeling?" Steve asked with a smile.

"Better," she answered and turned to face them. Jack tossed her the Tylenol bottle, and she drank a second full glass of water. "I guess we should go."

"We? I thought I'd lie down for a bit." Jack moaned.

"Not a chance. I need you where I can see you for a couple hours. No sleeping," she warned, and he sighed. There was no arguing with her.

They walked out to Steve's truck. He told them he didn't think they should drive and neither of them fought him. He drove slowly to the hall to lessen the bumps along the way, for which Everleigh was very grateful.

They were starting to feel sick again by the time they got to the Hall. Everleigh slid out of the back seat and saw a lovely licorice plant. Jack gave her his pocketknife, and she plopped herself on the ground next to the plant.

"What is she doing?" Steve asked.

"No idea," Jack answered. "With a witch, it's sometimes better not to ask questions." He rubbed his stomach, which was still not happy about what had happened.

Everleigh stripped the outer layer off two stems and stood up, leaning on the building. She handed Jack back his knife and one of the stalks.

"Don't swallow it. Just chew it a bit and suck on it," she instructed and did the same with the other one. She waited until he put it in his mouth and started walking up to the big doors.

"Good. You're here. I wanted to ask you about—" Tom began.

"Tom, perhaps we should wait? Do this tomorrow?" Carl suggested interrupting.

"Why wait if—" He turned his chair and saw them slumped together, Everleigh's head on Jack's shoulder, and Jack's head resting on hers. "Why are you chewing on sticks?"

"So we don't die," Jack mumbled. He was not someone who got sick often and this was a very uncomfortable feeling for him.

Everleigh smiled and took the stick out of her mouth. "One of the plants in the greenhouse bloomed. We didn't see it in time and ingested some of the spores."

"So, you're sucking on sticks?" Carl asked, clearly amused.

"She made me drink green mud. I think I threw up everything I've ever eaten," Jack mumbled again and closed his eyes. "Now I'm sucking on a stick. Why am I sucking on a stick?"

"Do you feel better than you did without the stick?" she asked. Jack moaned and nodded his head, ruffling her hair. "Then stop whining and no sleeping."

Carl couldn't help himself. He left the room before he started laughing out loud, but they could still hear him.

"If I had known. I am sorry. We can talk later," Tom said.

"No, it's alright. We need to stay awake for at least the next couple hours," Everleigh said poking Jack. "What would you like to talk about?" she asked sitting up.

"I wanted to ask if you had any thoughts about the barrier." Tom knew what he wanted to say but thought it best to go a little slowly, as opposed to his usual bluntness. "I only ask because we are due to get snow in a couple days."

"I do. I found the book earlier today, actually. I have all the herbs to make it, well, most of them. That's why we were in the greenhouse. There are a couple plants I need in there. I wanted to make sure they were still healthy, and they are." Everleigh was perking up the more she talked.

"A little too healthy," Jack mumbled, slumped on the couch with his head hanging over the back.

"But there is something I'm going to need a little time with. Is Carl coming back? This will interest him." Everleigh twisted her body and instantly regretted the quick movement.

Tom put his hand on her shoulder and went to find Carl.

"The symbols in the collar are similar to what is used in the barrier spell," Everleigh told them before they had a chance to sit down.

"Are you saying it's the same magic that powers both the collar and our border?" Carl asked.

"The symbols are different, but they have the same lines as runes." Everleigh sat straight up and was using her stick to draw in the air. "Runes! That's it! That's the power!"

Carl sat closer to her. He understood more about magic than most.

"In one of my books, it talks about binding the spells together. What if one rune could be bound to another?" Everleigh's head hurt but she couldn't stop. "If we could figure out what the individual runes are, maybe we can find a way to unbind them?"

"If the runes can be unbound, then perhaps the spells can be too?" Carl's excitement from the night before was being renewed. "We could figure out how that collar works if we knew the spells they used."

"That's great, but how does it help us with our time sensitive barrier issue?" Tom asked.

"If you can unbind runes, you can reverse-engineer the process and bind them back together." Jack groaned, with his head still hanging over the back of the couch. "Can we go now? I think I need a new stick."

"Open," Everleigh said, now standing over him. She took his stick and popped hers into his mouth. "Don't go to sleep!" she ordered and left the room with the other two following. "Is the collar still in the workroom?" she asked, clearly on a mission. Carl answered yes.

She grabbed the collar and took a good look at the markings on the inside. "Damn, I missed it. There are more than just the markings you can see. Just like on the stone, each one has a smaller symbol attached to it."

Carl gave her a pencil and paper and she redrew the runes adding the markings only she could see.

"You really see all that? What could it mean?" Carl asked looking at the collar again.

"I have an idea, but I don't really understand it." Everleigh stared at the extra markings. "I need to get home. The answers must be in one of the books."

"Steve, would you get Jack and take these two back to the cottage please?" Tom asked. Steve nodded his head. "It's been a long time since I've seen Jack that sick."

"I feel bad about it, I do, but it was the fastest way to get the spores of out of our system before they could cause any damage." Everleigh swayed and leaned heavily on the table.

"Are you alright?" Carl asked taking her arm.

"Still a little lightheaded, I guess." She smiled back.

"A woman's tolerance for illness far exceeds that of most men," Tom said watching her closely. "You do feel sick. I can see it in your eyes. I want you to rest. Let this pass and we'll get back to it when you feel better."

* * *

Steve drove them back to the cottage. Jack headed for the bathroom and Everleigh the bookshelf. She collected a pen, notebook and the three books she thought would be her best bet to find what she was looking for.

She was curled into the corner of the couch when Jack came out and lay down with his head on her lap. She stroked his cheek until he fell asleep, which didn't take very long, before going back to her books.

It took a couple hours, but she had worked out the rune combinations used in the barrier spell, and she had a pretty good idea how to work the magic that bound them together. She decided to try it on something small to makes sure she was right. The thing she couldn't work out was the small markings only she could see. That was going to have to wait. The barrier was more important right now.

She carefully closed her books and set them on the floor with her notes. Slowly she stretched her legs out around Jack, who was still sleeping. Resting her head on a small pillow against the back of the couch, she closed her eyes and fell asleep.

When she woke up, she was lying flat on the couch covered with a blanket and Jack was gone. She sat up and looked around. The front door was open, and she could hear faint voices outside.

The sun was low in the sky, and she was feeling much better. The headache was gone, as was the soreness in her throat and stomach. Her only complaint was that she was no closer to finding out what those markings were.

She was folding the blanket when Jack came back in. He wasn't smiling as he closed the door.

"What's wrong?"

"Sometimes I think the Brotherhood asked too much of Lilli and now you," Jack said. "I would be lying if I said the barrier wasn't important, but you just got home yesterday, and then the spores today. How can they expect you have all the answers so quickly?"

"And six months ago, I didn't even know magic was real, or that I was witch," she added, and he agreed, sitting next to her. "Jack, I do have the answer."

"Of course you do." Jack allowed himself to fall back against the back of couch. "There's a bit of a welcome home for you at the Inn tonight. Feel up to it?"

"I do. It'll be fun." She smiled and tossed her legs over his. "How are you feeling?"

"Much better, thank you." He pulled her head down to his shoulder and cuddled her. "You know you can take a break every now and then."

"I seem to recall you telling me this was a quiet village." She looked up at him.

"It was, before you got here." He kissed her shocked smile and pushed her legs to the floor. "I need to get to the Inn. I have tables to wash. Care to help?"

"I would love to."

* * *

As the night came to an end, Everleigh found she was exhausted. She had talked to so many people and given countless hugs, as Jack watched from his usual spot behind the bar. It was so good to be home and she realized that as happy as she was to be there, the villagers who had lived most, if not all their lives in Mallard Pond, were happy to have her there.

CHAPTER 17

"You are sure about this? It's not going to hurt, is it?" Sera wasn't sure how she felt about being Everleigh's test subject, but she did want to help.

"It's not going to hurt," Everleigh assured her. "Are you ready?"

"No, wait," Sera shouted. "What if you end up trapped inside?"

"I'm not going to be trapped inside." Everleigh raised her arms and recited the incantations with one small change. She used a different pass phrase.

She wanted to see if she really did have it right. The plan was simple. Everleigh set up a small area next to the cottage and roped it off so she knew where the barrier would be. She set the spell jars around the circle, and she was ready to test it out.

This was on a much smaller scale but, if it worked in the garden, there was no reason it wouldn't work on a scale large enough to encompass the valley. If Sera, not knowing the pass phrase, couldn't get inside the roped-off area, she knew the bind runes would hold.

"It's beautiful!" Everleigh said as she watched the barrier form like a bubble around her and disappear. "That should do it. Sera can you...Where are you going?"

Sera had started walking toward the path that led to the river. Everleigh quickly moved one of the jars out of position so the barrier would fall and caught up to Sera and stopped her.

"Everleigh, what happened?" she asked shaking her head. "One minute I was talking to you over there and how did I get here?"

"I think you may have been standing too close when the spells combined," Everleigh said with a laugh. "I guess that means it worked. Could you see it form? It was beautiful. Shimmery and rainbow-coloured, like standing inside a bubble wand bubble."

"I don't think I saw it. If I did, I don't remember," Sera said, almost disappointed.

"I want to try something else. If you're up to it, of course." Everleigh poked her.

She called Tom and told him she needed a couple test subjects to try out her mini barrier spell on. He assured her he would send her what he called her 'victims.'

Steve and Ken arrived, looking a little curious, and listened to what Everleigh told them would happen. Sera also assured them that she had been through it, and she was fine. They agreed, and Everleigh stood in the center of the area again. She had the men stand farther back than Sera had been and had Sera stand beside her.

Everleigh replaced the jar she had moved, told her the pass phrase and this time the girls held hands. Everleigh repeated the incantations and again, the bubble-like barrier formed, but this time Sera could see it too. The two men watched, confused as to what the girls were looking at.

"Alright gentlemen, try and cross into the circle." Everleigh requested.

With a quick look at each other they walked towards it. Suddenly they both started walking in different directions away from the circle.

One more test with their help and the barrier spell was ready. Everleigh had an idea.

She talked to Tom about her idea, and he loved it so much he sent a letter to every home inviting everyone in the village to take part.

Everleigh worked tirelessly for the rest of the day. It was agreed that she would only get what she needed from the killer greenhouse, and they would see to a proper clean up when the barrier was finished.

* * *

Everything was in place. The jars were buried in their designated spots around the hilltop that surrounded the valley, and everyone in the village was waiting in the Great Hall to find out what was happening.

Tom got their attention and room was quiet. Everleigh had never been comfortable speaking to large groups, but this time she was excited.

"I was trying to think of some way to thank you all for welcoming me, helping me move, and showing so much faith in me, even though I sometimes have no idea what I'm doing." She waited for the laughter to die down.

"Magic is a gift given to very few and it's my honor to use that gift to protect our valley. Today, I am going to reform the barrier spell and I have found a way I can share with you what I see, as it forms. I have tested this idea on a few of our bravest and I assure you it is safe and painless."

"And beautiful!" Sera shouted from somewhere in the crowd.

There were mumblings from the crowd. As much as the villagers liked the protection magic gave them, seeing it seemed a little unnerving.

"My family would like to see it." John stood up with Mia and Justin at his side.

"Me too." Scott stood next to Sera.

"That would be something to see," Martin agreed, with Margi nodding next to him.

Slowly, hands started going up until the entire room was excited to see what it would look like. Everleigh explained how they would need to work together and that they needed to watch the tree line and the sky so that everyone would see it.

"This is going to take time to set up, so we beg your patience." Tom joined her and took over the planning. "If you are near someone who will need a chair, and you are able, would you take one out to the square? We will get them put away after. Jack, Scott, and I will be assigning you a place to stand to make sure we can all join hands when the time comes. When Everleigh is ready, she will take the first hand to her left and begin the chain. This will only work if we are all connected. It will take time, but you must keep hold of each other. Once the chain reaches her right hand, Everleigh will begin the incantations." Tom waited a moment, but everyone seemed to understand. "Let us move out to the square."

The circle, once ready, wasn't much of a circle at all. With the entire village wanting to take part, the circle had to reach not only around the outer edge of the square but extended down some of the roads before looping back.

Everleigh looked around at the amazing sight. She had never before seen so many people working together like this. To her right and left there were chairs for the older folks, and she made sure they were close enough to each other to comfortably hold hands. She wasn't sure how long it would take.

When she took her place in front of the doors of the Great Hall, Jack was at her left side with Sera and Scott. Tom was on her right, with Marcus and Carl. She took a deep, centering breath and Jack held out his hand to her and the chain began.

"It's time." Tom held out his hand to her and smiled, completing the circle.

She closed her eyes and, just as the book instructed, she repeated the incantations three times. She slowly opened her eyes and waited.

It was taking longer than she expected, but from somewhere in front of her she heard someone say, 'there it is' followed by a chorus of 'look there' and 'it's so beautiful'.

Everleigh watched the faces of the people closest to her before looking up herself to see the bubble close high above them. The bubble-like rainbow disappeared just as she said it would, and the village was safe.

Cheers went up from all around her, a mixture of excitement, knowing the valley would remain safe, and awe at seeing for the first time the beauty of the magic that protected them.

"You did it," Jack said and hugged her tight. "I'm going to help get the older folks home. I'll see you later." Everleigh agreed and he was off again.

The crowd was thinning as people were heading off seeing about the rest of their day, so she began the walk back to the cottage. It was a warm late autumn afternoon. The sun was high and the leaves were in full colour, mixed in around the evergreens.

Everleigh knew magic was draining. It took energy to create, and magic on the scale she had just worked was exhausting. She understood why most witches preferred to work alone. When she got back to the cottage and opened the door, Grayling ran out past her and immediately found a butterfly to torment. She went inside but left the door open enough so he could get back in. She hung up her hoodie, kicked off her shoes, and went to bed to lie down.

When Jack arrived back at the cottage, he picked up the little cat and gave him scratch before setting him back on the wall and going inside. He hung his jacket on the hook next to hers, his shoes on the mat next to hers.

"Leigh?" he called softly so as not to wake her if she was sleeping. He went to the bedroom door and saw her curled up on the bed, legs tucked up as tight as her jeans would allow.

Jack went to the kitchen for a glass of water. Looking into the sink, he saw their plates from breakfast that morning, his coffee cup next to her teacup. He felt her arms slide around his waist and took her hands, holding them to his chest. She was resting her head on his back between his shoulders and suddenly home had a new meaning.

Home was no longer an ancient Hall with his Brotherhood of Darkvale Warriors. It wasn't the Travelers Inn where he had spent his youth working to earn his place in the village.

Home was a small cottage next to the river, with his beautiful witch, and ruled over by an ever-watchful, crazy, gray cat.

EPILOGUE

Richard paced between his desk and the large window that looked out over the city. The view gave him the feeling of a king looking out over his subjects.

"Where is that good-for-nothing son of mine?" Richard demanded.

"No one has heard from him for a couple days, sir," Egan replied from his post next to the door. "Would you like me to track him down myself?"

"You would think getting a collar back from a single Warrior would be a simple request." Richard was pacing again. "And where is Amelia? I asked for her an hour ago."

"She is on her way, sir," Egan said calmly as the phone on the desk rang.

"Yes, what is it?" Richard demanded.

"Is this Mr Richard Pullman?" the voice asked.

"Yes it is," he replied, not recognizing the voice on the other end.

"My name is Detective Mitchell. I've made several attempts to do this in person but your people at the front desk have been less then helpful."

"What do you want?" Richard snapped. "I am rather busy."

"As you wish I'll get right to the point," the detective replied in the same cold tone. "I'm calling about your son, Donald Pullman. There was an accident on a dirt road outside the city. I'll spare you the details. It took a few days to identify the driver, but we have confirmed, through dental records, it is your son. I am sorry, sir."

"Would you be referring to the vehicle fire a few days ago?" Richard asked.

"Yes, sir I am." Detective Mitchell softened his tone. "When you're ready please call and we can make arrangements with your chosen funeral home."

"I'll do that tomorrow. I'll have to talk to my wife first." Richard glared at the knock on his office door. "Thank you for calling, Detective Mitchell."

He hung up the phone and sat down at his desk. He nodded to Egan to open the door.

"I'm sorry sir, traffic was terrible." Amelia wasn't paying attention and continued talking. "Here are the reports you sent me to get. These are the two contracts you've been waiting for. The front desk said they were dropped off a few minutes ago and I stopped to get you a coffee and they had your favorite doughnut."

"Do I look like I want a coffee?" He stood quickly and hit the coffee so hard it flew across the room and hit the bookshelf. "I want your daughter. I don't care how you do it, but you will get her here or it's your head!" he shouted.

Amelia bowed and left the room as quickly as she could without breaking into a run. He was angrier then she had ever seen him, and she knew very well what happened to people who angered him. Standing in the elevator, she pulled up her the sleeve of her sweater and looked down at the scar on her arm.

ACKNOWLEDGEMENTS

A special thanks to Dan Vasc for allowing me to reference his t-shirt in the first chapter. Your amazing music has kept me company on long drives for years and will for years to come. You can find Dan at www.danvasc.com

ABOUT THE AUTHOR

Taryn wrote her first book, *Welcome to Mallard Pond*, in Southern Ontario, where she lives with her family. *Welcome to Mallard Pond* is the first book in the Mallard Pond series. To learn more go to www.tarynlwagner.com

CPSIA information can be obtained
at www.ICGtesting.com
Printed in the USA
BVHW031412021122
650793BV00018B/30

9 780228 883500